D0558674

BEING SOMEONE

Being *Someone*

A NOVEL BY ADRIAN HARVEY

urbanepublications.com

First published in Great Britain in 2014 by Urbane Publications Ltd
20 St Nicholas Gardens, Rochester
Kent ME2 3NT

Copyright © Adrian Harvey, 2014, 2015

The moral right of Adrian Harvey to be identified as the
author of this work has been asserted in accordance with
the Copyright, Designs and Patents Act of 1988.

All rights reserved. No part of this publication may be
reproduced, stored in a retrieval system, or transmitted
in any form or by any means, electronic, mechanical,
photocopying , recording or otherwise, without the prior
permission of both the copyright owner and the
above publisher of this book.

All characters in this book are fictitious, and any resemblance
to actual persons living or dead is purely coincidental.

A CIP catalogue record for this book
is available from the British Library.

ISBN 978-1-909273-09-2

Cover, text design and typeset by Julie Martin
Printed and bound by CPI Group (UK) Ltd, Croydon, CR0 4YY

urbanepublications.com

Contents

For Kitty

ACKNOWLEDGEMENTS

Writing can sometimes feel like a very solitary thing, but a number of people have helped immeasurably in the development of this book. Thanks are due in particular to Sarah, Liz, Billy, Ulla, Tom, Jo and Eleanor for their generosity and insights in reading early drafts; thanks also to Victoria Watson and Shyama Perera for invaluable editorial advice; and I want to thank Matthew at Urbane for being such a pleasure to work with. Finally, thanks to Katherine Heaton for her patience, support and belief.

"*This is what fools people: a man is always a teller of tales, he sees everything that happens to him through them; and he tries to live his own life as if he were telling a story. But you have to choose: live or tell.*"

JEAN-PAUL SARTRE, *Nausea*

THE KING OF MYSORE

The accident happened quickly, almost unseen. Only a handful of women caught sight of the body lying beneath the feet of beasts and men. Their shrill, sharp screams hung but briefly in the air before they were swallowed by the chatter and cheering of the crowd. Some of those nearest looked over, momentarily curious, but soon returned their gaze to the spectacle of the parade.

Such was the din, so fleeting the cries, that it would have been impossible for the young sergeant to have heard them. Later, explaining his ill-discipline to his superiors, he maintained that he had not seen the incident itself, only the aftermath. This he had glimpsed in fragments through the legs of those ahead of him. He made no mention of the shrieks of women and there was no reason to doubt his word. His superiors agreed that his vigilance was to be commended, as was his decisiveness and discretion: with a comrade, he had left his place in the parade to scoop up the broken and bloody corpse and carry it out of the sight of the crowd and of the Maharaja, who rode on the elephant above.

Over the days to come, the whole city would talk of nothing

else, yet in the moments after the event, only a handful of spectators and two of the Royal Guard were aware of the death. And Iravatha himself, of course. He knew most acutely of all what had happened and what it meant. Iravatha had known Annayya since their adolescence; they had spent the following fifty or so years together, growing old. Until today.

Today, as always, Annayya had led Iravatha from the cool stone of the Palace stable into the clear morning light, to bless the children who lined up as they did on each Vijayadashami day. As always, Iravatha had raised his trunk and softly touched the children's heads, had smelled the soapy clean of their soft hair. And, as always on this day, Iravatha had stood placidly as the great riding platform had been strapped onto his back. Made of solid gold, the howdah had pressed heavily on Iravatha's shoulders. But he was accustomed to its preposterous weight: he had participated in the Jamboo Savari over thirty times and he had been leading the procession for over ten years now, while other elephants might have been lucky to carry the golden howdah once. Over the decades, Iravatha had become the most prestigious elephant in the 400 year history of the Dasara festival. He had long been the Maharaja's favourite, and also the darling of the people. During his years of service, Iravatha had become the mightiest bull elephant in the Princely State of Mysore and his picture hung in the Durbar Hall of the Palace. He and Annayya had achieved their greatness together, and now Annayya was dead.

Annayya had been just fourteen when his father, also a mahout and the son of a mahout before him, had made the bargain with the district agent. The youth was set to work training the young bull, recently taken from the forest near Kakanakote. Under his father's guidance, Annayya began shaping Iravatha for work in the forest and possibly, in his more extravagant dreams, to take part in the festival of Dasara in Mysore. Annayya had accepted the task as his dharma, but had also known that this was his one chance to shape his destiny too, to become a person of significance through his own endeavours. With total dedication, he set to work with Iravatha, his first – and, ultimately, his only – elephant.

In the early years, before Annayya was married, he would often sleep in the forest with Iravatha, better to understand how the beast thought and behaved, to reinforce the authority and control that he had over it. But it was also out of affection – he found that he liked the animal, that he sometimes caught a glimpse of something in its eyes that might have been love, or simply respect. He was the third son and had only sisters younger than him: he liked the idea that something so powerful as an elephant might give him respect. But he also knew that he owed a great duty to Iravatha, that this was no ignorant beast of burden, even if it did spend its days clearing the forest, carrying timber. Within a couple of years, Annayya began training Iravatha once more, to prepare for the Dasara.

As with the more rudimentary training appropriate for forest work, much of this preparation relied on wielding the hooked ankus to drag Iravatha by the ear, mouth or crown to where the mahout wanted him to be. Annayya knew that this caused Iravatha great pain, especially when the ankus was used in the inner ear, where the skin was softest and most tender. He tried to avoid this wherever possible, only doing so when Iravatha was being particularly stubborn. Other mahouts in the district would mock his sentimentality, along with his grand ideas about Dasara, and sometimes, to shut them up, he would make a show of dragging Iravatha roughly with the ankus to the correct position, whether to push against a tree trunk or to bow delicately.

But when they were alone, Annayya preferred to cajole and nudge Iravatha, leaning his body into the elephant's flank. He would lead him by the trunk, not with a hook or a chain, but with his hand, like a Frenchman leading a lady in a quadrille. With Iravatha's trunk tip in his palm, Annayya imagined his every thought and instruction could flow directly, wordlessly, into the bull; that their spirits were water of the same pool. Leant against Iravatha's side, he imagined their movements had converged, that they were one organism, their flesh separate but one. Sometimes, Iravatha would resist Annayya's unspoken guidance and the mahout, remembering that they were simply man and beast, would push harder against the rough skin until the elephant moved suddenly, leaving the young man to fall heavily onto the dusty ground. Iravatha would tilt his head and look down at the prostrate Annayya, waiting for him to find his feet.

By the time he was married, Annayya had trained Iravatha in all the skills he needed to become the most productive elephant in the forest. Combined with his unusual size – Annayya had always ensured that Iravatha had the best food – this training made the bull the envy of the district. By the time his oldest son had taken his first tottering steps, Annayya felt that Iravatha had mastered the arts required to be considered as a participant in the Jamboo Savari, the pinnacle of the annual Dasara festival.

His father being dead, and having had no education himself, Annayya asked his uncle to intercede on his behalf with the district agent, the successor to the man who had assigned Iravatha's training to Annayya some nine years before. At first the agent was hostile to the proposal – there were enough procession elephants already, and no-one at the palace had contacted him to say otherwise. In addition, Iravatha had greatly increased timber production in his district. To waste that strength and industry would be criminal. But his uncle was a successful merchant, trading cardamom with the British, and he was able to persuade the agent.

After the rains, word reached the district, and Annayya prepared for the visit of the Maharaja's master of processions. He had always washed Iravatha thoroughly each evening, and fed him titbits to supplement his diet, but he understood that now he had to take additional steps to prepare the elephant for his audition. Bidding farewell to his wife and children, he set up camp near the forest station, taking with him provisions for Iravatha, some bought especially and others taken from home. He had resolved to spend the entire fortnight before the master of processions arrived tending to Iravatha.

Each morning, he prepared a mixture of peanuts, coconut, jaggery and rice, with which he supplemented a stem of bananas:

this he fed to Iravatha as a rich breakfast. He felt only a little guilt that this breakfast cost more than the three meals that his whole family would eat that day. Then, Annayya would spend the rest of the day training Iravatha, so that he would walk with grace and grandeur: his strength and character were already assured, gifts of the gods. And as the day's light grew golden, he would lead Iravatha to the river and, with a fistful of coconut coir, he would scrub the dust from his thick grey skin.

The district agent railed at Annayya for taking Iravatha away from forestry work, threatening to end his pay, to report him to the authorities, to see him charged with the theft of an elephant. But Annayya pleaded that it was only two weeks, and that if he was successful in having Iravatha accepted by the palace, then great honour would fall on the district, and therefore onto the district's agent. If he failed, then Iravatha would soon be back at work, and he, Annayya, would no longer have foolish dreams and would apply himself entirely to his work in the forest. The agent was a practical man and, despite his anger at losing Iravatha's muscles even for a short time, he resolved to bide his time until the master of processions had been and gone.

The day came. Dressed in a pristine white dhoti, trimmed with gold and emerald green, Sri V. Vishweshwariah stepped from his carriage and surveyed the forest station with both boredom and resentment. He did not expect to find a suitable elephant in such a miserable place. He glowered at the district agent, who immediately understood that the uncle's inducement might not entirely compensate him for the gentleman's displeasure. He bowed deeply, as much to hide his discomfort as to ingratiate himself.

Vishweshwariah approached, grasping the silver-capped cane that was passed to him by a servant – he was in his sixty seventh year and found walking an increasingly tiresome chore. The agent dragged Annayya forward with fearful haste and gabbled some fragments about the district, the elephant and about Annayya. Vishweshwariah fixed the young man with his rheumy, yellowing eyes. Then, looking above the heads of the two men before him, he asked of the forest, 'Where is the elephant?' His voice was surprisingly firm and solid, even as it was edged with exasperation.

For half an hour, Annayya worked Iravatha through the steps and movements that were the product of almost ten years, all of his adult life; Iravatha seemed also to understand that this was the point towards which his whole life had been moving. He responded by performing as he had been trained and with the grace he had possessed since his forest birth. His walk was controlled, delicate even, for an elephant standing over ten feet in height, and he knelt with precision, as if bowing to the watching dignitaries. Vishweshwariah and his entourage, along with the district agent, stood at the edge of the large clearing. There, they were joined by some of the local villagers and forest workers who had stumbled upon this show as they went about their business. They were grateful for some spectacle to break the monotony of village life, even if it was simply the fool Annayya and his stupid elephant.

Before Annayya had completed a final lap of the clearing,

at the furthest point of the loop in fact, Vishweshwariah turned and, leaning heavily on his cane, moved with surprising speed to his carriage. Recovering quickly from this unexpected departure, the servants scurried after him; the driver was able to dispose of the beedi he had been enjoying and open the carriage door by the time Vishweshwariah reached him. Across the clearing, Annayya put his hand on Iravatha's trunk and through hot, wet eyes watched the carriage disappear, back to the city.

It took twelve days for the letter to reach Annayya, although it had taken only five to reach the district agent. It took another day to find someone who was able and willing to read it. The agent had been elaborate in his protestations that reading the letter would be an inappropriate intrusion. This would have been a sign of his great virtue, had he not in fact read it immediately on receipt.

His uncle read the letter quickly and excitedly gave Annayya the news, pleased that his investment had not been wasted. Iravatha had been accepted by the master of processions, despite the need for considerable refinement in the rustic training he had hitherto received. Annayya had twelve months to bring a marked improvement in Iravatha's performance before one of the Maharaja's mahouts visited next autumn.

The next nine years passed quickly. An Empress died and, somewhere on the other side of the world, two brothers built a flying machine: two events that, as much as any other, opened and defined the century to come. But for Annayya, there was only an elephant. The money from the Palace helped to compensate both the district agent and Annayya's wife and children. Almost all of his and Iravatha's time was now devoted to preparing for the Dasara. Iravatha was drilled a thousand times in walking with precision, so that he would be careful in the procession, with all the noise and people and commotion – elephants are very big and people very small. The rigorous training Annayya imposed upon Iravatha, together with the strength he had gained through his routine work in the forest, meant that with each year's visit from the palace, the elephant became more accomplished.

By the time Wilbur Wright left the ground, it was simply a matter of waiting for one of the established elephants to make way for Iravatha. These last two years of anticipation, before Iravatha's first Dasara, were in some ways the hardest. Annayya started to spend one or two days a week at the house of the toddy man, drinking the sour liquor until late into the night. On the days following these lost evenings, Annayya would feel great disappointment in himself for betraying his dharma. With sour penitence, he would pursue a day of rigorous and bad-tempered training, before curling up under a tree to sleep like one of the village dogs, snarling lethargically. In time, Iravatha became famous in the district for his weekly visits to the toddy man, roughly hauling the drunken mahout out of the shady yard. The joke went around that Annayya had a second wife.

Eventually, it was judged that the elephant Mahendra had become too old and weak for the Jamboo Savari. Iravatha and Annayya moved from the forest station to the camp nearby, to join some of the other Dasara elephants and their mahouts.

There they began their final preparations for the procession that autumn, leaving the heavy work of the forest behind them. During the rains, Iravatha was able to roam freely, and Annayya returned to his wife and family, who were surprised – not entirely pleasantly – to see so much of their husband and father after all these years. But they were soon left to their peace once more, as Annayya returned to the camp and then for the city and his first Dasara.

Iravatha had developed an air of majesty and nobility during the long years of training and, combined with his immense stature and good nature, he quickly became a favourite of the children who lined the streets to watch the procession each year. Through the children, the whole city took Iravatha to its heart, and by the time he had completed his fifth Jamboo Savari he was a firm favourite of the crowds. He had also become a favourite of Nalvadi Krishnaraja, the still-new Maharaja. Even when the increasingly popular Iravatha was simply one of the fourteen elephants taking part in the procession, Krishnaraja would seek him out for some quiet words. And he didn't mind who saw him, courtiers or commoners, holding such conversations.

Part of Iravatha's ballooning popularity stemmed from his habit, from the very first year, always to walk the 70 kilometres from the forest to the palace gates in keeping with the old ways: Annayya refused the offer of a truck from the district agent, mistrustful of the new machines. As his fame grew, more and more villagers came out to greet the elephant as he made his way to the city, throwing flowers before him. At each village where they rested at night, the pair would be serenaded before being presented with a fine meal.

As his years as a procession elephant passed, Iravatha spent most of his time back in the forest, roaming freely, siring many calves. Each autumn, after the rains, Annayya would come to the forest to find him and to spend a few weeks with him to make sure all was well with his physical and mental health. The mahout had moved to the city and worked as an adviser to the other mahouts in the palace stables: he had refused to take on the training and care of another elephant. Each month, he would send money back to his family in the village, and each year he would visit his wife on the way to the forest and again when he accompanied Iravatha on the return journey. Sometimes he would stay for Diwali, if he was not needed urgently at court. But to all intents and purposes, his life revolved around Iravatha and the rhythms of the Dasara.

As Iravatha became more popular, so Annayya became a more noteworthy figure at court and in the city. He seldom paid for his own tea when he visited to the Devaraja Market, and on many evenings he would accept the hospitality of acquaintances and enjoy the cooking of their wives. When it was announced that Iravatha was to lead the Jamboo Savari for the first time, Annayya did not have to eat in his own home for a month.

It had been inevitable, of course, that Iravatha would someday lead the procession. He was the most accomplished, best natured and most physically impressive elephant that anyone could remember. The surprise rather was that it had taken so long. With each passing year that he continued in the role, people forgot that there had ever been another lead elephant. He had everything: looks, loyalty and flawless conduct; ears which met when brought together across his face, a long and hairy tail, freckles on his face, a graceful walk, and a long trunk that reached to the ground. This he would swing in time to the music which clattered from the Maharaja's marching band during the procession. Quietly, and with careful smiles, the people started to call Iravatha the King of Mysore.

This year had been the twelfth that Iravatha had led the procession, more than any other elephant in 400 years. It had started as the eleven before it had started, with Annayya mixing Iravatha's special breakfast before painting his skin and hanging his body with gold and silk. Then the children had arrived, and Iravatha had greeted each of them with the tip of his trunk, taking the coins they held out and passing each into Annayya's hand. Then the great metal platform had been loaded onto his back, the straps pulled tight, its weight settling onto him, forcing him to rebalance his stance, to re-find his feet under the pressure, so that he could walk as he had been taught through the years.

In the morning, the air had still been cool, fresh, but dry. By the time of the Jamboo Savari, the sky had turned light grey, and a thin drizzle had set in, punctuated by angry showers. There was often rain during Dasara, but these showers were heavier than in previous years: Iravatha savoured each drop as it landed on his back and ran down his flanks, his head, his trunk, grateful for the water's cooling under the great golden howdah. In the crowd, saris and dhotis and shirts and trousers were dampened, but not the mood of the people. Those who had occupied vantage points some three to four hours before the procession began had no intention of giving them up simply on account of a little rain. Some perched atop the roadside trees, others were seated precariously on bamboo scaffolding, while still others crammed the pavements: the entire procession route was chock-a-bloc with onlookers. They craned their necks to see the elephants, to see Iravatha carrying the Maharaja, sheltered above the din. Many threw flower heads before the procession; everyone cheered. But the noise and the crowd and the warm dampness and the soldiers and the weight of the howdah no longer bothered Iravatha. He understood that this was how the day was to be, and he was content within the confines of his role.

Annayya walked beside him, as always, neither nudging nor prodding him, simply indicating his intentions with a gentle tilt of his head. Sometimes he would glance up towards the howdah, but he couldn't see the Maharaja from beneath the shadow of the great golden platform. However, his attention was overwhelmingly focused on Iravatha, willing him to maintain his poise and swagger, knowing that he would. Only the slippers he was made to wear on Jamboo Savari distracted him – every other day of the year he walked barefoot, and had done throughout his 66 years. Despite 30 years of Jamboo Savari and slippers, he had not become accustomed to their constrictions. His eyes flitted between his estranged feet, Iravatha's eyes and the looming howdah above him.

No-one knew quite how it happened, but it was early in the route, as the head of the procession passed Hardinge Circle. Maybe it was the slick stones of the street, maybe the wilful slippers, maybe Annayya's old legs simply gave up. But he stumbled and fell heavily to the ground in front of Iravatha, who was in turn distracted by the shouting of the children in the crowd. A tearing crack, and the thick slow redness spread from the shattered skull. A woman screamed, soon to be joined by others, and then the confused sobs of their children.

Iravatha had felt the sudden give, the crack, as the skull collapsed under his left foot. He paused momentarily to look down at the prostrate Annayya, tilting his head, seemingly waiting for him to get up, to find his feet, to continue the parade amid the cheers and blessings. But instead, Annayya was bundled out of the way by some soldiers and Thimmu, the master's apprentice, had stepped up to Iravatha's side. Tapping his trunk with the short baton, he restarted Iravatha's barely interrupted progress through the streets.

What happened next is well known throughout Mysore and what is now Karnataka. News travelled quickly – aided by the coverage of events provided by the new wireless service that had commenced operations just a few weeks before the Dasara of 1935. This 'voice from the sky' carried the news of the tragedy far and wide. It could even be heard in the distant villages, if a radio set had been bought by a family able to afford one. It was in this way that Annayya's wife heard that her husband was finally dead:

Mrs Jayaraman, the postmaster's fleshy wife, had run panting into the little garden, sobbing out the grizzly news under the late afternoon sun.

Akashavani also carried the news, over the following days, of the Maharaja's sad decision. It would be inappropriate, he felt, for Iravatha to take part in Dasara in future. Given the nature of the unfortunate accident that had befallen his beloved mahout, Iravatha could not of course be blamed for the death and should not therefore be punished. However, in the light of events and after such a long time with the Jamboo Savari, now was a good time for the great bull to retire. So Iravatha was sent back to the forest at Kakanakote, making the journey in a truck for the first time. The people of Mysore, still holding their 'king' in great affection despite the inexplicable accident, were saddened by the decision, but agreed it was probably for the best.

For Iravatha, the return was filled with sadness. Pining for both his mahout and for the thrill of the Jamboo Savari, the foresters of Kakanakote noted that Iravatha had lost his spirit and virility. He seemed to shrink inside. Without Annayya, the bull was listless and aimless, his broken heart written deeply in his eyes. When he trumpeted, instead of a bold fanfare, there was only a plaintive, mournful lament. Stories of his melancholy spread around the district.

It was then that Iravatha became cemented forever in the hearts of all Mysore. The very year after the accident, he began his celebrated annual pilgrimage to the city after the rains. Walking alone the 70 kilometres to Mysore, he was once again feted by the villagers along the route until he reached the city. Police officers, initially nervous, allowed him to walk through the streets until he reached Hardinge Circle. There he stayed, standing in the same spot for days, living only on the food and water brought to him by the local people, until the Maharaja sent a truck to take him back to Kakanakote ahead of the Dasara festival, so as to save Iravatha's feelings.

Until his own death, Iravatha never forgot his Annayya and each year he would make the journey again. Fully five years, each time a little thinner and frailer, he made the long trek to the city, passing villagers whose earlier joy at his arrival turned into a sadness they shared with the elephant on his pilgrimage. Then one morning, in the autumn of 1940, the vast dead bulk of Iravatha was found slumped in the road by Hardinge Circle. It was such a pitiful sight that even the dogs and the crows did not approach. By 8am, a huge crowd had already gathered. People vied with one another for a last look and liveried men scurried around urging the crowd to keep away from the elephant. Yet the crowd pushed forward to see Iravatha, who lay stretched on the ground, grand and dignified. Even the Maharaja came to pay his respects to Mysore's best-loved citizen. From a hastily constructed platform, addressing the still growing crowd, the prince laid a shroud of sumptuous tribute over the crumpled corpse. He dedicated that year's festival, and every subsequent Dasara during his reign, to Iravatha, in recognition of the elephant's long service and, indeed, of the love, loyalty and devotion he had demonstrated to his master, even in death. It was, he said, an example of supreme fealty, from which everyone could learn.

...

The young man finishes his story. He is maybe eighteen years old, perhaps much younger. Uncrossing his legs from under him, he slides his feet into the plastic chappals which have lain undisturbed in the dust since he began and adjusts his loose cotton shirt, no longer white. It is worn at the collar and cuffs after years of dhobi washing. He watches my face, tracking my expression for interest, for comprehension. I try to emphasise both, keen to keep him here, talking. Since he found me, sitting on a bench in this little park across from the Palace, lush and well-kept – so unlike most of urban India – I have found reassurance in his voice, his story, in drawing on his authenticity. For the first time since I arrived in Bengaluru five days ago, I feel like I'm actually in India. Or at least, the India I remember, the place I idealised. The big city, with its call centres and shopping malls, felt stranger than last time, more alienating than I am able to believe, even now. Sitting in my hotel on the corner of Church Street and Museum Street, I had felt that the whole trip had been a mistake after all. But Mysore is as glorious as I remember it, and Maruti – was that his name? – has finally enabled me to land.

And I am grateful to him for that, for his gift. All the other exchanges I have had since I arrived have been transactional, not least in that great city of commerce. Finally to have something purposeless and personal to hang on to is somehow comforting. Of course, there may well be a scam, or a hard luck story, or some other reason for my trust being a mistake, but for now, it is enough.

When he introduced himself, I was sitting in the shade of a tree in this little park by Hardinge Circle. The playful spluttering of water from a nearby hose had been losing its battle against the roar of traffic, the putt-putt of auto rickshaws, and the brash intrusion of car horns. I had been similarly defeated by the noise and the heat and the dust of the road ringing Mysore Palace, and had sought refuge here. At first I had assumed he was selling or begging, or was simply going to ask: 'What is your name? What is your country?' in machine gun succession. But he hadn't. He had simply started to tell me about his city, about this long dead elephant.

He studies my face, and I am unsure whether he is looking for approval, or if he is trying to see if his story has given him an advantage on which he can capitalise: after the calm and safety of the story, I am suddenly jolted into a state of guarded unease, wondering what I will have to resist next. During previous trips to India, many of my conversations had occurred under this shadow of apprehension, waiting for the story of the son, brother or wife who needs medical treatment: apprehension at entering into a conversation, making myself vulnerable to a stranger with unknown motives, of opening myself to speculative scams; but also unease because I know the stories are probably genuine. Batting off the request for assistance only draws a thick red line under the distance between this world and my own. When the initial rebuff is delivered, there is usually a disbelieving glance and a despondent recognition of defeat. 'But Rs2000 – that is nothing to you!' And indeed it is nothing to me. And I know it is everything to them.

But Maruti's father appears to be fit and well. Instead of conjuring up the familiar ingratiating sadness, he continues in his role as official guide to the sights of the royal city.

'Have you been in the Palace already? They say it is very grand inside, with many hundreds of rooms, all decorated with tiles and carvings and pictures. The palace was built by an English man – you are English, yes? – for the Wodeyars. Only a hundred years ago, but it is still very grand, very beautiful. The Maharaja ordered it built after the old palace burnt down.'

'Yes, I visited earlier today', I lie.

In fact, I visited it the last time I was here, some eight years ago, and I have no intention of doing so again. I know that the palace, a hideous Edwardian reading of Mughal decoration, contains very little that could be described as beautiful.

'But you should see it tomorrow evening, when they light all the lights. There are a hundred thousand lights all over the Palace and tomorrow they light them all, and the people will come to watch and there will be a party in the grounds of the Palace – they open the gates, no need to pay, so all the people of the city can come to watch the lights. I think it is at six o'clock in the evening, maybe seven. You should go and see it, it is very beautiful, and there are so many people.'

I nod earnestly, checking the details with Maruti, even though I had seen the Sunday evening lighting up of the palace last time too.

'Do you know where the State Silk Shop is?'

We had failed to find it eight years ago, despite wandering the streets all afternoon, too afraid to ask strangers on the street. Too late of course, but I ask Maruti now, newly emboldened. And he does know of it, but of course he knows of a better, very special shop where I can buy some fine Mysore silk at the very best price.

I cannot now escape. I have brought this upon myself. I am condemned to 45 uncomfortable minutes, being shown every piece of silk in the shop – silk I have no interest in buying. Of maintaining equidistance between complete disinterest, which would be rude, and the merest trace of interest in any particular piece, which would open one-sided bargaining about the price of something I wanted at no price.

Already, Maruti is standing to escort me to the door of a shop some few hundred metres away, to guide me through the chaos of the Mysore street, past the crowd jostling to see the matinee performance of *Om Shanti Om* at the Opera Theatre cinema. A massive billboard cut-out image of Shahrukh Khan towers above the theatre, a gaudy Colossus. Beyond the Hotel Dynasty, we weave through the hot mass of people and into the cool, quiet compound of the Mysore Silk Emporium.

Maruti ensures that the shopkeeper – I can trace no obvious family resemblance – registers who has delivered the wealthy westerner to his store. Then with a last flash of that same broad, energetic grin with which he had greeted me earlier, he disappears into the seething crush beyond the courtyard. I walk into the shop, resigned.

...

I drop the packet onto the little marble-topped table by my bed – the two pieces of furniture in my hotel room. The packet, Rs 2500 of silk, wrapped in yesterday's Deccan Herald, stares at me accusingly. I stare back at it, and wonder what I'm going to do with it. I feel a fool. She is not going to wear it now. Fool. I am the owner of a frankly pointless, over-priced, emerald green silk shawl.

It's now 4pm and there is not much to do until I eat: I'm tired and there is only so much wandering through the tangled streets that I can face, only so much of the heady sights, sounds and smells of this city that can be absorbed before they become garish, overwhelming, sickly. It's not like it's my first time here – I've done the sights, got the measure of the town. After my weakness in the Silk Emporium, I think some time resting is best, all things considered. I kick off my sandals and slump onto the uncertain bed, the sheet still crumpled from last night.

My small, spartan room is at least clean: the grey marble floor is washed daily, the crumpled sheet is actually white, and the beige walls are largely free of marks. A fairly typical, good Rs 350 sort of place. Rs 2500, on a shawl? A shawl no-one, now, is ever going to wear? Clean and tidy, basic but friendly. Not a bad place to end up, but certainly very different from my last trip to Mysore. Then, rather than this budget affair close to the market, it had been a heritage hotel on the outskirts of town, set in a small palace. A palace much more tasteful than the monstrosity in the centre of the city, certainly. Not only had there been furniture, but decoration; not simply staff that are friendly, but that were helpful and efficient. It had cost rather more – about the same price as a green silk shawl – but it was much more fitting for that trip. And Lainey would have hated the Hotel Gayathri.

But she's not here, so it will be buses and Rs 350 rooms and dirty dhabas; seeing these cities and temples again, but from a different angle, a more authentic perspective, the way I used to see India, before Lainey. It feels strange to be here again, of course, without her. In this city, in Karnataka.

Maybe Richard was right. Perhaps this was a mistake; not a starting over, nor a moving on, after all. He had called it a pilgrimage. More a hopeless, poisonous return than a soul-saving reclamation. Like that elephant, revisiting my loss until it overwhelms me, saps the life and energy from me. Is this journey simply one more error on my part?

The elephant returns unbidden, without restraint. Maruti's story will not finish with me and, lying in the damp heat, I rake over the tragedy of their ending. The parallels to my own situation seem obvious, as if the boy had been sent to give me solace, or at least some explanation of my fall.

I close my eyes, head sinking into the pillow, and start to drift again into melancholy. Forcing myself into alertness, I open my eyes and turn my thoughts to practicalities, to where I might eat later. I pick up the guide book and flip through to the section on

Eating in Mysore, scanning the names and descriptions to see if anywhere sounds interesting, diverting. I am distracted almost immediately by the map at the start of the Karnataka section, absorbing the shape of the state and the names of its cities.

Without pausing to consider it, I pick up the phone by the bed and dial 0. A friendly voice answers and I ask if he can secure me a bus ticket for tomorrow to Badami.

2

GARBO

After the babble of introductions and the shaking of hands, there is silence. The carpet soaks up the last of the cordial exchanges, and all trace of conviviality drains into its depths. There is only awkwardness now.

I wonder how much a table like this would cost: how many cases won, how many contracts concluded before this expanse of walnut could be justified in fees. How much have these glumly smiling men earned in the few minutes since we were ushered into the still air of this boardroom? I know only that we aren't paying and so I am content to wait, taking in the view of the remaining scraps of London's Roman walls.

Time slips by. I have never been entirely clear about my role in such circumstances. I requested the meeting, on behalf of my client, so in many ways it is his meeting, to use as he sees fit. But Martin seems disinterested. I am not surprised: what did I expect from a man in his thirties who still doesn't know when it is appropriate to wear a suit. I look from his jeans to the crisp, dull tailoring of the three men facing us and wonder which of us,

Martin or I, look more ridiculous to them. There is at least an authenticity to Martin's clothes, while my suit cost less than one of their shirts. I wish I had worn a tie.

Finally, I decide. If the first move is not to be made by Martin, then who? Not by Chloe, she is simply the intern, brought only to demonstrate our seriousness, and even I would not expect her to take responsibility for this. I run my gaze lightly across the three faces across from me. They are impassive, content to watch and wait. There is, then, only me. I am the go-between, the pimp, the interlocutor. Regardless of precedence, it is for me to break through the dead air.

'So, should we get cracking? I know you guys must be busy and we don't want to keep you longer than we have to.'

Ever since I left home I have revelled in the ambiguity of my accent. Southerners think that I am from the north; everyone else makes wild guesses, but few people can recognise an East Midlands accent. For the most part, it amuses me that something that should mark me, locate and designate me, should in fact be a camouflage. In the dawning days at university, I soon gave up on the frustration at their confusion and ignorance, and began to enjoy teasing the southern girls from expensive schools. I found hiding behind myself liberating. But here, now, I am simply conscious that my voice sounds coarse. I can make no claim to this terrain and my insufficiency turns over in my chest.

'Yes. Yes, I suppose we should make a start. However, we are still expecting one of our colleagues, so if we could just wait for a few moments longer...

The door opens as if at their command; a gentle sigh as the air rushes in to equalise the pressure.

'Ah, Ms Driscoll. Welcome, welcome. Do come in. I think you know Mr Bradbury? And this is Mr Cooper.'

She shakes hands with each of the three men in turn, her arm moving with supple precision. I can tell from their nervous smiles and the sudden colour in their cheeks that they too are aware that Ms Driscoll is devastatingly attractive.

'Mr Lodge, Mr Townsend, Ms Stopes, allow me to introduce my colleague, Ms Driscoll. Ms Driscoll is over from our New York office, and I am sure we shall benefit from her expertise.'

'Please, call me Lainey. Very pleased to meet you.'

And then she is shaking my hand. The cool of her skin evokes the bisque porcelain bust of the young Queen that had fascinated me during dreary visits to my long-dead grandmother. The small scar above the knuckle of her middle finger is the only blemish on her otherwise flawless hand. Later, I will learn that it was the price of her obstinacy with knuckle-headed racists in Spanish Harlem during her college days. But here, in this first instant of our acquaintance, I can only think that it resembles a crescent moon, a celestial birthmark. I stand watching it while everyone else takes their seats.

'Mr Townsend? Maybe we could begin?'

I clatter my way into my chair without grace or dignity. Lainey Driscoll smiles discreetly in my direction; she holds my eye longer than any woman I have ever met. It is a quiet and intoxicating display of self assurance.

While Mr Barnard, the senior of the three grey skinned men, rehearses the details of the situation I remain transfixed by Ms Driscoll. I trace the loose strands of her copper red curls as they snake down from where she has piled them artfully; their wilfulness suggests a chaotic effervescence barely contained by the limits of her navy blue business suit. Her intervention is as surprising to me as it is to her senior colleagues.

'So, gentlemen, as I understand it, you are seeking permission to use images of the artist and of some of his works, the rights to which are the property of our client, in order to promote an exhibition of other works by the same artist, the ownership of which is not held by our client. Is that correct?'

Lainey's words seep only slowly into me, yet the way her collar bone shifts in the shadow of the open neck of her tailored white shirt strikes me like hot metal.

'Err, yes. That is a very succinct summation of the matter, yes.'

There is a small sigh, and an exchange of glances between Ms Driscoll and Mr Barnard.

'You do realise, Mr Townsend, that such permissions will only be granted by our client on certain stringent conditions of use as well as payment of an appropriate disbursement. It is likely to be a significant disbursement.'

Each syllable is clearly, deliberately enunciated, conveying some sense of just how significant the required disbursement would be.

'Mr Townsend, Mr Lodge, I'm afraid I can see no possible

reason for further negotiation on this point. The permissions you have been granted by, uh, Mr Liebowitz, the owner of the works you are seeking to display, in no way affect the rights retained by our client. I can, if I am honest gentlemen, see no value in continuing this discussion further. Application to licence the images can be made via Ms Hopkins in Mr Barnard's office.'

That we had got this far was incredible, a testament to my naivety and presumption and to my urgent need for this to work. Despite the near certainty that the outcome of this meeting will lead to me losing my only client, my biggest regret is that my meeting with her is soon to be over.

I watch her hands as she pats her papers into a crisp and orderly block. Beside me, Martin is shifting impatiently in his chair; his expectant eyes glare at me, but I do not turn to face them, choosing instead to savour the last of Lainey Driscoll.

Abruptly, she pauses in her preparations to leave. Head tilted, with something like a smile, she looks quizzically over at me.

'Forgive me, but I'm a little confused. Why don't you simply use the pictures you already have for your promotion?'

'That is a very reasonable question, Ms Driscoll, and I am confident that there is an equally reasonable answer to it.'

The answer, in truth, is remarkably straightforward: none of the paintings are all that good. I had not known that of course, sitting outside Martin's office six months ago. The contract with Martin's gallery had been the opportunity I had needed and that was all that had mattered. I had not expected to win the work:

the relocation of one of London's most fashionable galleries was properly the business of more established agencies, but I had pursued Interim relentlessly until they capitulated and invited me in to pitch. I still knew very little about contemporary art, had yet to learn its language and its memes and it was only as I waited to be shown through that I realised I had nothing to offer but speculative bravado.

It was then that I remembered the art collector I had been introduced to the previous year in New York. He owned some of the early work of a young artist from Brooklyn. The artist had died of a heroin overdose a decade before, but one of his pieces had just been sold in London for an obscene amount of money. There had been a well-received biopic a couple of years previously and that was still doing the rounds on VHS. His was the ideal name to mark the opening of the new gallery space, to provide a little stardust to smooth Interim's move from the West End to Bethnal Green, a place that is still a little off the beaten track for the people who buy art, if not for those who make it. I pitched the idea of a minor retrospective of the work of this young dead artist as the centrepiece to a promotional campaign. Martin liked it; the contract was won. It was then that I discovered that Ari Liebowitz's six paintings were early, minor works.

So, I raised the stakes. I had to. Interim was my first significant client in the year since we had founded the agency, and I had no others on the horizon. While Gareth had brought over a number of his more interesting clients from the PR agency where we had met, I had decided that I was going to start completely anew.

I had spent years writing banal copy for products I hated: for the first time since I had left the empty, deathly places of my childhood and youth, and had rushed headlong towards the heat and light of London's crucible, I was finally shaping myself, my life, and the world around me.

Like London, I wanted to make my own landscape, to free myself from the confines of the predictable undulations of my topography. The same low hills rippled across the ground on which London stood, but the city itself made mountains and chasms, valleys and cliffs, forests and clearings: the city made its natural foundations unrecognisable.

The idea of specialising in arts promotion – at the corporate end, rather than the dull and worthy world of Arts Council grants – had seemed the right thing to do, bringing a degree of glamour, of meaning and cultural kudos, as well as earning potential. That had seemed all the more prescient in the afterglow of the *Sensation* exhibition. It had to work.

Lainey is still waiting; everyone is waiting, even Chloe. But I say none of this, simply hold the moment, the luxury of her watching me. Martin breaks the spell.

'Well, thanks for your time gentlemen, Miss. We'll have a conflab about things and let you know how we want to proceed. You've been very clear about the matter, and I am grateful. Lots for me to discuss with Mr Townsend.'

The arcs of her eyebrows flash upwards fractionally, and I shrug in reply. In the jade glint of her eyes, there is mischief and empathy in equal measure. Then it is over. She stacks her papers, thanks her colleagues, and turns to the door. There is one last instant of intimacy as her hand closes around mine, but it passes too soon. I return to the office to await Martin's inevitable phone call.

...

The bar is reassuringly shadowy, sombre even. It is busy and there is a pleasant after work buzz to the place. The customers huddle around low tables on battered leather sofas and drink Eastern European lager and white wine from the New World. Almost all are in their twenties. Outside, the lights and vibrations of traffic, of buses and taxis and vans, shudder past the reeded window panes, set in pale wooden frames. This is a public house in the millennial style.

I am alone, drinking a lager I have never heard of from the Czech Republic. It has been a fraught afternoon: after losing the contract last week, I have been calling in as many favours as I can, pitching wildly, unsuccessfully, to anyone who will listen. Another failed attempt has just ended and, not wanting to go home, or back to the office, to talk to anyone, to see anyone I know, I have ended up here. It is a fine place to hide and to drink.

The voice pulls me back from my sour thoughts. She sounds like a movie. It is lighter, more mischievous, but it is undoubtedly Lainey Driscoll. I scan the darkened bar in the direction of the voice. It rises and recedes in the spaces created by the blandest of music, which I notice only now that it has become an obstruction. She is laughing, and it is the lightest, sweetest sound I have ever heard. I scan the faces, the shapes, of a small group standing at the foot of the stairs, but none of them is distinctly her.

I strain to hear their voices. Two British women, one definitely Scottish, and two men – I can't make out their accents, their deep voices are lost in the rumble of the bar. And there is the American. She is wearing a broad-brimmed felt hat, dark green, that obscures most of her face and her copper red curls. It hadn't occurred to me that she might wear something other than the rigid business suit, and I am startled to recognise her in the hat and camel overcoat.

I am excited and panicked. While I had hoped that I would run into her again, I didn't believe I would, and now that it has happened, I have no idea how to ensure that she does not disappear once more into the swirl of London. I am not feeling talkative and she is with people. Friends? Colleagues? Were she on her own, I pretend that it would be straightforward, an easy thing to do, to approach, to say 'hi', to begin a conversation that might not end in my humiliation. But she is not alone: I would be intruding, and I have no idea if she would welcome the intrusion. Frozen, I stare at the inch of lager in front of me and contemplate melting into the evening, avoiding the fool I might make of myself, even at the cost of losing her again.

'James? It is James, right?'

She has taken six long strides across the room and is beside me, her green eyes scanning my face from under the brim of her hat, looking down at my slumped and seated shape.

'Look, sorry if I'm interrupting anything, but I just saw you and wanted to come over to check there were no hard feelings after last Wednesday? You know, the Basquiat thing?'

She rocks minutely on her ankles and shoots a quick glance back to her colleagues.

'Of course, not a problem. We were completely out of our depth on that one, the gallery really should have done their homework. I'm just sorry that they had to drag you over from the States. Are you with Saunders' people?' I nod to the four figures by the stairs, 'You seem to be in civvies this evening, so I wondered... I like the hat, by the way.'

I want to suck the words back into me the moment they leave me mouth. She probably thinks I'm being sarcastic. About the hat. I'm not. I do really like it. It reminds me of one Greta Garbo is wearing in a photograph I like. I stand up, to make the conversation a little less tilted, and notice that our eyes are level. I want to look at her feet, to see if she really is this tall, but know how this would appear.

'Thank you,' she adjusts the brim needlessly. 'No, they're friends, good friends. Morag – in the blue – I've known for years, and that's her husband, with the beard. The other two I don't know, to be honest: friends of Morag, and I've only just been introduced. I'm terrible with names. Anyhow, I'm staying with Morag and David, just until I sort out an apartment. You see you didn't drag me over here; I've decided to give London a go for a while.' Another glance back to her friends. 'Why don't you join us? Unless you're waiting for someone, of course'

'No, no. I'm just hiding from the world.'

'Do you owe money?'

I want to tell her that, yes, I do owe money – to the banks, to my business partner, to my flatmate, and all on account of our previous meeting. But instead I laugh, and the laughter feels like a balm. The smile will not drop from my face; I do not want its lightness to leave me ever.

'Come over. Hide from the world with us. We're all fugitives ourselves, in our own ways.'

That beguiling boldness again; were I to want to resist, I would not be able. So I follow in her wake, as Lainey Driscoll parts the crush of drinkers and leads me across the bar. I wonder where such composure is made; how she can be so compelling with so little noise. And I wonder where my maudlin bitterness has gone.

'What have you found now, girl?'

'Now, Morag, play nice. This is James. I met him through work. He's in hiding.'

'Oooh, that makes you much more interesting. From the law? Or from a lover? By the looks of you, I'd guess lover. '

She wants me to pull my eyes away, to reveal my untrustworthiness, but I am good at this game.

'Neither, I'm afraid. Rather from the disappointments of the world. I find pubs make good hiding places.'

Morag laughs respectfully, and winks at Lainey. She allows herself to warm to me.

'The lament of the tragic poet down the ages. Hmm, you've a nice smile, too; you can stay. Don't worry, we'll provide you with sanctuary.'

Lainey's hand is on my arm, and it is warm now: I can feel its warmth seeping through my shirt and into my skin. It is the same cool hand that I had shaken only a few days before, but here, in the conviviality of this bar, it carries now a heat that had been absent, or hidden, at our first meeting.

'You'll have to forgive Morag: she's a journalist. As is David, but David is much better house-trained.'

We shake hands and I note that there is none of Morag's mischief in his eyes, no playfulness at all. He is weighing my soul.

'Nice to meet you. And how do you know Lainey, David?'

'Through Morag. I'm married to Morag. She's known Lainey longer than she's known me, which rather makes us all 'Johnny-come-latelies' to this party. They're very close.' Scottish too; a heavy, slow voice. 'So, are you a lawyer too?'

I am conscious that, behind me, Lainey and Morag are now tightly bound in conversation, that there will be no easy way to break in and that I will probably spend the next hour or so talking to David. It is a heart-sinking prospect. I look to the other two in the party, in the hope that maybe one or both of them will be able to rescue the evening. But the woman simply stares at the glass turning in her hand and will not catch my eye; the man watches me nervously, his eyes darting away every time I look in his direction.

'No, not a lawyer. Actually, I'm in the art business.'

David tilts his head, inviting me to say more. There is something hostile in his expectancy, and I know enough about journalists to bide my time, to wait for his next question.

'So, do you paint? I mean, it's an interesting turn of phrase, the art 'business'. Funny to see art in those terms, isn't it? Paul, is that common parlance these days? Paul is a reviewer, writes on the arts pages at the paper.'

Paul relaxes now that he has been included in the conversation on familiar and comfortable terms. A smile stretches across his face like a cat settling into a favourite chair.

'Theatre reviewer, David, theatre. Not necessarily the line that James here is in, you know. But, to be honest with you, in my world, it's very common to describe the business as, uh, a business. There's no business like it, as they say.'

He chuckles, supremely pleased with himself. I take the opportunity to introduce myself, first to Paul, then to his colleague. Claire looks fleetingly in my direction while we shake hands, but returns immediately to the study of her drink.

'Indeed. What about you, David. What's your, um, talent?'

His face flexes and I wonder if I've gone too far in my choice of words.

'Not sure I'd call it a talent, but I write about politics. International affairs, mainly.'

'You're hiding your light as usual David! David is one of the country's leading international correspondents. He won last year's Orwell Prize for his reporting on the war in the DRC.'

Paul's intervention causes David to dip his head, almost bowing, hiding his satisfaction in his beard. I notice that Claire has now left her drink unwatched and is beaming at David in something like awe. Even though I have no idea what any of these things mean, I realise it is a big deal and offer my congratulations.

'Are you bragging about your award again, my love?'

Morag's arms fold around the thick torso of her husband. Claire's eyes return to her glass and David roars with genuine laughter.

'Of course, my dear. As you know, I never cease. Now, I think it's your round.'

I take the opportunity of Morag's absence to free myself from David and to return to Lainey.

'They're nice. I'd imagine it's fun at their house.'

Her face blooms with recognition, and she swallows what's left of her wine with a flick of the head. The hat has gone, rested somewhere, and some strands of hair escape; she tucks them carelessly back up into the pile on top of her head. I long for her to touch my arm again, but she does not.

'It is! But I kind of knew what to expect. We shared an apartment in New York, you see, when she was over doing her post grad at Columbia. I was still a Bachelor's student, final year, and I guess we should have been working hard a little more often than we did.'

Still more of the rigidity in which I had dressed her at our first meeting melts away. I picture her as the carefree, student Lainey, fizzing with energy and curiosity. She is light and open, but never wanton; tipsy, not drunken. In her awakened memories, her lightness shines even in this dim-lit London bar. I realise I am grinning, and straighten my face.

'Why law? If you don't mind me asking.'

'I don't know. I guess because my dad's a lawyer. It never occurred to me that I'd be anything else. It just seemed like the right thing to do with my life. Not the intellectual property thing. Not that. God, no. That just happened. I had debts to pay and, well, you know how it goes, right? Besides, I wanted to stay in the city and a job came up, so…'

She tells me that, after a decade long romance with New York City, she wanted to try somewhere else before she turned thirty. London had seemed sufficiently alike and sufficiently different; her firm's branch office here had made it all remarkably easy. It was inevitable that, once she had crossed the ocean, she would move into Morag and David's dilapidated house on Clapham Common.

'I met David for the first time just before their wedding. I came over a couple of weeks before, to help Morag out. They'd met on the paper: he was the rising star, and she was the bright new cub reporter. It was a whirlwind romance, very sweet.'

Morag is back with the drinks just in time to laugh a caustic laugh on the word 'sweet'. I will her to leave us to each other, but she takes up her position at Lainey's elbow, a jealous chaperone. Morag watches her ward with scepticism.

'It was too. Even Jake thought it was a beautiful wedding, and he doesn't have a scrap of romance in him.'

'Jake?'

I try to maintain an air of casual disinterest, but Morag knows, is studying my face as soon as Lainey mentions his name, before my too hasty question.

'Jake? Um, my ex. Well, I guess he's my ex now.'

Morag smiles and waits, the same hostile expectancy as David had displayed earlier. Why did both of them so want me to reveal myself as inappropriate, unwelcome? I will not give them the satisfaction.

'That's often how it goes when you change cities. Love can be quite site-specific. It's rare for it to translate easily, and it is intolerant of distance. It doesn't have to be like that of course, but that's how it's been for me, thus far at least.'

Morag's scepticism is now turned on me, but she was not my intended audience, and Lainey has softened further. The rest of the bar, of London, no longer matters; everything is to be found in the green of those eyes.

'David said you were something in the arts. But he thought you were a dealer, not a poet.'

Again. I am tiring of their inquisition, but respond with a laugh.

'No, Morag, I'm not a poet: I read enough of those at college to know that that was not where my talents lay, no matter how hard I wished. Nor am I a dealer. No, I've got a little arts promotions agency. Not as lucrative as dealing, nor as exciting as actually painting, but it keeps me near something I love, but in a capacity for which I have a talent.'

Of course, two of us know that those talents are limited, but Lainey does not mention Interim. She has retrieved her hat and is turning it slowly by the brim, as if she is waiting for something, considering carefully her next move, my next move. Her coyness is unexpected, perfect. We both watch her lithe fingers manipulate the soft felt brim for a moment. In forgetting Morag, I realise what to do.

'Actually, you know, one of my clients is having a private view next week. It's pretty good work actually, if you're interested in art. A little place in Shoreditch: think Williamsburg, that sort of area. I could get you on the list, if you wanted to come, see something of non-corporate London?'

A glass drops to the floor behind the bar. There is a cheer and then laughter. I hear the barmaid swear gently, feel her embarrassment under the glare of the customers' mockery. Only slowly does the hubbub return to its former familiar rumble and all the while I watch Lainey and Lainey watches me.

'That sounds like fun. I'd like that, James. I'd really like that.'

It is after closing time when the four of us finally leave. The evening is already chill, the warmth of the day having slipped from the city's stones into the darkness above. Claire and Paul had disappeared as soon as the clock edged past ten, so I walk with Lainey, with Morag and David lost a few paces behind, as far as the tube station. They say their goodbyes at the bottom of the escalators and rush for the southbound platform and the train that has just arrived. There is no time for hugs or handshakes.

I stand for a moment, waiting, in case Lainey decides to turn back, to throw herself at me, let me take her home with me. But she doesn't, and I become embarrassed to be standing in the middle of the concourse, awkward and inebriated. A couple of minutes after the southbound train has left, I turn towards the other platform.

Waiting, I consider my daydream. Was there any basis for the thought that Lainey might come back for me? She had given me her phone number easily, willingly, and had agreed to see me again. But we had barely touched, certainly not kissed. Her interest in the private view might simply be an interest in art. Her willingness to talk openly about her pathway to London, her openness to being befriended, might simply be the openness that all newcomers feel when they arrive, isolated, in a strange city.

As far as I could tell, her only friends on this side of the Atlantic were Morag and David, and through them a handful of others. Why wouldn't she seek to widen that circle? She had met me in the office, so I wasn't a complete stranger, was probably not dangerous, and in any case she had had her friends with her. Why not talk to me, tell me about herself, ask me about my London? All of this would be consistent with a dislocated person rebuilding themselves in a new location, a woman crossing the Atlantic to develop her career, to realise her potential: her displacement had been to expand her horizons, not to close them down. The train arrives and I board, casting one last look along the platform.

3

BALM

Friday shudders to its end. There is still no replacement for the Interim contract; no work at all, to be honest. What had seemed like a foolproof way to make money was proving perfectly fallible for me. Gareth was at least billing something, having retained some of his lower key clients. Me, I had thrown it all over for the cultural grand event, for Art. And now, staring at the dying minutes of Friday late afternoon, I have one book launch and one private view left on my horizon.

The private view. The angry red ring around the date reminds me of the other great failure of my week. It is now three days since Lainey Driscoll had given me her number, written in a fluid hand on the back of her business card, and I have still not phoned, not wanting to add yet another fruitless call to the list of the week's fruitless calls.

But something about the week's closing stirs in me the memory of the lightness I had felt talking with her. I want more than anything to feel it now. I pick up the phone and, with neither commitment nor enthusiasm, dial the number she had given me for her office. Before my self-pity solidifies into a decision to hang up, her voice is in my ear, prim, business-like. There is no trace of mischief: not like a movie at all.

I start to explain who I am, to establish in her mind the reason why I might be calling. Hesitancy frays the edges of my words and she interrupts before I can stutter my surname. There is something that sounds like excitement in her voice and I scan it to determine whether it is real or simply my willing it. I give up, it being my turn to say something.

'How've you been? I hope you don't mind me calling. At work, I mean. But I just wanted to see if you were still interested, maybe, in going to the private view I mentioned on Tuesday.'

There is a pause. A little breath.

'That would be great, James. I was really hoping you'd call. The show sounds like it will be fun.'

We arrange a time and a place to meet and say our farewells. As I replace the receiver in its cradle, my grin breaks wider; I dance a little in my chair.

'Tell me that was a client, James. Please, send me into weekend with some good news."

I had not realised that Gareth was coming back to the office this afternoon; he had been out at a client meeting in the East End. His diligence feels like a rebuke.

'Afraid not, mate. Actually, I was making a date with a very attractive American.'

'Now that is interesting. Give me details!'

One thing that could always distract Gareth from concerns

about the business was the merest hint of gossip, particularly of romance. Whenever he was berating me for failing to bring in work, respite required only a little invented indiscretion on the part of someone we hardly knew within the industry.

'She's drop-dead gorgeous, of course. But it's not just that: she's got this composure about her. I've never met anyone with that degree of self-confidence who hasn't been an arrogant sod. Not a trace of it. What I wouldn't give to have one tenth of that certainty about myself.'

'I think she might be a little out of your league, Jim Bob, but I wish you well. Where'd you meet her?'

Despite the extravagant smirk, Gareth's observation feels all too perceptive. Dampening down my resurgent doubts, I manage a sour glare in return.

'That's the thing. She's a lawyer. Works for Saunders. She's the one that sank the Interim contract....'

'Sleeping with the enemy, huh?'

'Oh god, I hope so.'

...

Those first weeks were an undefined sequence of encounters and partings, late nights and endless weekend afternoons. Every minute was spent either with Lainey or thinking about being with her. We had started moderately enough. As we had spilled from the gallery into the darkness, drunk on the cheap wine and the absurdity of Shoreditch, she had turned to me, falling slightly from her heels and throwing her arms around my neck for support. I never worked out if she had really stumbled, but we had kissed nonetheless. There had been desire, and her eyes had sparkled when finally the embrace was broken; I could feel her breathing speeding towards abandon, but I had put her in a cab headed south and made my own way north, alone.

But restraint, physical and emotional, had not lasted. The affair had become a relationship in a matter of days. The progress from doubt to open abandon and back to doubt again seemed familiar, despite its dizzying pace. I convinced myself that she regarded me as something other than simply another node in her growing London network shortly after I had played the breathless, girlish answer phone message that awaited me when I got home that night from Shoreditch. The message earnestly hoped that I had had a good evening, and that I still wanted to see her again.

The following days, weeks maybe, had been emotionally dramatic: anything seemed possible, and everything wonderful. My desire and affection for her grew exponentially and in that perfect, halcyon moment, they were indistinguishable, the one feeding the other. Only a dim but growing awareness of all the reasons why Lainey could not feel as strongly as I did, could not regard me as uncritically as I did her, clouded my euphoria. I could taste on the wind the beginnings of the creeping conviction: it was obvious why I was with her, but less so why she was with me.

The geography of the relationship meant that I needed most of my creative energy and organisational capacity to ensure that I was on the right side of the Thames at the right time. I carried a travel tooth brush and change of underwear in my bag each morning, in case a quick drink after work turned into another night spent in her room in Clapham. Within a month, I could dispense with the travel toothbrush, having installed a brand new, full size one in Morag and David's bathroom.

...

Lainey is late, or maybe I am early. She is still assiduous in her work, despite our own whirlwind romance. I admire this at least as much as I resent it, but now I simply wish that she was here. The noisy conviviality of the bar would ordinarily distract me sufficiently, but not today. Gareth has driven me from the office with his too familiar questions about the likelihood of new clients. But, rather than shaming me for my failure to win work, to really want to win work, he has simply made me ashamed of the work itself. Even here, in the safety of the Liberties Bar, the tawdriness of my working life refuses to leave me be.

Despite my claim to higher things, I am simply trying to shift units on behalf of whichever cretin in skinny jeans is prepared to pay the fee. That I am not very good at it does not alter the essential baseness of my trade. Maybe it is art itself that I do not like: most of the work that I am supposed to package and present I hate in any case, in itself. Why doesn't anyone use paint anymore? Richard paints. He paints things I can recognise: people, places, emotions. There are the echoes of life and pain in his work. Wanting something that is authentic, human, does not make me hideously outmoded. We are both, Gareth and I, charlatans who have sold our souls for a pile of shoddily-stitched plastic and unwanted timber and tin. Not even for the chance to create something, no matter how pointless, but simply to sell it.

If the business is essentially one of shovelling shit, does it really matter if it goes to the wall? Aren't there more important things? Why not go back to the agency, devise campaigns for deodorant? It is as valid, and better paid, than this.

'Sorry I'm late, honey. Am I late?' Lainey checks her watch and shrugs. 'Guess not. Can I get you another? Actually, how many have you had already?'

I hold up one finger and try to slump a little less. She has an energy and joy about her that could only ever refresh me. The familiar business suit no longer seems to constrain her, now that I know how she moves into and out of it, seamlessly, fluidly. Her eyes flash in the lamplight and ignite my first smile of the day. She crosses the room to the bar and her movement provokes a sweet and heady excitement that sustains me until her return.

This time I rise and embrace her, and while we kiss London holds its breath. Peeling away, she smiles, but an imprint of the day's work clings to her, a wound inflicted by yet another engagement with relentless, unforgiving commerce. For all my dissatisfactions, I know that she too has her share. A lawyer, yes, but not one acting in the high halls of justice. She serves the integrity of commodities, rather than people: intangibles maybe, but commodities none the less. It does not make her happy, even if she is rather more successful at her trade than I am at mine.

'God, am I pleased to see you. Gareth was being an arse again. Wants me to take on some idiot's show, but it's rubbish. Utter, utter rubbish. There are times, you know, when I just want to chuck it all in. If I'm going to sell my soul, I might as well get a good price for it.'

The beer swims down my throat, to drown the incipient self-pity. I know she understands all this at least as well as I do. While my job leaves me empty, it at least has a sheen of glamour, a trace of creativity, an aspiration to higher meaning.

'There's not a lot of solace in that, trust me. And at least you're around something you love. And making money isn't an unfortunate by-product of work, you know? Sometimes you might have to settle for something instead of nothing, or work harder to land those contracts that you think are good enough for you.'

It was going to be different. In a bar very much like this one, I had sat with Richard, my oldest friend, plotting out my route to fulfilment in art. He had encouraged me, not quite realising that his very existence was the only encouragement I needed. His realness, his integrity was sufficient incentive. Through those formative days of Mercury Associates, I clamped close to my chest the knowledge that all I was doing was attempting to be more like Richard.

'How do you do it? I mean, I know you hate your job too, that it makes you unhappy. You're a talented lawyer, you're so smart: you could do anything you wanted.'

She had described it to me, how her life might have been, while we were locked in the languid embrace of twisted sheets and drowsiness. Two weeks into our affair, we had finally found ourselves in bed together, naked and unguarded. In the undertow of passion, her uncertainty surged out into the dark air. Carried on the slow rhythms of her heartbeat, her head rising and falling on my chest in time with my breathing, she told me about the wrongs she had dreamed of righting, the good she had planned to bring to the world. Not for her the fiery justice of her vainglorious college comrades; she saw herself as an instrument of rationality and reconciliation. But money and things had left her only with due process and the rights of objects, rather than of people. I had lost my fingers curling through her hair and she had slept, leaving me to guard over her sadness. Even her sadness was nobler than mine.

'It's not that bad. A little like you. Some of it is what you hoped for; the rest, well that's the price you pay. I'm not sure anyone gets it all: not even David, with his purity and the privilege of his writing. I bet the office politics are dreadful.' She laughs and everything sparkles. 'I know, let's go see some art at the weekend. Something good. Something old. Something in oils.'

And with that she dissolves the day's dissatisfaction and carries me back into the light.

4

Velocity

I'd always known. From the first time she had looked into my eyes with possibility rather than containment, with a smile, with vulnerability, I'd known that there would be hurt, pain. It was a certainty that formed in me at the very moment that we had fallen towards each other. There would be hurt, unforgiving hurt, and despite the easy blooming of our shared intimacy, the giddy joy of it all, I knew that its arrival was inevitable.

But despite my certainty, I had not tried to step from the inevitable line that would lead there, had not held back from its embrace, from her. Of course, my certainty had been that she would hurt me. It would be my hurt, my pain, rather than hers. And perhaps it had been that, the knowledge that I would be the victim, that had made bearable the shadow of certain, unbearable hurt.

Of course it is easy to say with hindsight that I had known from the very beginning. But I stand by the claim, even though there are no witnesses, never were. It was a secret conviction. Maybe that fatalism, conceived at exactly the same time as the relationship itself, had secured its own inevitability. Was this the moment at which the relationship started to die? In knowing that loving Lainey led to immeasurable hurt, I had set about creating a relationship, a story of the two of us, that could lead only there. Perhaps travelling hopelessly can only ever deliver you into despair; to reach a place of happiness, maybe you need to set off in the conviction that that is where you are headed. Maybe next time I will remember that, will be able to begin the journey as an optimist.

But back then, despite my conviction that we were bound irrevocably to a future of hurt, of hurting each other, I threw myself willingly into love with her. If we were to end in pain, I was going to suck every drop of joy out of the meantime. With reckless abandon, I flew towards her.

...

Most of the leaves had already gone from the trees and the earth was still wet from several days of rain. But a few patches of grey dryness, drab supernovae, were forming in the darkness of the asphalt along the pathways. It was a bright day, unusual for that damp autumn. The low sun arced across a clear sky, and people were scattered across the Common, walking off their Sunday lunch as we were. But they were relatively few in number and the low rumble of traffic along South Side disappeared into itself, creating a sense, in London terms, of intimate seclusion.

Lainey had called to suggest lunch at the pub in Clapham Old Town, and I had rolled down the Northern Line to meet her. Like her growing taste for whisky, her embrace of the Sunday roast signalled to me that she was assimilating successfully, making the transition from one context to another with ease, becoming essentially European, while retaining of course the exoticism of her foreignness. I liked this cultural ambiguity, this dexterity.

There was something about the day: she had held me longer and closer than usual when I emerged into the sunlight at Clapham Common station, and had tightly bound her arm through mine as we walked the short distance to the Old Town. I welcomed the closeness and leant into her, gently but steadily, not allowing any space to come between us.

'It's like a late autumn day in New York – makes me think of home.'

'And that makes you happy?'

Why was I doing this? Laying a trap for her, a chance for her to hurt me? I wished the words unsaid, but the snare was already set. Lainey, of course, was too smart to blunder into it: she brought us to a halt and slid around to face me, never once letting her hand lose contact with me.

'Of course it does. Doesn't mean I don't want to be here with you, if that's what you mean. Those days in the City were happy, just like today. I'm thinking of home because it's a place full of happiness, just like right here, right now. You know?'

'Not really. Different sort of family. But I would like to meet yours. See where you came from; how you got to be so lovely.'

She pulled me closer and, her face nestled in my neck, I could swear that she was purring. After a minute of two, I slipped her embrace and, clutching her hand, guided her towards The Sun.

Heads bowed like conspirators, our conversation over lunch had been a blizzard of quiet confidences. The busy pub barely intruded, and when it did press its way between us, we each responded with a frosty aversion, until we had forced closed the door to our private exchange. Our capsule accompanied us on our walk later around the Common. We talked about our families, our fears and our fantasies. We had both explained our frustrations with the furniture of our lives, how far we were from what we had hoped to become; we speculated on how we might yet be all that we could be. We talked about the mountains and the sea and what kind of happiness could be found in each. We talked about god, happy to discover that neither of us had much room for him – she the only daughter of East Coast liberal academics, me the second son of agnostic, middle class Midlanders with other things to worry about. And beneath the threadbare trees we confessed our unique love for each other for the first time, as if revealing a fundamental truth with peaceful dignity.

The day's light was almost gone by the time we made it to Lainey's, its warmth sucked up into the clear sky. We kissed like teenagers on the step before she slid her key into the lock and the door swung open. I had been in that hallway many times before, but there was something different that afternoon: an expectancy hung in the thickening air. Noise and light stumbled from the kitchen and we made our way towards it.

David sat at the broad table, lost in the creases of the *Observer*, while Morag busied herself at the stove. Invisible behind their respective distractions, we watched from the doorway until Lainey's discomfort at her intrusion overwhelmed her and she made our presence known.

"Man, something smells good. Is that your bolognese, Morag? My god, James, Morag makes the best bolognese. The best. Please, M, tell me there's enough for me?'

Morag was already across the room, her arm around Lainey's shoulder, and a kiss for me. David sang his hellos from his seat, the paper rapidly folded into asymmetric leaves and tossed into the basket by the fridge.

'Of course, hen. Enough for James, too – are you well, James, by the way? You look well. To be honest, I was getting worried you'd decided to stay out to eat, that we'd miss you. You see, all this is in aid of a celebration. We've got some news. David, get the fizz out will you, love?'

As he filled our glasses, David explained that he had landed a book deal, giving him leave of absence from the *Guardian* for a couple of years. But the champagne was in another cause. The new job had opened up other opportunities it seemed, the chance to do something they had long wanted to do. They were leaving London to return to Scotland, had bought an old farmhouse in the middle of nowhere. They were going to rebuild it, while David wrote polemic and Morag raised vegetables.

'We always knew that we'd go back someday, and this is just the right place for us now: somewhere that David can write, not too far off the beaten track; I can be in London in just four and a half hours, door to door. And it's beautiful. You'll come and visit?'

Lainey threw her arms around Morag, only just holding onto the tears that she wanted to shed, conscious that she did not want her loss to contaminate her friend's excitement. I left them to their communion and joined David, to shake his hand and pour us both another glass of champagne.

'Congratulations, on the book and the move. I wish I could take a couple of years out to pursue something like that. I am very jealous.'

'Really? You wouldn't miss London? You know, I find it hard to imagine you not in London.'

'Maybe. What about you? Are you not going to miss the cut and thrust of the newsroom? The energy? The excitement?'

David simply shrugged and disappeared into the middle distance, draining his glass. As I topped him up, Morag called us all to the table, and the evening began its slippery glide towards midnight. The food all gone, the wine too, we left the debris for the morning and made our way upstairs; Morag and David said their good nights at the first landing, while Lainey and I carried on up to her little room at the top of the house.

'Well, you were right, that bolognese was phenomenal. I am stuffed.'

I lay on her bed watching her hang tomorrow's clothes on the wardrobe door,

'Yep, Morag is some cook; her food got me through the roughest of times at Columbia. God, I'm going to miss her.'

Later, when the tears were gone and she had pretended to be consoled by the mere five hours that will separate her from her friend, I asked her what she planned to do. She didn't immediately grasp the meaning behind my question.

'When Morag and David have gone, I mean. Where will you live?'

She turned to me, brightening, a smile spread across her naked face.

'That's the thing. While you were getting drunk with David, Morag asked me if I'd be willing to stay on here. They don't want to give up this place, and they don't want to see me on the street either. Of course, I'll miss them, but isn't it marvellous? I mean, I can't afford the rent on my own, but maybe…'

• • •

I snap shut the notebook. All the other passengers have disembarked, but I am anxious to be moving, willing the driver, through my simple presence, to start up the engine and continue the journey north. But he, sitting on the back seat of the bus, is entirely focussed on the newsprint parcel of cold rice and dhal, which he transfers with his fingers to his mouth, relentlessly, rhythmically. He hunches over his meal, knees apart, feet planted firm and flat on the chronically gummy floor. He stares down the aisle, not at me but through me; I turn back into my seat, pushing the notebook into the top of my rucksack. I had refused to let the driver throw my pack onto the roof of the bus and, in the chaos of the KRSTC bus stand, he had conceded, exasperated. I look through the barred window at the other passengers, who are drinking tea and eating vadai and pakodas, fried up at stalls around the bus stand. Four hours into the journey, and another four until Hospet, where I will have to sleep tonight before catching a bus to Badami in the morning.

I am tired already. The alarm woke me at six. Forty five minutes later I had left Hotel Gayathri and set off through the cool morning air towards the bus station. Once past the market, already busy, I had made a detour down to Bombay Tiffany's, where for once, there were no other tourists. The canteen was serving tea and idlis. I joined the locals but ate the small fluffy pillows, drenched in aromatic sauce, with a teaspoon rather than my fingers. Sucking in the hot, sweet, thick tea, I felt my head clearing, becoming focused. Looking up, I noticed fully the extent to which the men around me were ignoring my presence. I simply didn't matter to them.

My invisibility was both welcome and hateful. The insistent attention that had accompanied every previous moment in India was an irritation, an annoyance, and it had marked my difference, my novelty. But even so, being in the spotlight, on stage, being an object of fascination, had always made me feel special. Exceptional. The constant questions and the sensation of eyes, hundreds of eyes, following me along the street had fed the need in me for recognition. Its absence that morning in Bombay Tiffany's simply saddened me.

When Jess and I had visited India, when we were still together, she would have done anything for such anonymity, for this silence. We'd been living together for a couple of years before the trip, after meeting in the hedonism of London's bars and clubs in our mid-twenties. Dark hair, dark eyes, and a job at the Arts Council: Jess had stumbled into my life, and we had ended up in a one bed flat in Tufnell Park. At the time I was merciless in my mockery of her work, but it was through her contacts that I would later be able to make Mercury a reality.

As the months rolled into years, her mother had become increasingly expectant. Yet we had never spoken directly about marriage until we planned that trip to India, when I had claimed another's wisdom as my own and suggested that for convenience's sake we should pretend to be married while we were away. We even bought a cheap ring and, while she laughed, I slid it onto her finger with mock solemnity.

I had first visited India, between A Levels and Reading, with two forgotten school friends. I had fallen for the country, but after two months of chaos and hard work in Rajasthan, I insisted that Jess and I head to the south, where things were more relaxed. She missed out on the Taj Mahal and the pink light of Jaipur, but I assured her that their charms were lost among the crowds and the hassle in any case.

And the south was more relaxed: I was able to re-gloss my earlier experiences in the subcontinent as profound and beautiful, safe in the temples of Tamil Nadu, or drifting on the Keralan backwaters. It was in Tamil Nadu that I first encountered elephants close up. I developed an incomprehensible affection for them. I had kept the photo of me, smiling astride a temple elephant, for another two years, until I left it in Tufnell Park, with Jess.

I was able to replace the picture a few years later, when I came to Karnataka with Lainey. Shortly after I had agreed to move in with her, I had suggested that we should go to India for a few weeks. I loved the country, and I wanted to share it with her, show her the sights, smells and sounds. As Christmas drew nearer, my suggestion became more insistent, although Lainey was preoccupied with the Holidays themselves. She had had her ticket back home for a while, but was agonising over whether I should join her at her parents' home, rather than my own, for Christmas and New Year. I made the trade willingly, buying a ticket on the same United flight, abandoning my mother for a woman she had not met. I bought two tickets to Bangalore on the same day.

5

VERTIGO

His father had woken him early and the night was still dark. They washed and dressed in lamp light while his mother prepared idlis for breakfast. Still half asleep, he ate quickly before he was thrust out into the black street, his father's strong, unforgiving hand pressing into the back of his head.

The pace was stiff and Annayya stumbled over the rough ground. By the time the great ball of the sun had slipped loose of the scant trees to the east, burning away the morning's mist, they were already miles from the village. In the day's growing light they plunged into the forest, following the loggers' road into the heart of the trees. Annayaa wanted to complain about his tiredness, about the pains in his feet and his need to rest, but his father's determination sat angrily on his face. There was no conversation. The boy knew not to ask, nor to offer opinions or observations. He was the youngest son: he knew he owed his father the most perfect respect. So they simply walked relentlessly into the wakening forest.

It was 8 o'clock when they reached the forest station.

The sun's heat had begun to hang heavily in the air. They had walked for four hours to reach this clearing, these few wooden houses and stacks of felled trees, and Annayya was pleased simply to stand still, to rest in the fringes of the forest's shade. After a brief greeting, his father exchanged some words with the agent, a weary man whose age had spread from his eyes, across his face and into his white hair, and was now making its assault on his sagging limbs. With a glance over at the boy, the agent spoke quickly into his father's ear and it was agreed. The three of them walked across the clearing and a little way into the trees.

There, a young bull elephant was clearing whatever vegetation he could reach. Chained by the left forefoot to a large tree, the bull became agitated at their approach. Turning to face them, he raised his trunk and shook out his ears defiantly, before returning to the depleted bush beside him. Once more he began stripping its leaves, wrapping his trunk tightly around the young branches and plucking a green posy to be pushed into his mouth, chewing it down while the trunk went in search of other branches.

He was already over ten feet tall, but despite the young bull's bulk, Annayya was transfixed by the cold amber eye, terrifying and yet immeasurably sad. The boy peered cautiously around his father, his tall, resolute father, behind whom he cowered. At his father's bidding, and with a gentle push in the centre of his back, Annayya approached the bull and placed his palm on the beast's trunk, which was already searching his clothing for the bananas it could smell. Gingerly, Annayya held out the fruit, initially for the searching, irrepressible trunk. As his confidence grew, he pushed bananas directly into the loose triangular flap of a mouth, the sudden tongue pushing each one deep into the grinding jaws.

The visits to the forest became more regular and within weeks Annayya and his father would spend two or three days at a time among the trees, the foresters and the elephants. The daylight hours were spent walking with Iravatha, watching his father instruct and reprimand the beast. In the evenings, Annayya would help out around the station, fetching water, collecting elephant dung for fuel, its smoke dense enough to keep the mosquitoes at bay. In quiet moments, he would slip out into the darkness to check on Iravatha, chained at the edge of the clearing. It was in the quiet of these evenings that the boy began talking to the animal, sharing with it his secrets and dreams.

Later, once they had become better acquainted and Annayya had lost most of his fear, when he had learned the commands and become accustomed to handling the hooked ankus, he had hauled himself up Iravatha's flank, using the elephant's raised knee and the chain that hung around his shoulders, to scale and conquer the elephant mountain. His father had shouted instructions from below as he shuffled gingerly across the secure flatness of Iravatha's broad back, edging forward along the narrowing neck, urged on from the safety of the ground. The rough skin grazed the inside of his knees and the hot pain sent tremors through his already quivering legs. At last, and terrified, Annayya reached the point just behind the elephant's skull, his shins tucked in behind the surprisingly powerful ears, which Iravatha flicked with a broad, hollow slap every now and then. Over the previous weeks, during which he had come to know Iravatha, Annayya had gained a respect and admiration for his massive bulk, but now, from here, perched precariously on the neck some twelve feet in the air, he hated it, hated his father, hated his weakness.

At his father's urging, he planted both palms flat upon the twin domes of Iravatha's broad skull, fingers splayed between the sparse, coarse black hairs. To his surprise and giddy pleasure, the elephant's head was warm and soft. Iravatha stopped his ticks and fidgets of irritation, and Annayya believed that the warmth and softness of that point of contact had suffused both their hearts.

'Mal!'

Kicking gently at his ears, and issuing the command taught to him by his father, they moved forward together, slowly but with purpose. Iravatha's massive shoulder blades pushed into Annayya's buttocks with every step, threatening to send the boy crashing to the red earth below; with every turn of the head, flap of the ear, or step, Annayya thought he was certain to fall to his death. But the terror was mixed with a heady blend of awe and wonderment.

...

Eight thirty, on the platform at Bangalore train station. It is thirty minutes until our train departs for Mysore. The station is less frenetic than I had anticipated, although this only increases the persistence of the two beggars working the platform. Lainey takes photographs, captivated by the romance of Indian train travel, and we drink hot thick tea, the essence of tea, stewed, sweet and brick red, served in cloudy glasses at the Milk Stall on the steadily filling platform.

Below us, Hooded Crows hop across the tracks, while mice dart around the benches of an empty second class carriage, stationed at the next platform, awaiting an engine. Bright sunshine spills through the unglazed, barred windows, creating spotlit shafts through the dust and onto the bare wooden boards, stark against the dark interior. I toy with Lainey, claiming that we will be travelling in that coach or one just like it.

Only twenty four hours ago, Lainey had watched with relief as the taxi pulled out of the hotel's driveway and into the grinding chaos of the city, leaving us in the cool tranquillity of the well-mannered compound. Lainey had become unnerved as soon as she had stepped from the relative calm of the airport building into the crucible of the taxi station beyond. Once inside the cab, sealed off from the madness, she had become absorbed by the senseless ebb and flow of the traffic, the eddying of the people and livestock between the vehicles. She had allowed herself to smile at the strangeness of her surroundings, safe there behind tin and glass, edging herself closer to embracing the riot of colour and sound that hung safely at arm's length.

We were ushered by the turbaned doorman into the hotel's reception, to air-conditioning and clean calm. There was even piped music. It was still only 7am, but the young woman behind the desk was pleased to be able to let us into our room. She smiled disarmingly as she handed me the key card, all precise movements and demure professionalism. She was Indian, naturally, but looked uncomfortable in the cream and purple sari that the company required of its female reception staff.

After a shower and a couple of hours of sleep, we walked out of the hotel's leafy precincts to see the city. We took an early lunch on Church Street, then found a rickshaw to take us to Lalbagh, the botanical gardens laid out in the eighteenth century. There, we had ambled through the wide spaces in the shade of trees and lake-cooled breezes, letting the vivid colour of the country and the people be absorbed in relative calm. I watched as Lainey had relaxed into India, and I speculated about what might be next for us, contrasting how I felt now with every other moment of my life so far. When I took her hand, she had looked around urgently but did not pull away. She even let me steal a kiss.

The train pulls in and I usher Lainey towards the 1st class AC carriage, through the sudden throng, a melee of passengers trying to disembark and embark at the same time, the clear voice of a passenger, a middle class Indian woman, giving advice, instructions and a commentary on the chaos.

Somehow we are on the train, and find our seats. Sinking into the upholstery, Lainey sighs long through pursed lips.

'Well that was real!'

'Nah, that was nothing. One time, I was getting this bus, up in Rajasthan, and… and nothing. You're right: intense. A bit feistier than the Northern line, wasn't it? Welcome to India, sweetheart.'

Through the milky glass of the window, the station platform

slides from view and is replaced by Bangalore's suburbs, then countryside, indistinctly green and blurred. While Lainey dozes, I watch the colours smear by, trying to make out trees, houses, landscape, anything.

Then Mysore. We wade majestically through the countless, insistent offers of taxis and rickshaws and take our pick: the oldest rickshaw, with a bulb horn and an ancient driver to match. We exchange looks, both knowing that this is how we want to arrive. Somehow the luggage is squeezed into the spaces around us and we set off, slowly, up the long hill out of town, towards the hotel: a small palace built as a rural retreat for the Maharaja's daughter at the turn of the last century.

The next days are spent in and around the royal city of Mysore. We queue with the crowds waiting to watch the Palace light up with a hundred thousand light bulbs, and the next day we walk barefoot through the gaudy palace itself. I dismiss the enthusiasm of an awestruck Indian, who challenges me to name anywhere in Britain of such grandeur and antiquity. Lainey scolds me afterwards, once the crest-fallen man has walked away, offended. We visit the elephants at the palace temple; an amenable mahout is willing, for a price, to let us get closer to the beasts and we duck under the fence and have our pictures taken with them. I am mesmerised by them, and claim a moment of communion looking into one of their eyes, all sickly yellow, morose. Seated on the broad back behind a pink freckled face, I feel the coarse hair and unexpected warmth of her skin; I feel vulnerable, and immensely privileged. We wander around the grounds, watching Brahminy Kites fight in the sky above the palace.

In Devaraja Market, we deflect the sellers of incense sticks, preferring the lanes filled with baskets of flower heads, piles of vermillion, stacks of banana stems. We taste lemon salt and jaggery at the spice stalls. We search for the Government Silk Shop, which refuses to be where it should be. Instead, we stumble on a yard off a tangled street of warehouses. The smell lures us in, Lainey leading the way, urging me to forget my English reserve and follow her under the dark arch and into the brilliant white light of the courtyard, maybe fifty metres long and twenty wide. Across every inch of the concrete floor are small blue and white stones, that aren't stones but are ginger roots, drying in the sun. The air is intoxicating and we stand smiling like idiots and don't notice the two men who emerge from the warehouse until they shout. But as we shape apologies with our bodies and turn to leave, they beckon us over and show us around, explaining in barely comprehensible English the process of drying ginger and the spice's manifold medicinal benefits. They smile broadly throughout, shaking our hands repeatedly, insisting on taking our picture in front of the yard full of pungent roots, the heady aroma warming our hearts in the heat of the day.

On Chamundi Hill, among the temples and crowds, the monkeys and cows, we dodge the burning shards of smashed coconut, dashed into the road as offerings to the gods. The boy asking for specific UK coins to complete his collection, before naming every European capital city in alphabetical order. A monkey snatches a bag of fruit from a family sitting under a tree and proceeds to eat it, piece by piece, just out of reach of the irate father, who curses, then scowls, as he chews his way through what is left of the picnic. Children everywhere asking our names and where we are from.

We leave Mysore with a sense of immovable well-being, wrapped in an emotional intensity that leaves no space for doubt or questions. We are seamless, integral. As the car pulls away from the hotel to begin its marathon of temples and palaces, all the way to the coast, I take Lainey's hand and squeeze it, smiling to myself. I do not need to look at her to know that she, eyes lowered, is smiling too. As the Ambassador builds up speed on the main road, we bounce on the over-sprung back seat, my head thumping into the swirling velour of the ceiling, and we laugh loudly, ignoring the driver's eyes in the rear view mirror.

A week later, we arrive at the sea. The Malabar Coast is as I remember it: a line of yellow powder and palm trees and surf all the way to the vanishing point, interrupted only by colourful wooden fishing boats. We drive north, every now and then interrupting a town or village: on through Honavar, Kumta and Mirjan. We cross broad rivers running down to the ocean from the uplands of the northern reaches of the Western Ghats. Coconut and banana grow everywhere and the landscape is painted to a verdant iridescence by the brilliant sunshine. At Madangeri, we turn west out to Gokarna, then along a dirt track to Om Beach.

...

'Do you want to move on soon? Maybe head inland, find some more temples?'

It has been three days and already I am restless, bored by the beach. The triple curve of the bay, with its low rocky headlands, is far beyond picturesque, and it has been good to relax amid its beauty, to simply sit in the sun, to watch the waves and do very little. But I am twitchy to move on – I do not want to be around the teenagers and travellers, the achingly self-satisfied Europeans, any longer.

'They're not that bad. And you've got to admit this beach is gorgeous. I say we give it another couple of days, yeah? See if we can't get you to relax a little?'

Lainey's toes dig deeper into the soft sand, pushing up little crumbling mole hills around her ankles. She is lying flat on her sarong, only her knees are slightly raised. She is soaking her already golden skin in the sunlight – within days of landing in Bangalore, her complexion had transformed directly from pale and delicate, almost fragile, to supple and honey-toned, and in the three days at Gokarna the rest of her has caught up.

Still horizontal, she turns her head towards me, eyes hidden behind large sunglasses, her left cheek resting on the soft cotton of her sarong. A strange, sideways smile fights against the gravity that smears her face from right to the left, up to down. For the first time since I have known her, she does not look beautiful. Her face distorted, I can see the shape of her skull beneath her stretching and sagging flesh. Just a skull, not cheekbones and jawline, but basic, bloody bones. With her mouth pulled to the left, I imagine her as Lainey after a stroke, Lainey mortal, Lainey dying. Frantically, I search her face for the reassurance of her vital beauty. She sits up, leaning on her elbow, and raises her sunglasses, revealing a frown, quickly rearranged into a concerned smile.

'Are you alright? You look horrified. Honey, I don't want to make you unhappy. Look, we don't have to stay any longer than you want. I just don't think it's as bad as you seem to.'

With gravity restored, I can see her again as the live and lovely Lainey I have known these five months. But the memory of the other woman, plain, degenerating, who only moments before had been lying next to me on the beach is stubborn and I reach out for her free hand, resting on the sand. Once I have found it, I run my index finger gently, slowly, along its length, as far as the first knuckle of her middle finger. I fix my eyes to hers.

'No, you're right. It is gorgeous here. We should give it a bit more time. And I'm not unhappy, honestly. I was just thinking out loud, daydreaming. There's so much to see here, it's such a big country, it just makes me think we should keep moving. I guess I need to find a better balance between the excitement of anticipation and the enjoyment of being there. So, yeah, let's give it another couple of days. Just so long as I don't get stuck with Yvette and her dreadful boyfriend...'

Lainey laughs spontaneously, guiltily, and her laughing face, creased and stretched, is beautiful. I am still stroking the back of her right hand, and I squeeze it gently, in communion, in relief.

'He's not that bad. I mean he's bad, but he doesn't mean any harm by it. He just tries too hard to be serious. I think it's sweet. At least he's not one of those people who's been everywhere, done everything. Dan just thinks that everything you've done or might like to do is inauthentic, not the real India. Not that I've seen too many real Indians who are dope heads with dreadlocks.'

She has pulled her knees up tighter to herself, warming to her theme, and the twist of her body accentuates the curve of her hip. I feel a dart of desire. I watch her knock the sand from her now free right hand and pick up her paperback, before she turns onto her front. As she settles, I look along her lithe body and down to her pale heels, reliving a thousand shared intimacies. Reassured that my beautiful Lainey is real, I return to my own book. Seeking out a position in the sand conducive to reading, I catch her eyes, which are sparkling with mischief and realise that she watched me trace her form with my gaze. Embarrassed, flushed, I smile a timid response; but she mouths the word 'later' without inhibition, then returns to the page in front of her. Unable to concentrate on reading, I drift into dreaming for what feels like a few minutes.

When I once again open my eyes, the sun has grown fatter and more golden. It hangs low over the ocean and lends a compelling lustre to the sand and to Lainey's skin. It is now that the boy arrives on the beach. Lost under a huge bundle, he moves methodically over the sand in the late afternoon heat, pausing at each couple or group of barely clothed Europeans, exchanging some words, moving on at the shake of a head, the raise of a hand, the shrug of shoulders. Occasionally, he drops down and starts to unwrap the bundle of carved wooden things, wrapped in lungis and kurtas and salwar pants, before moving on, weary European politeness exhausted. Once or twice over the past three days, he has managed to show everything, and once to actually sell something.

Lainey pulls on a beach dress, as she has done every day when Thom has arrived on the beach. He is 14, maybe 15, years old and has adopted the name Thom for professional reasons. On our first day, as he took us through the items carefully unwrapped from his bundle, Lainey had asked his name, then what his real name was. He had smiled, saying that as much as it mattered, his real name was Thom. The name his far away mother had given him was too complex, too cumbersome for a man starting out in this business, a man already weighed down with that bundle: better to lose what encumbrances you could.

At the end of his round, Thom drops his bundle beside us and falls to his knees, sending up a small cloud of sand. He holds out his hand; we each shake it firmly, and then offer our own embarrassed 'namaste'. Thom says good afternoon. I offer him some achappam from the enormous bag we bought by the level crossing in Madangeri three days ago; as usual, he declines. He wipes the sweat from his face with his loose fitting shirt and smiles broadly.

Normally, idle chatter about the weather, business, or the sky suffices, gives Thom the chance to catch his breath, to cool off, without appearing to be slacking. To any watching eyes, he is working, talking to tourists, showing them the products, trying to make a sale. I like to think that maybe he also enjoys the conversation, the human exchange, the inter-cultural encounter, as much as I do; but I know that that is unknowable, and that ultimately it is pointless to determine, that it is enough that the small talk serves both our purposes, whatever they are.

But today is different. Yesterday I promised to buy something today and Thom is confident that the investment he has made will pay off, that I won't betray his trust. So, after we have agreed that yes, today is hot, he sets everything out, the garishly patterned fabrics and the carved wooden figures. I look to Lainey for help. Since I want nothing he has to offer, I hope she can spot something to rescue us from this situation. Lainey is watching Thom intently as he presents each of his treasures, explaining their origin, use and virtue. He shakes out each garment, and reverently smoothes the fabric on the sand, stroking it like a son's cheek.

Then suddenly he's telling me how beautiful Lainey is, what beautiful eyes she has, and as I am snapped back from his hands and start to think that he has crossed some sort of line, strayed too far into familiarity, he holds up a green kurta to her face and triumphantly exclaims that it is the perfect match for her eyes. I look at Lainey and her eyes, at the soft emerald cotton and am astounded to see that it is a perfect match. Thom says that I have to buy it for my beautiful wife and Lainey smiles impishly and nods, her green eyes ecstatic in the perfection of this resolution: alongside the exchange of goods and rupees, everyone gives and everyone receives, from each to one another.

Relieved, I say, of course, it is the perfect match, it was made for her, and I pull my wallet from the small bundle of clothes that I have been using as a pillow. I am increasingly satisfied with the purchase: we had failed to find the green silk shawl we had wanted in Mysore and, while neither silk nor a shawl, this is the perfect shade of green.

As we discuss a price for the kurta, I notice a small carved wooden elephant, gloriously plain compared to the rest of Thom's statuary. Less than two inches high, and carved from a pale sandalwood, the form is simple, almost minimalist, a slight and suggestive rendering of such a substantial animal. Beside its overly-coloured, clumsily wrought neighbours, it is a modest work of genius; even alone in my hand, it is a small masterwork. I hold its smooth, short back to my nose and inhale the woody aromatics. I look up at Thom and ask how much he wants for it. He tells me it is very fine sandalwood; I tell him that I know what it is, but that I do not know how much he wants for it.

He is thinking, weighing up the cost of the piece against the potential number on which I am willing to settle. He senses that this might be a genuine negotiation: not an embarrassed haggling over the price of awkwardness and the insistence of need, but rather about the value of the piece itself. His young mind races behind an excited, placid, fearful, triumphant face for a moment, then he bobbles his head – perhaps mimicking an uncle, for reassurance – and says reluctantly that I can have both the kurta and the elephant for Rs 400. I know this is utterly reasonable but make a counter offer of Rs 300, so that he does not feel that he has massively miscalculated, so that his confidence in negotiation is not diminished. There are two or three minutes of hurt looks and reluctant sighs, before we settle on Rs 350.

'What on earth were you doing, arguing with him like that? It was just fifty rupees, for god's sake.'

Thom has just disappeared beyond earshot, heading up the beach, smiling, finished for the day. Lainey is angry and open-mouthed. Her anger startles me.

'That's what you do. You haggle. I mean, I don't want him to think I see him as a charity case – I just thought he'd want to prove himself, as a businessman, you know...'

'I think he'd rather have the fifty rupees. Prove himself? He's just a kid and he's living on his own, on his wits and god knows what pressure he's under. Whoever's supplying him with his stock is going be expecting a hefty percentage, and I doubt that's all. Prove himself? I think he's already proved himself. Jeez!'

I feel the sand skitter across the back of my hand, and can't help myself from looking, expecting to see an insect or worse. There is nothing, of course, just sand and hair and skin.

'Are you sulking, James? Really? Look, I'm sorry for shouting. I know you're not a bad person. I know you thought you were doing the right thing. We can see things differently, you know? James?'

'Yeah. Yeah, I know. It's just I've never seen you angry. I mean properly angry. At me. I really did think I was doing the right thing. Maybe I stuffed up. I don't know. Maybe. Really, I thought it was the best thing.'

'OK, enough already. It's done. Over. OK? Let's go get a beer, take in the sunset.'

She is up in an instant, knocking the sand out of her sarong and rolling it into her bag. Offering her hand, she pulls me to my feet, then runs her palm down my cheek, to signal that everything is good between us, everything is understood. While I struggle with my shorts and t-shirt , she slips into her sandals and sets off up the beach.

The beach bar is a rudimentary affair. The ill-matched tables, decked in blue and red cotton covers, are simply littered across the sand in front of a small shack made from plaited panels; those customers nearest the shack benefit from the shade of an awning also fashioned from coconut fronds. Two young men loiter by the entrance. As we approach, one of them rushes forward, suddenly animated, welcoming us, pulling out a chair for Lainey, then for me. He presents a sheet of A4 paper, printed on one side with the food and beverages on offer. But we do not need to read it, and simply order two bottles of Sunny Beaches. While he fetches the beers, I take one of the squares of hard pink tissue paper from the pot at the centre of the table and knock the debris left by a previous customer onto the sand. Satisfied that our table is as hygienic as is it going to get, I watch the young man to returning with two glasses and two large bottles, while Lainey watches the sea.

'Hey guys. Good day?'

A voice crashes in from behind me. I shoot a glance at Lainey, but she simply shrugs and smiles. It was inevitable, I suppose.

I ready my own smile and gulp at the beer as soon as it is poured.

'Hey Dan, Yvette. Come, join us.'

Lainey is her hospitable best. They take the two spare chairs at our table, Dan dropping a colourful cotton shoulder bag in the sand. He spreads himself wide in cargo shorts and hemp shirt, while she sits constrained, awkward in her shalwar kameez, clothing that does not look as if it were her idea. They are gap-year kids, maybe fresh graduates at most. Their youth is most apparent in Yvette's tender, awkward features, in her flawless skin and imprecise lips.

'We just had a quiet day on the beach. You know, lazy. Really nice though. James failed to make it into the sea again. Didn't see you down there. What did you get up to?'

'We were in town, taking a look around, buying some stuff, you know? It's pretty like, but I got so angry. There was this one shop there with such a massive mark up on everything for non-Indians. India is changing, man. Everyone's trying to rip everyone off.'

Lainey fixes me with eyes that tell me now is not a good time to mention my earlier dealings with Thom, and I do not interrupt.

'I mean, I'd understand it if it was just for tourists, but, you know, we don't look like tourists, do we? We're students, skint.'

With a sweep of his arm, he herds his wayward dreadlocks behind him. Yvette nods emphatically but does not speak. It occurs to me that I have seldom heard her speak. I want to tell

him that the simple fact that he could afford the airfare means he
is not skint at all, especially not here. But I can see in his eyes the
disappointment at having arrived in India only to discover that
they were too late. The halcyon innocence they had imagined in
planning their trip was nowhere to be found, no matter how hard
they looked. The boy's sense of loss weakens my scorn for him,
diluting it to pity.

'I doubt it was ever quite like you imagine it to have been.
I first came here ten years ago. Rajasthan. There were plenty
of scams and rip offs then too. It was cheaper, of course. But
you could still get a pint in London for a couple of quid then
too, so...'

'Talking of pints, shall we get some more of these?'

A suddenly smiling Dan brandishes an empty bottle of Sunny
Beaches and holds up four fingers to the young man by the shack.
We settle in to drink and eat until the blackness of the subtropical
night blots out all the world's worries and dissatisfactions.

Eventually, we pull ourselves away, using our age as an excuse.
As we make our way back to the cottage, Lainey and I hang from
each other, almost staggering, laughing with each stumbled step.
The ocean and the sky are spectators to our lightly tripping joy,
our pure pleasure in each other's company. Before the door, on the
little veranda, I feel Lainey's hands explore me, erasing any trace
of my error with Thom, any residue of my awkwardness with
Dan. She pulls herself so close to me that there is no distance at
all between us. Somehow I find the key and manage to open the
door. Lainey takes one last look at the moon, huge and yellowing

over the ocean, and follows me in, shutting the mosquitoes out of our room.

Another two days pass before we find a car to take us back inland, by which time I do not want to leave. We see Thom only once more: he visits our little camp on the beach late on the afternoon of our last day. He looks more relaxed, more assured, and we briefly talk about how hot it is. He tests my appetite for more sandalwood, but without vigour and, hearing that we were leaving the next day, he simply wishes us well on our travels and hopes we come back through Gokarna. We shake hands, knowing it is the last time we will do so, each of us preferring to maintain the pretence.

...

Lainey did not try to mask her disappointment. The room was both shabby and characterless: neither a Taj nor a heritage hotel. We had arrived on the outskirts of Badami and checked into the Royal Court Hotel after a long drive through the farmlands of Karnataka. I had insisted on coming to the town, and this was the only place within fifty miles that had sounded vaguely appealing. It wasn't dreadful: it was clean, even the bathroom, which had hot water, an actual shower and a bath tub to boot; the sheets were fresh and white; there was AC that actually worked, and the windows were sealed against the mosquitoes; the view across the garden gave directly onto the cliffs that hung above town. But Lainey barely conceded these virtues until a waiter, stiff in his still not yet accustomed collar and tie, brought tea and snacks and fruit and the most welcoming of smiles. Lainey brightened and, from the balcony, we watched the sunset turn the cliffs blood red.

'I'll be honest: there've been times on this trip that I've hated India. If it hadn't been for you, keeping me safe, I would have turned back at the airport. Daddy always told me that it was a big world, full of marvels, that I should get out and see it, but I've never really strayed from the safe and the comfortable. Thank you for making me come here, for giving me the courage.'

I wanted to tell her that she did not want for courage, that I was perpetually in awe of her confidence, but I simply kissed her instead, charmed by her unfamiliar vulnerability and intoxicated by her unwarranted gratitude. Her fragility made her yet more precious to me and even the clanking of the AC unit and the shouts from the street could not break the spell.

In the morning, we took an auto rickshaw to town, through the dust and chaos of the main street, past the bus station and market, and to the gate below the caves. Badami town had little of interest, save the pigs in the street, the monkeys in the trees and the complete absence of white faces. But the temples, hewn into the living red rock, were breathtaking. Deities and animals and human figures, lion-faced men and buxom women, emerged from pillars and niches, fresh and sharp despite their 1400 years. Each cave was fronted by a platform, and each platform was bustling with school children: a party of seven year old girls in beige pinafore dresses and burgundy ties; young women in crisp colourful saris; boys in navy blue trousers and sky blue shirts. Below the caves, in the horseshoe of the red cliffs, nestled a brilliant green lake. Women in saris washed clothes on the steps that led down into the water, filling the world with an explosion of colour; a hundred different oranges, blues, and yellows, set against the overwhelming green of the lake and red of the cliffs. Standing in the timeless tranquillity of the temples, surrounded by the exuberant riot of the present, Lainey turned to me and said quietly, definitively, that, OK, she got it. A smile broke across her face, her green eyes sparkled, her red hair shone.

...

A slight breeze blows over the plateau on which the north fort stands. Below us, a cascade of cliffs, with temples set on unfeasibly neat, lush lawns painted onto rocky sills. From the caves, we had walked past the ghats where the women were washing saris and dhotis, and I can see their earlier work spread out across the steps to dry, great rectangles of brilliant white and vibrant colour. We had climbed through the narrow canyons, natural corridors that lead up through the cliffs to this perfectly defended fortress, leaning over the lip of rock above the dusty town and brilliant green water.

Monkeys sit precariously on the cliff walls, watching. Certain they are our only witnesses, I take Lainey's hand and press my lips gently against her cheek. I am the king of the world, this is my mountain fortress and this is my queen. Still with her hand in mine, I nod towards the temple perched higher above us, on the next plateau. Despite the day's heat, she smiles and nods and we leave Tipu Sultan's empty treasury, and climb up to the seventh century Shivalaya Temple. Two green parakeets fly past as we reach the upper ridge.

Across a small green water tank cut into the rock of the plateau, the temple looks down on the town. We sit on the stone steps, to catch our breath, to cool a little in the breeze.

'Bloody marvellous, isn't it?'

I indicate the view, which extends far across the flat farmland, but I am referring more to the sensation of being alive, of being with her. She smiles and stares off into the haze, nodding slowly, reaching for my hand.

'I can't think of anywhere I've been that is more remarkable. This place, up here, it almost makes you believe in the gods.'

She turns her head over her shoulder to face the temple and whispers 'no offence'. I look around too, at the temple, the stone. I reach out and pat the head of a brutally eroded elephant, its neck and trunk still joined to the living rock. It's smooth, reduced shape reminds me of my sandalwood elephant, bought on the beach at Gokarna, of the green of Lainey's eyes, the slope of her neck. Suddenly, I am awash with memories of all the moments of intense immediacy we have shared. I am taking both her hands, and I am turning to face her, searching her features for something: for promise, for reassurance, for safety, for adventure, for love. My mouth is moving with the certainty that this is absolutely the right thing, the only thing, that could possibly be happening now and I am asking Lainey to marry me, to be my wife, to stay with me forever, to share all of this, to share everything.

She is staring at me. The confusion on her face is anchored

in a small smile. For an endless instant, she is going to say no, to laugh or curse, to stand up and walk quickly from this site of embarrassment. I hate my mouth for its recklessness, her for her heartlessness. But her mind and body and heart reconvene, find their fulcrum, their equilibrium. Her small smile is broadening, then breaking into a grin and then she is throwing her arms around me, and saying yes, her breath hot in my ear, and everything else in the world has disappeared.

6

ELYSIAN

The chill steals in through the gaps around the windows, a pack of ghostly hounds chasing out whatever warmth and comfort we can put into the house. It scurries through the kitchen and into the living room, a foot above the carpet; it cascades down the stairs, filling the hallway with its malevolence. I am standing in its midst, cursing Morag for choosing to put the telephone here.

London in late February feels a long way from Karnataka. In the two weeks since we have been back, my skin has never fully thawed, even wrapped in as many jumpers as I can muster. There are two duvets on the bed, but even so, moving fractionally from the area already warmed is painful. Lainey's feet are, it goes without saying, icy. We hold each other without passion, despite our hunger for each other, in the simple pursuit of physical warmth.

A voice, at last, on the line. Richard is hesitant, suspicious. I know he has been staring at the phone all the while it rang, hoping it would stop, would still itself of its own accord, as he debated with himself whether he should answer it. He really should get an answer phone: then he would not have to guess blindly at which calls to take and which to leave. But his mistrust of telephones extends to all technology related to them, and he refuses to consider the possibility, preferring to play his waiting game with the raucous device in the corner.

His voice becomes less hesitant when he hears that it is me who has disturbed his solitude, although he retains an awkwardness that is never present in the flesh. In real life, Richard is open and fluent; he rushes headlong into human encounter, clasps the world in a bear-like embrace. Only on the telephone does he become distant, diffident, even with me.

At school, Richard had drawn caricatures, imagined landscapes, or faithful, brutal, renderings of dead animals he found beside the road. I had envied his certainty as much as his creativity. While others at my suburban comprehensive made themselves through sport or bookishness or disruption, Richard was not simply making himself, he was making a world as he wished it to be.

It was entirely unsurprising when he went off to Art College, while the rest of us either left to find work or stayed on in sixth form in order to avoid it. I kept in touch after he left, neglecting the friends I still had at school until Richard became my only friend. Later, he became the first person I knew who actually made a living, or something approximating a living, from painting. Over the years, our friendship had taken an erratic course, but he was still my best friend. I likened him to a comet, disappearing into the cosmos for a few years, only to reappear unexpectedly and stick around for a few weeks or months until it was time for him to vanish again.

Warily, meticulously, he responds to each of my questions about the twelve months during which I have not seen him, before he cordially returns them to me. I rattle out my news, the only news that matters to me, as if a second's delay would break the spell.

'But how can you marry someone I haven't even met?'

'If it's any consolation, my folks haven't met her either.'

Richard is not surprised and does not intrude further. I know he thinks that the distance I maintain from my family is the result of some terrible fracture. In reality, I am simply stubborn, and I will not forgive them their own remoteness. I am punishing them with my own withdrawal. But to admit that would mean losing the mystique of my original pain, the only thing of interest that I bring to our friendship.

'Have you set a date yet?'

Richard is easing the conversation back to the reassurance of the mundane. I tell him there is no date, and confess that we have yet to come to terms fully with the idea. It's only been six months, and even I recognise things are moving quickly.

'Don't worry, you'll be the second to know. And you'll meet her soon enough, assuming you agree to be my best man.'

He is, of course, delighted to accept the responsibility, and I tell him to stand by for further instructions. He warms to the idea of this being some kind of clandestine operation, of being a great adventure, and his warmth seeps into the frozen hallway.

...

Spring has reached even this far north. Lainey is smiling a childlike, wondrous smile in the passenger seat, the same smile that she has worn since we threw our things into the boot of the car in the black night of the early hours. Under the cover of darkness. Even though there was no-one to censure us, to hold us in London; even though we made all the arrangements a fortnight ago, had asked Morag to take charge of the wedding supper, had made sure Richard knew how to find Morag and David's place. We are eloping, and these things need to be done properly.

So we had driven like fugitives over the river and on through the empty streets and suburban bypasses of the commuter lands; by the time the pinking sky signalled the arrival of dawn, we had already reached the motorway. When the sun broke from the shroud of mist, somewhere near Solihull, Lainey had half woken and we had looked on nature's glory like Iron Age farmers watching a solar eclipse. She drifted back into sleep as the cities and towns of England passed by unseen, their names remembered only in *Transport Medium* stencilled onto blue plaques. It wasn't until after the road had squeezed its way between the Howgills and the Lakeland Fells that she roused herself finally for the day.

It is now almost ten o'clock, and I am starting to become hungry, aching to get out of the car and unravel my limbs. With excitement and relief, we watch the last of England pass, then the low, drab roofs of Gretna Green. We will be back here in a little over two hours, after we have dropped our bags, eaten, and washed the journey from our skin. Then we will be married.

I slip my hand from the gear stick and run my palm down Lainey's thigh, squeezing gently when I reach her knee, murmuring 'happy?'

'Ecstatic', she breathes, and pushes herself back into the upholstery and closes her eyes, still smiling.

Despite my anxieties, the elopement seems to have been a good idea. In the first few weeks after our return to London's chill, Lainey had spent excited hours on the phone, telling friends and family about our decision, carrying the thrill of it all on our behalf. Meeting friends she had not told, she would drape her left hand across the table such that they could not fail to notice the glint of diamond, and then she would stoke their excitement into a bundle of embraces and effusion.

But under the spotlight of returning daylight, she grew more cautious. Plans had still not been made, the wedding remained a loose idea yet to be articulated, let alone realised. By the time the clocks went forward, the rushing, euphoric intoxication had dissipated and Lainey seemed mired in the sobriety of the logistics and the logic of marrying.

'Look honey, there's no harm in slowing things down. A wedding is a big deal, you know, especially this one. We don't even know yet which side of the Atlantic it's going to be on. There's still so much to think about.'

She dressed procrastination as seriousness and told me be patient, sensible: grown up. Things this complex take time to get right. I understood her caution, of course, but it choked me none the less. I feared that the momentum of the relationship might falter, that the excitement of courtship risked simply slumping into boredom. Without momentum, like sharks, we would drown.

Moreover, I was impatient to mark this relationship as different, distinct from those that had preceded it. I wanted to show Lainey, and to prove to myself, that this one was the one, that it would not after all end in failure as had all my other relationships. I didn't need to wait to be sure, and I did not want the intricacies and gravity of a grand transatlantic operation. I wanted the immediacy, the lightness, of Lainey unclothed.

And she was naked when the idea of eloping came to me: a late spring Sunday afternoon, lost in the folds of sheets and limbs, cocooned in drowsy contentment. She'd laughed at first, then caught the determination in my eye, realised I was serious. She had wrestled against her suppleness to make solid her reservations.

'But what about my parents?'

'We'll sort out a big party over in the States later in the year, I promise. But for now, just leave everything to me, I'll take care of it.'

Once the decision had been made, the forms completed and submitted, the urgency and excitement re-established themselves, and the world was only us again. These last fifteen days had melted into this single bright morning that inevitably leads to Lainey and I together. We arrive at the farm and Morag waves to us as she checks her watch. Richard is there too, proud and awkward in his unfamiliar suit. This is really happening.

...

Later, under the night's sky, the darkness studded with a million points of light, we sit wrapped in coats and scarves, hats and gloves, and each other, watching for shooting stars. Morag, David and Richard, all have gone to bed, despite the early hour, to give us the space they know we want. And we have all of space, stretched out above us, a limitless ocean of possibility. The bonnet of my car flexes under our weight as I shift to pass the champagne to Lainey; she rises on one elbow, lifting her chin from my chest, and tips her head back to pour wine into her mouth. The heavy lip of the bottle rests on her own lips: they are pink now, where a few hours earlier they had been scarlet, and the rose aurora matches that around my own mouth. I watch her drinking until she notices my gaze. Embarrassed, she stops abruptly, covering her mouth with the back of her free hand to prevent the fizzing liquid forcing its way out. She unbalances and starts to slide from the bonnet, powerless to stop herself from falling. I try to catch her and we both slip from the hard metal to the soft, damp ground, landing in the unkempt grass where we giggle uncontrollably. Every wonder of the vast universe pauses to watch us, smiling benignly on our drunken laughter.

Like the wedding itself, the evening has been intimate but no less special for it. Just the bride and groom, the best man, the maid of honour and David, who filled in for Lainey's absent father to give her away. First had been Morag's table, heaving with food and wine, and toasts and speeches, one from each of us. Then there had been dancing, the furniture pushed back against the wall, Richard's mix CD on repeat. Later, meaningful, forgotten conversations with David and with Richard over too much whisky, while Lainey and Morag shared their own secrets. I had never felt so complete, nor such a sense of belonging, been so overwhelmed by the warm conviviality of other human beings. The world was here and it was glorious.

'Do you think it will ever be this perfect again? You, me, the stars, our friends, our very best friends, the very best friends anywhere: all right here, for us, only for us.'

'Are you drunk James? I think you're drunk.'

Lainey wrestles with the ground for a few moments, trying to stand, or at least crouch against the car bumper. She gives up, defeated, and slumps back into the grass, sitting on her heels, her knees tucked up in front of her. The skirt of her dress falls in a rippled cascade of green silk to reveal the tops on her stockings. A still moment hangs over us and I gaze at my wife. She is beauty, its very essence and allure. I am not blind to her awkward, twisted position, nor to her collapsed stack of wayward hair, nor to the three inch run in sheer silk. These are part of her loveliness, reminders of her vital lightness of being. Even in her drunken disarray, she is the most perfect, adorable woman I have met, and I am reminded that this is my wedding night. I run my fingertip over the ladder in her stocking, catching fragments of her satin skin between each silken rung.

'Of course it'll be this perfect, if we want it to be. I love you, and you love me, right? Morag and Richard, they aren't going anywhere fast, and the stars sure as hell aren't. Stick with me kiddo and I'll give you the moon on a stick.'

Her nose wrinkles, and her stifled snort breaks free as unquenchable giggling.

...

The air is scorched in the clear white Mediterranean light, bleaching out the remaining colour from the wood and stone and scrub land that surrounds me. Under the sun's hammer blow, only the shimmering water retains any intensity of pigmentation: iridescent turquoise set in the flat low hills that surround our bay. There is a savage beauty to the parched landscape, an unconscious brutality that sears a happy numbness into the eye. Even through the warm brown haze of my sunglasses, the early afternoon light is relentless, without compromise or compassion.

I pause to absorb the murmuring breeze and the gentle lapping of the waves against the rocks below. A tiny rivulet runs over my knuckles from the dew-wet bottle of rosé, the reason for my exertions. Clutching it, and the two squat tumblers, I restart my descent, bouncing with long, lazy steps down the roughly flagged path to where I left Lainey reading in the shade of an olive tree.

Reaching the turning before the little terrace, with its deckchairs and dining table, I pause again to watch Lainey, lost in a book, behind sunglasses. The dappled light through the tree makes the pattern on her beach dress appear as if animated, a perpetually shifting dance of shapes and colours. Her hair is pulled back and tied in a band, revealing the line of her cheekbone. Captivated, I sit on the low wall to watch her, to drink in the lines and curves, the slow precise movements, willing her to remove her sunglasses so that her eyes can also be mine to see.

These last weeks, I have often found myself mesmerised by her, unable to look away from her. That someone so beautiful should have agreed to be my wife continually astounds me. The thought of being able to look at her forever is the most perfect satisfaction that my life can offer. Since we left for Paris, I have been storing and cataloguing images of her, mental pictures that I can draw down when we are apart, in my sleep. I want to tell everyone I meet that, yes, she is my wife and, yes, she is the most beautiful woman in this city, on this island. Before Sardinia, the route of our honeymoon had led us through Paris and Rome. Two cities with pretensions to beauty and romance. But a small town in upstate New York trumps them both, in the slender, supple form of Lainey Townsend, née Driscoll.

I had at first suggested that we go somewhere more exotic for this trip. Maybe back to India, or to South America. But Lainey had explained that, for her, Europe was exotic; that, from her East Coast cradle, Paris and Rome were more magical than Zanzibar, gilded by the mythology of Hemingway. So we had worked our way through the crowded galleries of the Louvre and the Vatican, around the Musée D'Orsay and the Villa Borghese; we had walked, triumphal, along the Champs-Elysees and we had lain on the floor of the Pantheon, marvelling at the ancient immensity of the vaulted dome. We had meandered around the Marais and Trastevere, discovering secret bars and restaurants, where we had painted ourselves in the indulgent glow of candlelight; and in all of them I had been oblivious to my surroundings, captivated only by her.

In the gardens of the Palatino, looking down onto the Forum, we had talked about permanence, about legacy, about art and law, and the tiny mark we leave on the world, the insufficiency of mortality. I had felt the terror of inevitable loss, the relentless necessity of death and decay and ageing. She had seen the possibility of children, and we had talked for the first time about our shared, hesitant hopes for an abstract family of our own. As we walked through the narrow streets of Campodoglio to find lunch on the Via del Fienili, she had put her arm through mine and clung to me, despite the damp stickiness of our skin, fired by the June sunshine. The restaurant, painted onto a perfect triangular piazza, had been shut. We'd taken turns to peer through the window into the dusty darkness, until Lainey had deduced, deciphering the notice written in a language neither of us knew, that the place was closed for refurbishment. With only a laugh and no need for discussion, we had set off for the Ponte Palatino and the familiar ground of Trastevere. The world was ours to wear lightly, seamlessly. We had glided, frictionless, all the way to Sardinia, and whatever setbacks there had been were simply points of interest along the way.

It's been maybe five minutes, and she hasn't seen me. I want to stay here forever, watching her breathe, watching her smile gently at some phrase or imagery in her book; take in every nuance of her golden, slender limbs as they flex and stretch and shift by fractions. Only the slow warming of the wine pulls me grudgingly to my feet and down the remaining steps, breaking the spell of my voyeurism. After four weeks of married life, I am thrilled as if for the first time at seeing Lainey as a stranger, as a person not yet known. The simple contemplation, unnoticed, of the length and line of her thigh from hip to knee can leave me breathless. This glimpse now of the curve of her neck, its sweeping fall to her clavicle and beyond, is laden with such uncertain, giddying promise that I can only stand stupefied by her deckchair, until she finishes her paragraph and looks up quizzically. I can think of nothing to do, but to hold out the bottle and glasses in mute offering.

···

All through that summer and autumn and into the dimming of the passing decade, the passing century, I remained entranced by the idea and the reality of my wife. We knew each other's thoughts and no silence was awkward. Irrationally, I took this as an omen, like an absence of rain on St Swithin's Day. My relationship with Lainey continued to move breathlessly forward on the same trajectory as before, the whirlwind still swirling at the same intense pitch. There had been no distance at all between us during all those days and nights.

At the same time, the world of matter and of money arranged itself for our benefit. Work started to work, and Gareth relaxed. The business did well. It wasn't that I worked harder to find work, more that the work found me. The optimism of the time was infectious – a still young government, a buoyant economy, a sense that Britain, and London in particular, was the centre of something, of everything. People started to believe in the future again. We slid towards the new millennium and people wanted to define themselves in terms of the new, as sophisticated, cultured beings. Importantly, they wanted to buy art.

I no longer had to pursue reluctant clients. Instead, an impressive list of saleable artists and the most fashionable galleries gathered around Mercury. Not only could we pay ourselves and employ staff, we could even, to a degree, pick and choose the clients with whom we wanted to work. Gareth still couldn't understand my preference for painting, especially figurative work. The money and the excitement lay with the conceptual stuff that was leaking from every disused commercial building in Hackney: kids with asymmetric haircuts making flesh of puerile jokes in driftwood and plastic bags and abandoned shopping trolleys, aching to find a shark of their own. Yet I was finally able to pursue clients who spread oil onto canvas, and my work made sense to me as it never had before. I became content, reconciled to my career, to my life; I could at last see possibility, meaning, in it.

Things went well for Lainey too, but her heart was still not in her work. When her London contract was made permanent, she reacted with horror, as if it meant she had to stay at Saunders forever, as if the temporary terms under which she had been working were not an unwelcome insecurity, but a promise of release. When they promoted her that autumn, I bought champagne, flowers and a corny card and although she had smiled and buried her face in the freesias to inhale their fragrance, her eyes betrayed her dissatisfaction.

'Tell me.'

'Tell you what, James? You already know. You know that I wanted… not more, just different. The money just doesn't make up for it. I should be doing something that matters. But it's pointless to say this. You know it already.'

'I know, but I want you to know that you can say it, can scream it, even, if you want.'

But she didn't scream out her frustration, the pointlessness of being exceptional at something on which she placed no value; and instead kept her discontent, her pain, close and closed. Only later, when the bottle was empty, did she drift into hazy regrets and a slurred despondency that only lifted in the morning. Sleep, not my clumsy flattery, reconciled her to her progress.

More money, especially from Lainey's promotion, meant that we had at last been able consider with confidence the idea of buying a house, rather than continuing to rent Morag and David's place in Clapham. Over the summer, we had had fairly regular visits from Morag – down from Scotland to do some interviews or to research a piece she was writing – and sometimes, David. For the most part these were pleasant interludes: I liked and respected Morag, and seemed to have the ability to charm her. But I had come to resent their visits to their former home, their unspoken disappointment at the changes we had made, their sense of propriety over both the house and Lainey.

The prospect of finding our own place, then, had energised me and I had taken time out of work to trail the streets of south London's middle class enclaves, viewing houses on dubious streets and in various states of disrepair. Our budget, although relatively generous, did not allow me to pursue my hope of returning to north London. Since we were not prepared to give up on the idea of a house, rather than a flat, even Clapham itself was beyond our means. I had only been to Balham a few times, to meet some friends of Morag and Lainey, but that was where we found the house we were to buy, to make our home.

...

Her hair is piled onto her head with an opulence that masks the precision of its arrangement. I am mesmerised by the elegant sweep of her neck, its smooth whiteness cool in the yellow lamp light. Her dress, cut just above the knee, skims her body's contours, revealing then concealing her smooth sensuality with every twist and turn as she readies small dishes of macadamia nuts and salted pretzels. The short string of pearls around her neck clanks as she turns to ask me to uncage the glistening bottles of Prosecco standing on the kitchen counter. I want the guests not to arrive, to leave us to our home, our bed, each other.

The doorbell rings. Morag and David are the first and they bustle in, fizzing with nervous excitement, carrying a vase and two bottles of Veuve Cliquot. Lainey takes them on the tour, while I anxiously nudge small, suddenly unfamiliar objects, whose provenance and purpose I have forgotten, until they hang perfectly on the fir tree in the corner of the living room. I gulp at a glass of cold effervescence.

Before the tour is over, others have arrived: Gareth and Daisy from the office; some people I vaguely recognise from Lainey's work; Morag's Balham friends; others I have never met.

'Well, despite it being south London, I have to say, it's beautiful. I take it Lainey decided on the décor?'

'Now, Gareth, don't be so mean. It was a joint endeavour, wasn't it darling?'

Lainey arrives and circles my waist with her reassurance. I am grateful for her rescue, for puncturing Gareth's presumption. While Lainey introduces Morag to my business partner, David asks about the house, the details of the mortgage, plans for extending into the loft and I am struck, as if for the first time, by quite how dull I find him. When the door bell rings, I gratefully take my leave.

'Well met, hail fellow! Here, take this and put it somewhere safe.'

Richard thrusts a bottle of single malt into my hand, more as a housewarming present than as a contribution to the party. His solid build brushes past me in the narrow hallway as he makes his way to where the light and life is to be found. He greets Lainey with a kiss.

'Lainey, my dear! Ravishing as ever, I see. And Morag! Lovely, lovely to see you again. How're the wilds treating you?'

His embrace engulfs Morag's slight frame, and then he is shaking David's hand as if they are long-lost friends. Before I have a chance to talk to him, he submerges himself in the conviviality of the gathering. I watch as strangers and acquaintances alike hang from his heartiness and marvel at his ease in the world.

Time passes, blurred by wine. Still more people arrive, friends I didn't know Lainey had, all here to congratulate us on our new home, on our marriage, and to enjoy a last London congregation before the festivities drive everyone back to their families, salmon returning to their origins, reverting for a brief moment to the people they were before they found their London selves. I enjoy the attention, talking rapidly, repetitively, about the house and the wedding and Lainey to whoever will listen, which is everyone. Fulfilling my duties as host, I move steadily through the crowded spaces, making sure everyone is enjoying themselves. Occasionally I cross paths with Lainey, who carries two bottles of Prosecco, ensuring no glass remains empty for long. I brush my hand across her lower back, her hip, and steal a kiss before we pull apart to continue on our oblique orbits.

The back door is open. The aromatic trace of cigarette smoke nudges in through the gap. I take a bottle of wine from the counter top and step out into the cold air. Daisy is sitting alone on the low wall at the top of the steps that lead down to our malnourished lawn. She is smoking. A packet of menthol cigarettes and a blue plastic lighter sit on the bricks beside her and her empty glass. My arrival drags her back from wherever it was she had disappeared, and she smiles apologetically, as if her presence in the garden in some way offends me. It is a look she wears sometimes in the office: she has that youthful insecurity that seems so common to bright women graduates these days.

'Swap you?'

I hold out the bottle and nod towards the packet of cigarettes.

Amused, she holds out the cigarettes and lighter in one hand and her empty glass in the other. Once the glass is full, I sit next to her and light one of the cigarettes, inhaling deeply, holding the pressure in my lungs until I can feel the nicotine doing its work, then release the smoke in a long heavy exhalation.

'I didn't know you smoked. I mean, you don't, at work. Well, I mean, I've never seen you smoke. Or smelt it on you.'

'No, I'm one of those social smokers who prey on the good graces of real smokers and steal their cigarettes. Normally, it's just in pubs, but also sometimes at house parties, or in bloody frozen gardens. But never before in my own bloody frozen garden at my own house party, so you were just unlucky. Sorry.'

She laughs, as I hoped she would. It is a warming sound, welcome in the frosty air. Daisy doesn't laugh much in the office, maintaining a studious frown as she stares at her monitor, terrified of being insufficiently serious. This is her second job, and her first in the field she wants to be in. She is young and pretty. I like her, think she is able and talented and hardworking. I wonder if she has a boyfriend, if he knows how lucky he is.

I ask her if she's enjoying the party, if she's met some interesting people. I'd invited her in part to bring her out of herself, but also to demonstrate that the company is an informal, friendly affair; that we, Gareth and I, are normal human beings too. I'd like her to feel comfortable around me, around us. She assures me that she is having a good time, that she appreciates the invitation. And she really enjoys the job, hopes that we think she is doing well. She looks up coyly; I tell her I think she is fantastic and she takes the compliment meekly, gently nudging my shoulder with her forehead.

'There you are. I was looking for a corkscrew: the one that was on the kitchen counter has disappeared, and there are some thirsty people in there. Me, for one.'

Morag is scowling at the cigarette in my right hand, at my wilful betrayal of Lainey's trust. To distract her, I introduce Daisy. As they shake hands and exchange names, explain how they know me, and comment approvingly on the house and the wedding, I crush the offending stub into a flower pot. Even as I do so, Morag is asking Daisy if she can take a cigarette; I am impressed that Daisy offers another to me before she makes her excuses and returns inside, to mingle, to be sociable. Morag and I are left outside, smoking, complicit, sitting side by side on the low wall. I am grateful for her act of solidarity, the demonstration in smoke that she won't tell Lainey about me smoking, grateful that I had invested the time and energy in making my wife's best friend like me.

'I hate this time of year. I mean, I'm looking forward to the time off and everything, but we've got David's mam and dad coming to us this year. That's going to be a barrel of laughs: if you think David can be a bit dour, you should meet Duncan. God! What about you two? Spending it here, in your swanky new place?'

'Ha! No, we'll be over in the States again.'

'Not your own folks? You didn't see them last year, either did you?'

I shift uncomfortably on the cold stone of the wall and turn the conversation back to her and her life. I ask how things are in glorious isolation, whether she and David have adjusted to country life, and she smiles slowly and nods into the middle distance: they miss London of course, but the farm is a great place to be for writers. No distractions, nothing to get in the way of what's important.

'I'll be honest, James, I wasn't sure about you at first. Lainey is a serious girl, with an open heart, and you seemed a little, well, frivolous. I wouldn't say I thought you were a player, just that you attached less importance to things than she does. A bit too bright and breezy. But I guess that's what serious people need: a bit of brightness, and bit of breeze.'

She draws deeply on what is left of the cigarette, and disappears briefly into herself.

'You know, you're the first guy that's been able to open her up, bring her out of herself. I've never seen her more... more serene. Hold on to that, James. Hold onto her.'

We chink glasses in a moment of communion. I start to say something mawkish but stop myself in time and instead I put my arm around her shoulders and pull her to her feet, moving her back towards the light and warmth.

'It's bloody freezing. Shall we?'

Later now and all but the hardiest, the closest, have gone. Empty bottles crowd the floor around the kitchen bin, empty glasses the sink. One by one, the taxis arrive and the living room vigil becomes more sparse. Morag and David are the last to leave, and we walk with them down the few feet to the gate, waving as they fall into the minicab waiting by the curb. We turn as it drives off and look back at the three storey façade of our Edwardian home. Lainey's lips pressed hard into my cheek, her hand pulling into my waist, squeezing out the night's chill.

...

It was the second year that we had spent the Holidays in the States, but it was the first time that Lainey's parents had seen us as a married couple. The previous year I had been an unexpected house guest, quite probably a transient element in their daughter's life, a temporary and therefore amusing distraction; now I was a fixture. The atmosphere in the lakeside house was a degree cooler than on my previous visit: they had taken our secret elopement badly, and Lainey's mother in particular seemed to blame me for robbing her of her thirty year dream.

Since they had not been able to attend the wedding, we arranged a dinner on Boxing Day for Lainey's parents and all the relatives and neighbours. It was intended as a reprise of our wedding, but on a much larger scale, fifteen instead of five. It was not the large party I had promised, but Lainey accepted it graciously, nonetheless. We showed the video, passed around the photos and, after the profiteroles, we shared the preserved top tier of our stale wedding cake. Lainey's cousins, aunts, uncles and childhood friends made a polite and determined effort with it before I declared it inedible and fetched the cheese, a Stilton I had found in Syracuse.

The house was filled with an ocean of affection for the

returned daughter, niece, cousin, neighbour. Lainey blushed while her father boasted of her professional achievements, of the likelihood of his daughter being made a partner in the next year or two. She attended to their questions about the detail of her life in distant London, of her wedding, of her trip to Europe. I was overwhelmed by the tender attachment each felt for her and ate cheese from my own place of origin, unable to understand why I felt such a stranger there now. Lainey had left her home town, her state, her country and her continent, had married a foreigner without the involvement of her family and friends, and yet she was as natural here as the Sugar Maples that mark the passing of the year in their cascading colours. I had merely travelled a hundred miles down the M1 and yet would never be able to find my way back. Watching the universe orbit Lainey, I had imagined how this dinner would have looked in Leicester, with my family, the few neighbours that knew my name, and I felt so very alone. All I had left to me was to find a place in the light, the warmth, that radiated from Lainey.

Over the following couple of days, I tried to make amends for stealing Lainey in the dead of night, and to recompense Lainey for being given away by David instead of her father. My fault, my impetuosity, my romantic impulse; a promise that we'd come back in the summer, that they should come to London to see the new house. By the end of the visit Lainey's parents had seemed to have forgiven me. It took a while for me to understand how generous that forgiveness was and at the time I accepted it thoughtlessly, as if my glib explanations and easy assurances were sufficient, that their absolution was the least they owed me.

We took the train down from Syracuse to the City for New Year's Eve. Lainey's mother had asked us to stay over, to see in the new millennium with them. When I'd explained that we'd already made plans, Lainey's father had placed his hand gently on his wife's forearm, had shaken his head so slightly that the movement passed almost unseen. With our bags nestled in the station wagon, I lingered awkwardly in the snow while the Driscolls hugged on the porch.

Lainey was quiet on the train until we reached Yonkers in the late afternoon. From there, we got our first glimpse of the Manhattan skyline. The familiar shapes awakened a childlike excitement in her and she talked freely about her time in the city, her friends, her favourite places. We went straight from Penn Station to Brooklyn: we were to stay with friends from Lainey's days at college. They still lived in Williamsburg: activists, dissatisfied, resentful. To me, they were relics, forever lost in their juvenile struggles; but it was clear that Lainey saw in their unbroken passion something that she felt she had lost; something she had betrayed rather than left behind.

Despite their principled disapproval, they grudgingly agreed to join us as we squeezed into Times Square like tourists, wearing sunglasses fashioned into the shape of '2000'. We waited anxiously for the ball to drop, for the world's computers to fail and the jets to start falling from the sky – Jenna and Bob had been especially convinced, hopeful that the bug would bring down the system. They at least were disappointed when nothing happened.

Bob only cheered up when we arrived, frozen, at a house party. Jenna disappeared to find friends with grass. Bob warmed his legs on a radiator and tried to force the alcohol from his synapses so that he could dredge his fading memory of a book by someone called Adorno to harangue me.

'Look, Jim, I don't think you're engaging properly here. Through your day job, you're complicit in the commoditisation of the products of human creativity. That's tantamount to... to the commodification of the very essence of what it is to be human. No, hold on for a minute, this is serious. D'you see? Your business is trading in people's souls.'

'Bob, I mean this with the utmost respect, but that's bollocks. Art has always been a commodity. Do you think Caravaggio gave his stuff away for free?'

'Now you're being facile. Of course art has always had a material value, but Caravaggio, Frans Hals, whoever, they were selling their product on their terms. There was no middle man making a percentage.'

'Again, with respect, what I do in no way - in no way – undermines the authenticity of my artists' expression of their soul; it liberates it.'

'Fuck authenticity, Jim, I'm talking about the expansive logic of capitalism.'

Jenna returned with the weed and Bob's concern with critical theory dissipated into smoke. She brought Lainey with her, and I realised how much I'd missed her during her brief absence.

'Your friend, Bob? He's a bit, uh, intense, isn't he?'

'Actually, he's really sweet. And incredibly smart.'

To halt my inevitable objection, she pulled me to her and kissed me with an intensity of her own. While Bob and Jenna danced downstairs and lurched through the early hours with the rest of the party, Lainey and I found a quiet corner in a darkened bedroom and welcomed the new era privately, wrapped in each other and a mountain of coats.

...

Through the chill darkness of London's late winter, life bloomed without inhibition. Perhaps, during my years of restless dissatisfaction, I had simply failed to notice that there had been something missing, but Lainey appeared finally to have completed me. The unexpected but not unwelcome realisation that I was now more than I had previously been beguiled me completely. Unannounced, the giddy thrill of it all would race through me as I waited for the Tube, sat at my desk staring at the stark sky, or woke just inches from her warm softness. There was no other explanation: I was happy.

Without noticeable hardship, I had also become successful. Somehow, I received an invitation to the opening party of Tate Modern. I never found out who had put me on the list, or who had failed to include Gareth, but I took it as a sign of my specialness. I moved around the vast space of the Turbine Hall cocooned in entitlement. With my arm around Lainey's shoulder, our hips pressed together, I could feel with each step the curling and uncurling of her spine, the steady, fluid movement of her present physicality telegraphed directly into my bones. Even in the fierce glare of the glamorous and exalted, I was luminous; when she melted into the crowd, I could feel her light reflecting upon me as I talked with people infinitely richer and more celebrated than myself; and later, as she made her way back to me, I could pick her shape moving through the others, calm and confident, weaving her way towards me. Only towards me.

By the time the summer had finally arrived, we were one of the most successful agencies in town. The late spring and early summer saw a series of successful openings; the last, at the end of July, had something of a celebratory atmosphere, if only for Daisy and I. She had worked closely with me on each, and this was the last show of the tour. It was just a small space, an opening in Clerkenwell, nothing fancy. But the gallerist had come to me directly, on the recommendation of the artist, a painter whose work I actually rather liked. Unusually, I quite liked him, too.

My passion for painting, for seeing shapes on canvas, remained undiminished, maybe even strengthened, by the lack of interest in it shown by London's wider contemporary art world. I had grown used to the idea that painting could only be taken seriously if it incorporated elephant dung, but now that even the street artists were using stencils, I clung to shows like this all the more, allowed them to justify my comfortable obstinacy.

Lainey, away for work, was not there. Gareth also stayed away, deciding that the fee did not merit both of us. The rest of

London seemingly felt similarly, and the room never really filled. While I explained to the gallerist that late July was never a good time for this kind of event, even if it did mean that media interest was likely to be higher, Daisy fastidiously checked each arrival against her list. She busied herself the rest of the time by pouring wine and arranging bottles and glasses into evermore elaborate configurations. Afterwards, when the few who had showed up had left and the remaining bottles of indifferent white wine had been returned to their cartons, I walked with Daisy out to the Farringdon Road to look for a cab.

'Thanks for helping this evening, and for everything else. Sorry it wasn't the most glamorous end to the season. If you've not got anything pressing on your desk, make sure you don't turn up too punctually tomorrow.'

Since the housewarming, Daisy had blossomed, filling with the confidence that flows from competence. Her initial coyness had evaporated with the returning daylight of spring. She had also become my secret smoking buddy, and we had stood in the cold on the office steps, smoking Consulate and talking about music and bands I did not know.

After one too many menthol cigarettes, I had broken my moratorium and started buying my own. I had become a proper, if part-time, smoker again; in lucid moments I realised that this was a secret from no-one, that it was simply tolerated grudgingly, silently, by Lainey. But the myth of secrecy strengthened Daisy's belief that I had confidence in her; in turn this fed her professional and personal self-assurance. Twice she had taken me up on my invitations to come around for dinner, and the four of us – Lainey and me, Daisy and her boyfriend Greg – became comfortable around each other, sometimes going for a drink together after those events that Lainey was able to attend. Daisy in particular seemed to regard these evenings as special, to regard Lainey and me as special.

'No bother, it's been fun. You know that I'm really enjoying work at the moment, don't you? I just want to thank you for giving me the chance, and for being so nice to me, giving me your time. You and your wife. She's great, you know? I think you and Lainey are cool as fuck.'

Her woozy inebriation was suddenly apparent. She had obviously been busy with the wine herself. I laughed and threw an arm around her, kissed her forehead, thankful to her for saying something so sweet. As I squeezed her shoulders, I realised that she had managed to capture in a t-shirt slogan from my time at Reading exactly how I felt about my wife, about me, the two of us together. The naming of it, having it named by someone outside, filled me again with limitless self-satisfaction at my life.

My right arm still around her, I raised my left to flag down the taxi, complete with orange light, rolling down the hill towards us.

'This one's yours. You going to be alright getting back from here?'

She shrugged out of my embrace.

'Oh no, I'm getting the Tube. My boss doesn't pay me that much, you know? Bit of a skinflint actually. But you enjoy the ride home.'

With that, she turned and started down the hill and past the Betsy Trotswood towards the station. I shouted 'Expenses!' after her, but she only looked back over her shoulder, giggling, before throwing me a wave with the back of her hand as she disappeared down Farringdon Lane, into the gathering darkness of the evening. And I thought about how lucky her boyfriend was, about how lucky I was to have Lainey, to have London, to have this enormous adventure stretching before me. Almost quivering with excitement, I opened the cab door, told the driver the address and sank back into the seat, to let the seemingly endless wave of possibility wash over me.

7

Because I Can

'You can't make me! I want to get off. Please! I can't believe you're doing this to me. Please!'

I can't see the girl. She is sitting some rows in front of me. Even if I opened my eyes against my drowsiness, she would still be invisible. But even from this distance and through the quiet roar of the plane taxiing to the runway, I can taste the genuine terror and despair that is straining her young voice as she repeats her fragments of pleading and protest.

'I want to get off. You can't make me.'

Not so young - maybe eight? - but young enough to not yet understand that, in fact, yes, they can make you and that, in any case, this far in it is already too late to get off. Not until the final destination. Until then, the route is fairly well fixed. What's more, there is much worse that they can, and will, make you do. The time to run away, to avoid this terror, is past.

As the engines raise their voice and flight BA119 to Bengaluru makes its giddying lurch forwards, I think it odd that she should find this anything but exhilarating. As a child, flying was to be treasured, being as close to space travel as my eight year old self could imagine. And space flight was the pinnacle of my dreams at that age, until it was supplanted by the compelling and, to me plausible, idea of time travel. This happened sometime during an adolescence from which escape was simply not enough; only complete reinvention – the ability to begin again, somewhere, somewhen, someone else – would erase the catalogue of failures and flaws that I had amassed in my short life.

In the absence of a time machine, accepting that the future would not arrive soon enough to save me, I turned to more straightforward means. I embarked on a programme of photograph burning, covering my tracks, incinerating the residual traces of my life, a process of creative destruction, designed to free me to become whatever I thought I could be. Alongside the flames, I began a campaign of lying – to strangers, friends, family, anyone – about anything I could get away with. To disguise myself, to recreate myself in a shape that I could find a way to like, I obscured even the mundane facts of myself in untruths, half-truths and in the absence of truth. I practiced invention to compensate me for the many disappointments of technology and for the impossibility of time travel.

The banal tedium of flight fully established itself in my imagination long ago. Now I feel neither fear nor excitement as the plane hurtles forward and, then, just in time, upwards; simply a dull indifference to the time to be wasted between takeoff and arrival. I feel a brief pang of envy for the girl's terror, the intensity of her sensation, as the plane continues to climb, turning eastwards, and I resign myself to ten hours of confinement.

...

I am sufficiently self-aware to realise that the disillusion had appeared, had started its pernicious advance, long before I closed the door behind me at the house in Balham and felt the slow certainty that the keys I clutched in my left hand were now useless, would no longer work, could no longer grant me entry to the place that had been home for almost seven years. It was no longer home; just a house, a building that would be occupied and reoccupied by people with whom I had less and less connection, until I was utterly eradicated from the memory of the floor boards, the plaster, the very particles of air that filled the once familiar rooms.

I had known every inch of that house, had invested its corners and spaces with the substance of my life. But it had become a stranger to me then, instantly, at the precise moment the door clicked closed. All I had left was the fossilised house, the imprint lodged in my memory, and only in my memory. No-one else had that house, that version of it, and its uniqueness condemned me to isolation, separateness. I could never live in the house in my head with any living person, only with the persistent memory of Lainey, whose ghost was now my constant companion in its fading, imagined rooms. When I had been with her, I admit it had sometimes been easy to forget about Lainey. But now that she was gone, she was always in my mind. In her absence, she became a resolute presence.

...

This should feel like some sort of liberation. I am a male human being, alive and in my prime at the beginning of the twenty first century; I am in town without my wife and there are no chores to be done, no errands to run; I am under strict instructions not to go home until after closing time. I am free to make the most of this most cosmopolitan of cities and I am awaiting my oldest and best friend in one of my favourite pubs.

Yet it does not feel like a liberation. Rather it is an exile. While Lainey and Morag occupy my living room, I am banished to the outside, to the elements and strangers. I could have timed things better, or at least demonstrated some imagination. Only half a mile away are some of the finest works of art that Europe has produced, freely available even at this hour. It is somewhat shameful that the possibility of spending this unaccounted hour imbibing of that treasury did not occur to me until now. In place of the glories of *Rain, Steam and Speed* I have spent these precious minutes watching the market debris collapsing in the Soho drizzle.

My window seat at least provides me with a distraction from playing the part of someone forsaken by a would-be lover. In the busy bar, shared between the fashionable young and the determinedly craggy and independent, no-one seems that interested in me, only in the chair that I am defending for Richard. He is often early and I hope today will be no exception: I am not confident that the chair will still be here if I have to go to the bar once again, and my second pint is nearly done. To conserve my drink, I light a third cigarette, confident that I can blame the tobacco imprint on the pub or on Richard, should Lainey decide to notice later.

'Can I have one of those? Please, I mean.'

A blonde woman, early thirties, is standing across the table from me, appearing unseen from the crowd by the bar. Her voice is resonant of breeding and privilege and a complete lack of embarrassment at either. I push the packet and lighter across to her, with a small bow of my head, a courteous 'of course'. There is a pronounced flick of the head, which clears the hair from her face, before she struggles with my lighter.

'There's a knack. Let me.'

Standing, I lean across and hold my cupped hands close to her mouth. She draws in heavily and the cigarette flares briefly then glows red. She expels a long straight stream of smoke towards the ceiling above me, then looks across at me, smiles and says thanks. She winks.

The wink stays with me as I watch her walk away. I interrogate its meaning, its significance, and am convinced that my preferred interpretation is undoubtedly the correct one, that this was one of those occasions that are the stuff of fiction and fantasy. As the promised possibilities recede across the crowded bar, I reflect upon a lifetime of hesitation and inaction. What if I called after her, what if she fell towards me, yielded, gave me everything, her devotion and her desire? Would that make me happy?

'You have the look of a man in need of a beer. What are you drinking?'

Richard is there, already claiming the vacant chair with his familiar suede coat, his snaking purple scarf. I tell him the name of the Czech lager I have taken to drinking in recent years, using the crisp consonants to drag me back into this moment; I repeat the word until Richard can pronounce it with some degree of confidence. He shakes his head and ambles to the bar, Dr Marten's pulling at the sticky carpet.

He has been wearing those shoes, or ones just like them, since art college; the black jeans too. Over a decade. Richard has remained a constant for over a decade, while I have metamorphosed countless times. I envy him his good fortune in being able to pour his creativity into his work rather than himself. To have decided so young that he would do this, be this, liberated him in ways that my fluidity could never achieve.

'When did you start drinking that pish?'

Richard is looking suspiciously at my lager. He has never held with it, drinking bitter since he was fourteen. We would sneak cans of beer from his father's cupboard and smuggle them to the raggedy fields beyond the suburban cul-de-sacs that defined our world, to the spinney where that world would dissolve and we could weave new ones, unseen, drunk on McEwan's Export. By the time I left Leicester, that spinney was lost beneath new cul-de-sacs and I could only wonder where those children that came after went to dream.

'A pleasure to see you, too. Successful day?'

'Yeah, the gallery seem really up for it. The space is perfect, and Ged knows what he's doing. Which is reassuring, because

I've forgotten: can you believe it's been three years since I've exhibited?'

I had never really understood how Richard made a living, given how infrequently he showed his work. Of course, he produced great stuff and he was sufficiently well-known to sell on reputation alone. I had offered to help, to use some connections, pull some favours, to get him a high profile show in London, but he had always declined, content to move at his own pace, in his own way. And now he has landed a show at one of the more exciting galleries of the moment. All without my help.

'I'd be happy to do the PR for you, you know. Mates rates and everything. Fuck, I'll do it for free.'

Again, Richard declines: the gallery has it covered; my services are not required. There is no point in restating my case. He would probably let me help him if I persisted, but I will not be subject to his pity. I have given him every opportunity.

'Another pint of sheep dip, is it?'

...

The journey home collapses like a telescope, and all at once I am at my door, key in hand. Inside, there is no Morag, only Lainey. She is sitting on the sofa, her feet tucked under her. A glass of whisky is cradled in her hands and the bottle stands on the floor beside her. While there are no signs of tears, there is a distinct smell of sadness in the room, strong enough for me to notice it through the beer and self-pity.

'She's gone. We had an argument and she left. Said she

couldn't stay any longer. I think I might have lost her for good, James, I really do.'

Her eyes now fill with tears, and I sit on the sofa, close enough for her to reach for if she needs me, far enough away not to crowd her. I struggle to shift gear, to shelve my ennui and to find the right tone: soft but calm, not wanting to confirm her apocalypse or to deny it.

'I'm sure that's not true. Tell me, what's happened?'

Lainey does not respond, merely keeps her eyes fixed on the coffee table where an empty wine bottle and two glasses still stand, ghosts of the evening already passed. Uncertain, I shift the few inches along the sofa that change me from a friend to a confidante. I try again, coaxing. She says only that there had been an argument, something about David, Scotland and me, that it is probably irrevocable. She clasps my hand with hers and pulls me towards her. I fold my arms around her and we sit there for an hour maybe, the rhythm of my rocking interrupted by the irregular jolts of her sobs, until she pulls away, lowers her face and dabs at her eyes with an already damp tissue. Looking up, she apologises and mumbles something self-evident about the importance of Morag in her life.

'She's just always been there for me, ever since school. She's my big sister. We've never fallen out over anything before. Even when she was dating this real jerk, we didn't fall out. Even when I told her that he was a real jerk. And worse.'

'It strikes me that one of you, sooner or later, is going to have to say sorry. Which is it that owes the other one an apology?'

'Oh, I don't know. Maybe both of us? It was a very personal kind of exchange and I don't feel like I like her much right now. She probably doesn't like me much either. I really don't think it'll blow over like you say, James, I really don't.'

Stroking her hair, I try to reassure her that, in the calm light of day, their friendship will be fine, that Morag will calm down, that she will calm down, and that all this will be put behind them; a friendship as solid as theirs cannot be broken by one argument. She tries to believe this, to see beyond her immediate anguish to the permanence of friendship, of love.

Rising to go to bed, sighing, her hand trails out across the room towards me, but I decline to take it, with a tilt of my head. Sadly, she accepts that I am not accompanying her, and leaves the room. I pick up her discarded glass, pour out some more whisky from the bottle on the floor and sink back into the sofa to wallow in my own dissatisfaction.

I know that what I do, I do without joy. The success of the agency, now that it has arrived, has simply left me empty. If my pride would allow me to admit it, I would say that I am bored. The pointlessness of my success, not the disappointment of failure, has robbed me of the possibility that I might yet save myself. I have achieved what I set out to achieve. But I am still filled with an emptiness, one which I can no longer seek to assuage through achievement: there is nothing left for me to do to fill the void. I am too old even simply to reinvent myself once again. I am this person and I have no option other than to pretend to like myself, to distract myself from the boredom that I cannot admit. As I drift off to sleep on the sofa, I think about my hollowness, and about the woman with the cigarette.

...

The view from the top is amazing. To the south, the bay and Staten Island and the Statue of Liberty. To the north, all of Manhattan stretched out, with the towers of Midtown framed against Central Park. I had wanted to get a reservation for *Windows on the World*, but they had nothing this weekend. I had left it too late as usual, so we make do with a hot dog from the food court. Lainey seems captivated by it all in any case. All those years in New York, and she never once came up here. I squeeze her hand, two excited children, as we hurry from window to window, pointing at buildings and streets we recognise, Lainey reliving her time in the city through the memory prompts of familiar places laid out like a map. She is happy, I think.

I'd convinced her to take some time off work, to spend a week or two of late spring in New York, the City and State. So we were spending a couple of days catching up with friends in Brooklyn, doing the tourist thing in Manhattan, before we head upstate to spend a week with her parents. I would leave her there for a couple of days, in the nurturing embrace of her family, while I came back down to do some business with a couple of galleries in SoHo before we flew back.

She still isn't talking to Morag. The silent feud has dragged on for two months now, and I have learned not to ask too many questions about it. But I do know that she feels crushingly alone, stranded in a foreign country without her best friend. I'd thought that, if I couldn't fix Morag and Lainey, then a trip home might help. And for once, I appear to have been right. She feels closer to me now than at any point since the fight with Morag.

...

Lainey's parents' house sat in modest grandeur by the water's edge, off the East Lake Road that leads down from Skaneateles town. Spacious, set apart from its neighbours among the trees, this time I'd seen past its immediate and impressive physicality to understand that it was Lainey's home, the place where she was forged. She had been shaped among the trees and lakes and small towns in this most liberal of homes in this most liberal corner of the States. Political dissidence and non-conformism had been in the water she'd grown up with: the abolitionists of Skaneateles competed with Syracuse itself for the title of the great central depot on the Underground Railroad. Her mother and father were both on the faculty at Syracuse University, she a lecturer in sociology and he a professor of law. Her origins in the comfortable embrace of self-confident and untested security explained her composure and her self-confidence. Her mother's earnest honesty and incongruous light charm had also left their mark on Lainey, as had her father's impatience with trivia and the trivial.

By this fourth meeting I believed I had convinced him that I was not trivial. The frostiness of the first Christmas after we were married had now thawed. Peggy in particular still regretted missing our wedding, but both she and Barnes had washed the resentment out of their regrets. Their progressive rationalism had led them to conclude that the speed and secrecy of the event was simply a given, a feature of the natural world, not a deliberate snub to them. They had raised Lainey to be independent, to follow her own path; it would be bad faith on their part to chastise her for it now.

We spent the days sitting on the deck, looking across the lake, talking, becoming a family; once, Barnes had suggested that I join him out on the lake, to do a little fishing, leaving the women to catch up. We had taken the small launch out into the middle of the water, waved off by Peggy and Lainey standing at the end of the little jetty. While Barnes fished, he attempted to re-describe my work in terms he could value, or he talked about Lainey as a girl, her brilliance and charm.

'I don't regret not having a son, you know? I'd always thought, even as a young man, that that would be my completion: a son. When Peggy found out that she wouldn't be able to have more children, it seemed like the end of the world for both of us, but only briefly. We had Lainey, you see, and she was more than enough joy for one man.'

'Enough for two, sir.'

'I hear you James, I hear you. What about you? How's that brother of yours?'

I thought of my brother, a man I hadn't seen for three years, hadn't spoken to since I'd rung him, back south from Scotland, to tell him I was married to a woman he hadn't met, hadn't even heard of, had no prospect of meeting. He had been sullen, disinterested, bitter, but had wished me well, then asked if I had told our parents. I hadn't.

The closeness that Lainey had felt, still felt, among her family – uncles, aunts, cousins too, but especially Peggy and Barnes – awoke in me a huge resentment. There was guilt too, of course, for effectively cutting my own parents, my brother, out of my life. But primarily a sense of injustice that I had not been given the same richness of relationships that Lainey enjoyed. For years, my isolation had seemed like a strength, but there, out on the lake with Barnes, it felt more like a bereavement, an irrevocable mistake.

I was staring at the fractal skin of the lake, spring sunshine electrifying the surface, framed with the new green of waking trees, when Barnes spoke again. His voice dragged me from my self-pity with prosaic instruction, and we cast our lines into the air, breaking the tension, plunging into the hidden waters of Lake Skaneateles, and I wondered why this was the first father that had ever tried to teach me to fish.

For an hour maybe we fished, saying little, catching less. Then, with a look of quiet satisfaction, Barnes had started the engine and turned the launch back towards the shore. There was no greeting party when we reached the jetty, no wives waiting for the return of their men. While Barnes tied the boat, I sat on the deck, unwilling to trespass into the house and intrude on the secrets between mother and daughter. I sat there alone for some time. Barnes found things that needed tying or moving or lifting or sweeping, and I was struck by the diligence with which a man of letters devoted himself to tasks of mundane physicality. Lainey and Peggy did not emerge all the while Barnes worked on the boat and the garden, while I sat watching him, watching the sky and the water and the trees. I grew bored and I grew thirsty, so I crept into the kitchen through the garden door, and poured myself some juice.

I could hear voices, muffled, in the living room. Some words crawled under the door, but did not carry far enough for me to discern the nature of the conversation. Caught between a desire to be a part of their conversation and a distaste for eavesdropping, I stood motionless, poised between a noble exit and taking my now empty glass to the wall. Eventually, my fear of being discovered collided with the certainty of my otherness and I took the side stairs to the bathroom, making as much legitimate noise as I could, to alert Lainey and her mother to the presence of another within the house.

When I came down, I heard Lainey call my name as an enquiry and I went through to them; she gave me a hug and asked how I liked fishing, whether I'd caught anything.

'Now, honey, you must be famished. What can I get you?'

Peggy nodded a smile in my direction, and her eyes betrayed no trace of coolness. She bustled into the kitchen, shouting back choices and possibilities. Lainey beamed contentment from the couch.

'So, what have you been saying about me to your mother?'

'Ha! Get over yourself, will you? Not everything is about you, you know.'

The next morning I drove the five hours down to the City, leaving Lainey alone with her parents' love. I had lined up a series of meetings with gallerists in the Village and in SoHo, the rationale I had used to justify the trip to Gareth; I called Daisy to check arrangements for the next three days of meetings and lunches and viewings, to make sure that the fact I was working was noted, recorded.

...

Miriam is eating *gambas a la plancha* when I arrive at the bar. She is already a third of the way down a bottle, the ghost of her lip traced on the wine glass in a whisper of oil. I challenge her inability to wait for me with mock indignation; she simply kicks the chair out for me and pours *tempranillo* into the empty glass on the table. She is smiling, affecting an air of apologetic powerlessness, shoulders shrugged, hands upturned.

'A girl has got to eat, sweetie. And you're late for once.'

Sitting, I tear at a piece of bread, then take one of the shrimps, raising my eyebrows roguishly.

'Gentleman's prerogative, my dear.'

Shrimp demolished, the debris of its exoskeleton its only monument, I agree that it has indeed been a while and ask how the gallery is going. She says 'fine', and adds that she is heading to London in the autumn, to see some of Brit Art's second wave. I smile: that one of the more fashionable galleries in New York is looking for the next big thing in my town, rather than in Brooklyn, tells the story of our success.

'But Miriam, my dear, that conceptual bullshit is done already. That kind of post-modern, ego-driven art has become lost in a cul-de-sac of its own idiocy. You can't play games of novelty forever: sooner or later people are going to get bored of being shocked. Now, what you should be looking at is the work of a new crop of British artists. They provide a much overdue counterpoint to Brit Art's constant striving for public recognition, and its concomitant, constant fear of failure. The Stuckists are all about the amateur, about doing it for the love of it. Theirs is a quest for authenticity.'

Miriam smirks but holds her tongue for a few moments more.

'Their manifesto centres on the crucial insight that art is not art if it only becomes art in the sterile white of the gallery – art needs to be alive to, to be rooted in, human experience as it is lived. What's more – and I think this is really refreshing – they paint.'

The central importance of that one distinguishing truth causes me to pause for breath.

"Hell, James, did it hurt? Swallowing that manifesto? You still haven't got a clue about this stuff, have you sweetie? But boy, can you say it like you mean it!"

Miriam is a mass of dark hair and darker eyes. Older than me, maybe even forty, she is what a New Yorker should be. Where Lainey is controlled elegance and nuance, Miriam is brash, exhilarating energy. I have spent two and a half years learning to read Lainey and still she is too often a mystery, her feelings, motives and fears hidden. But Miriam, Miriam's whole being screams its essence to the world, doesn't care who sees or what they think. If she was unhappy with something, you knew what it was. Like when a PR spouts two year old propaganda at her, a gallerist, for a non-movement that doesn't sell and, more than that, advocates taking art out of galleries. Didn't I see why she might not be interested in that? While she thinks it sweet that I am still hung up on paintings, she refuses to believe that I can really be that naive.

'How's that painter friend of yours? Rick, isn't it?'

'Richard. I don't see so much of him, but he's around. He was my best man.'

'You're married? You? When did this happen? You, sweetie, never fail to deliver a surprise.'

She politely asks how married life is treating me, but is unconvinced by my description of domestic contentment. She is studiously bored by Lainey's profession, upbringing, likes and dislikes. She pours more wine while I try to make my news seem relevant, interesting.

'But are you happy? I mean, you're stuck now, that's it, your life is this. Sure, you've got your job, you can take up hobbies, but essentially, you are tied to this woman until one of you dies, or until you get divorced. Which, let's face it, is going to happen much sooner.'

We had slept together, once. A few years ago. I'd been in New York for work, towards the end of my relationship with Jess. Miriam had simply been there, fizzing, compelling. She'd told me that she'd never married, never would, and the way she spoke, as much as what she said, suggested that she moved from one erotic engagement to the next with a robust vitality. She had made it clear to me that that night in Manhattan was just a night, that it would not be allowed to interfere with the relationship between us, professional or personal. There would be no 'us', just sex. It had suited me at the time, and I had professed the same view of relationships. No wonder the news of my marriage seemed inauthentic.

'Oh sweetie, I'm only upset that you never asked me. A girl can get cranky when she's hurt, you know?'

She is smiling a faintly mocking smile and strokes the back of my hand with her short fingers in feigned contrition. I know she is playing with me, but I do not want to pursue the matter further, do not want to challenge her false concession. Sometimes I have the feeling that she understands me better than I do myself, that she can see me as I am, while I am caught in my own blind spot. So instead, I let her patronise me about art until the bottle is dead.

...

I have been trying to reach Lainey on the phone all afternoon, ever since Daisy looked up from her computer screen and said simply, 'Oh my god'. It had been a normal, dull Tuesday, ripped apart by news from across the Atlantic. There are rumours of tens of hijacked planes in the air, and London still twitches awaiting its own impact. I am safely tucked away in low-rise Soho, but Lainey is in the City, practically in the shadow of the NatWest Tower and I can picture the dust as it collapses, filling the streets, burying everything. She has probably been on the phone herself, to friends in New York, trying to get through the storm to hear a familiar voice, alive. An afternoon of redial, alternating between her desk number and mobile: one rings out, the other goes straight to voice mail.

...

Lainey had left for Scotland straight from work on the Friday, leaving me to my own devices for the weekend. She and Morag had made up, were friends again. Morag had called as soon as the news about the World Trade Centre had come on the radio: a colleague at the newspaper had called through to alert her to the breaking news, and she had immediately thought of her friend, and the friends they shared on that small island. It was inconceivable that the two friends should not talk on that afternoon of all afternoons, and they had spent two hours on the phone, first checking the other was OK, then running through the likely movements of each of their friends and relatives in and around the city, around the whole Eastern Seaboard, and finally addressing why it had taken this to break the silence between them.

Lainey had announced her intention to go visiting alone that evening. David was going to be absent too, so I wasn't to feel specifically excluded. They just had a lot to catch up on, as she was sure I could understand. I did of course. Morag was Lainey's only real friend on this side of the Atlantic – and, with no flights, that effectively meant her only real friend. Add to that the six months of antipathy between them, and it was perfectly understandable that she would want to spend a weekend in the Borders. I was the epitome of understanding.

In Lainey's absence, I had caught up with friends and

colleagues in New York, watched old films, drunk too much. I enjoyed the freedom to be unproductive without the unspoken censure I was sure Lainey felt towards my indolent self. I enjoyed the freedom in general: Miriam had giggled when I had told her that on the phone, and I was so pleased to hear her laugh, in spite of everything, that I did not feel the need to challenge her. Her gallery was in Greenwich Village, not far, but far enough, from what journalists were already calling Ground Zero. She had left the city, running to relatives in New Jersey, where she intended to stay until things got back to normal. If they ever did. There would, of course, be no trip to London this autumn, no flying ever.

Lainey got home on Monday evening – she had gone straight to the office from the station. She was effervescent, the joy of rediscovering her friend overflowing from her excited form, dousing her fatigue. She looked glorious and I felt a profound satisfaction that she was here, with me. Without removing her coat, she ricocheted through the events of the weekend, haphazardly building up to the crescendo, to the news that Morag was pregnant. She was only a month gone, and Morag didn't want to tempt fate, so we had to keep it secret for now. I demurred that we didn't know anyone in London who knew them, but the pettiness was drowned by Lainey's breathless excitement before she noticed it, rose to it, and I was swept willingly to agreement that it was great news.

And it was. I was genuinely pleased for Morag and David. I had thought at the time that their relocation to the middle of nowhere had been in part to this end, and I was glad that it had finally happened for them. A broad smile across my face, I tell Lainey that the news called for a celebration, that I would pop down to the High Road to get a bottle of something suitable, or that we could go out, if she wasn't too tired.

She hugged me, told me she loved me, then thanked me for being so understanding about the weekend. Squeezing her tighter to me, I told her that there was nothing to understand.

'Sweetheart, I know how hard it's been these last few months. Given what happened in New York, of course you were going to want to see her: I wouldn't have dreamt of intruding on that. Mind, I wish I'd been there for Morag's news – that must have been some celebration! David must be chuffed.'

I could feel her hands moving over my body, seeking a way through my clothes to find me, my warmth. But I pulled away, with all the tenderness I could muster; my smile felt unconvincing, even to me.

'This definitely calls for some fizz. Won't be long.'

As I pulled on my coat, she looked suspiciously at the tidy kitchen and asked if I had been behaving myself. I laughed an assurance that, aside from achieving no more than killing a bottle of single malt, I had done nothing reprehensible.

···

Across the churchyard, on another bench, a homeless man is the only witness. His beard and waxy overcoat are incongruous in the bright June afternoon, and a thin line of sweat cuts through the grime of his cheek. It is the only sign that he is part of his surroundings. He sits motionless, staring at the slabs of worn York stone at his feet, mumbling threats and imprecations into his chest. Maybe it is we who are the intruders, invading his sanctuary under Centre Point's long shadow, rather than his intrusion into our private moment. Maybe it is he that resents our presence here, in this last resting place on the way to the gallows.

Sophie leans forwards from the bench, her right leg tucked awkwardly under her left, to grind her cigarette into the paving slab. Short, rounded nails, painted a rich and pristine crimson, fresh from the manicurist. She regards the stub, the black mark, tear-shaped, burned into the stone, before lifting her eyes back to my face. She sighs.

'You're not a bastard, James. You just can't make choices. At least, not the right ones.'

There is no hint of tears around her face, just a weariness, a sudden tiredness, a subtle, fleeting shake of the head. She had known this point would come, we had spoken about the limits of our relationship at the outset. I had been determined that I would at least do this with some honesty. That had been part of the deal, the moral justification for the betrayal, a betrayal forged in the self-serving ellipse that had occurred to me as I woke on the morning after I had first kissed her: I can because I want to; I want to because I can. It was a limited transactional arrangement, and I had made sure that I had been clear, honest, about the terms of engagement before we had become properly embroiled.

But despite knowing its inevitability, the timing had clearly winded her. To be fair, she had forced the issue. With the impetuousness of the young and beautiful, she had decided that a line had been crossed, that it would now be impossible for me to return unchanged to my former way of being, to the regular rhythms of before, to my wife. She had made no ultimatums, had made no threats. Simply, something had changed in her. A belief in the possibility of transcendence, that maybe our initial contract had been superseded, that now there might be some way of turning a shallow, lurid affair into something of more substance, something that could stand up to daylight.

Now that I have shattered that emergent faith and gone further, giving the coup de grace to our relationship, to my infidelity, she is trying half-heartedly to argue for a return to our former illicit arrangement. But even as she makes the case, claiming that she would be content simply to keep things simple, she knows that she is once again carrying the pain for a man. No, not a bastard, she had said that, and I have no reason to doubt her sincerity even as I doubt the truth of her conviction. But irresponsible certainly, capricious and self-serving. Without malice maybe, but also without empathy.

She lights another cigarette, not offering me one, as she has so often in the past. I feel a pang of loss for that and for every other liberty she has granted me since we'd fallen into each other in a dark alley in Clerkenwell, her yielding easily to my drunken exploration of her form. I hesitate momentarily in the grip of that thought, but quickly remember Lainey and that this is wrong. Wrong.

She is saying 'so', passing the responsibility for what comes next to me, when she notices me looking at my watch. With anger rising, she apologises for keeping me, and the spell is broken. She knows now that there is no reason to want me any longer, and in the relief of release, the tears come. Only a few, but enough to harden her, to raise contempt in her, panic in me. I know that whatever power I had here is now spent and when she tells me just to go, I retreat like a bested animal, leaving her to finish her cigarette, damaged but impervious to further pain. The homeless man watches me leave, his head tracking my exit, slowly, steadily, imperiously.

8

DEAD AIR

Lainey is in the passenger seat. She is pale, shaking, and silent.
I am only driving, no longer trying to reassure or distract her:
I know it is pointless, it is futile. Her reddened eyes are locked
into a thousand yard stare and it occurs to me that I have never
really understood what that expression means until now. She
looks through the windscreen, through the south London streets,
through every material thing in front of her and stares into
what I can only believe is her soul. The tears run constant over
those perfect cheeks and it is the saddest sight I have ever seen.
Occasional sobs break her trembling paralysis.

It is five hours since we were last on this road, bound then
for the hospital rather than home. Then the car had been filled
with noise, anxiety and delusion, not silence and horror. Now
it seems obvious that we should both have known what the
blood meant, the cramps, the abdominal pains. But at the time
we had gripped each other in a frenzy of optimistic denial.
The babbling layers of our voices, constant then so that there
should be no space left for the waiting terror to bulge and spread,

are now stilled. The terror is gone too, leaving only a horrific emptiness.

One in five pregnancies end like this, the doctor had said. Most often in the first twelve weeks. No-one is to blame; it can't be predicted, guarded against. The explanations, the context and the platitudes cannot deaden the howl roaring through Lainey's now hollow body. We are lucky, there is no lasting damage, no need for surgery, for a D and C, we just need to go home and rest. And in six to eight weeks, we can try to conceive again.

But I know we will not. The clumsy, stilted months that had led us to this point, the fumbling negotiations and overwrought reassurances, now seem too arduous to repeat. The pregnancy had arrived before the full emotional terms had been agreed. Loss and recrimination will tear us further apart. It is not a question of simply picking up where we left off: we would need to go back to the very beginning, and we have changed since then. Moreover we have been changed by today. Lainey's silence, I know, is only the still surface sheen of a deeper silence that will prevail between us for all time.

Paused at traffic lights, I turn to face my wife. The shell of my wife, her absence. I need to find some words to fill the deathly void filling the car, to pull her back into the world, back to me. But there are none. The risk of choosing the wrong word is greater than saying nothing, of leaving her to her mute agony. Instead I gently rest my hand on her shoulder. She seems to flinch at my touch, her entire frame clenching, shrinking further from me. I recoil, burned, bereft.

9

She Paints

Sophie Jane Lamb. She simply appears in the gallery. Not on the guest list, I'm sure of that: she has the look of an interloper. A supremely confident one, but an interloper nonetheless. The confidence of youth. She can't be more than 25. Possibly younger, but her rich blue eyes are painted so opulently that her freshness, her innocence, can only be glimpsed through close study. Cropped, dyed-blond hair, a haphazard parting revealing a few millimetres of dark roots. The short fringe is combed straight across, framing those dark, heavy eyes; a slightly crooked, but otherwise textbook button nose sits over lips glossed a deep red. She doesn't eat, at least not often.

I excuse myself from the artist, who I have been cultivating as much to impress a potential client as out of any great love of his work, and move towards the door to check with Daisy, to see if the interloper is in fact on the list. Miss Lamb is a late substitution apparently, here instead of her boss. At least I have her name.

That she gave her full name intrigues me. Either she is so

uncertain of her right to be here, or she is so convinced of her own specialness that she believes she deserves to be named completely, precisely, so she cannot be confused with any other Sophie Lamb. Curiosity piqued, I present myself before her with a smile.

'I just love his work, don't you?'

I nod and repeat the same empty words that I have been using for weeks, with journalists, sponsors, anyone who'll listen. Then I introduce myself, and pause long enough for her to do the same. Interestingly, this time she is simply Sophie Lamb, here in the place of Candida, the director of a gallery on Hoxton Square, where she has just started to work. Candida is down with some bug and is very sorry not to be able to make it; Sophie Lamb hopes, with some apparent anguish, that it is OK that she has come instead. I assure her that as far as I am concerned her presence is more than fine, but since it is not my party – I nod towards the middle aged woman in a burgundy trouser suit, with a serene smile and an explosion of wiry grey hair– my blessing really is of no consequence in any case.

I ask if she would like to meet the artist whose work is scattered around the roughly-finished walls of the reclaimed warehouse. He works mainly with paint on canvas, a habit which much of the trade press regard as either quaint or passé, but which, I confide, is the only interesting thing about him. She giggles gently and briefly, wrinkling her nose, then nods in quiet excitement, her eyes remaining fixed on me. The whisper of a smile, even if it is laced with suspicion, passes over her face.

She was going to bring a friend along, since she knew she

wouldn't know anyone here, but she couldn't make it in the end, so Sophie Lamb is really happy to have run into me, to have someone to talk to, to introduce her to people; she had been worried that she would have ended up standing alone and awkward in a corner, simply watching the beautiful people. This she told me as we crossed the room to where the artist was holding court with potential patrons. I did not rise to her bait – could she really be that innocent? – to tell her that there was no way that someone that looked like her was going to be left alone in a room full of the hangers-on to the second division of London's art establishment.

I introduce her to the artist, emphasising which gallery she represents. This is sufficient for him to devote twenty minutes to her. I do not take the opportunity to disappear; rather I endure the artist's bombast as best I can, protecting her from whatever dangers may be circling. I am rankled that Sophie seems captivated by his pomposity and, spotting two friends across the room, female, also artists, I make our excuses and guide the startled Sophie briskly in their direction, my hand on her elbow, steering her away from the dull dauber.

While not celebrated, not even known, the two women are *bona fide* artists, with whom I have frequently bitched about the rest of the art world over warm white wine at openings just like this. They know, or at least know of, everyone. I leave them to further Sophie's education in safety, while I do the rounds of the room, ensuring that my paid-for responsibilities are fulfilled.

Later, as the room thins out, I find her again. She has made her own circuit, and is clutching a small bundle of erratically shaped business cards. She has had a great time and is so very grateful to me, for taking her under my wing and introducing her to the artist, and to those fascinating women. I feel briefly distinguished to have found a protégé, a bright young thing whose induction into the London art world falls to me. But it is too paternal a role, and I shy away from its inappropriateness, its limitations and its underscoring of generational difference. Instead I warm to the notion of us as co-conspirators, both on the fringes of this world, but within it, guiding each other with native intuition around its absurdities.

She asks if she could get on the list for other events like this. She is simply a marketing assistant at the gallery and she would rather not be reliant on Candida's health to access this world. She only took the job at the gallery to meet these people, people like me, to get an understanding of how this world works; it certainly wasn't the salary. She doesn't plan to be in marketing for ever, she has her own work, her own vocation to pursue. She paints and a job in a gallery, promoting the work of others, is just not enough.

She is sufficiently astute to see the flicker of hurt ripple across my face, but not perceptive enough to avoid compounding the injury. She asks me about my own work, by which she means painting, or sculpting, or whatever form of artistic production it is that I pursue. I tell her this is my work, I am first and foremost a communicator, and I choose to work around art because I like it, not because I have a compulsion to produce it. Of course, I admire those who do produce it, and I stress that I really want to hear more about her painting, maybe even see some of it, but I am no artist, I understand my limits. I tell her about the time I had been persuaded to attend a drawing class, omitting to tell her it was a birthday present from my wife; I describe it as drawing for the terrified.

'At the end of it, I still couldn't draw an ellipse – it was just a badly drawn circle with a kind of squashy bit at the bottom. When the tutor suggested I signed up for a follow-up class, it was pretty clear that it was not because she had any belief in my potential. More a mixture of pity and horror.'

She laughs at this, pleased that her *faux pas* has elided into light-hearted self-deprecation. She is giving control of the conversation back to me, and I take the opportunity to assure her that I'll put her on the list for future events, if she has a card or can give me her contact details. In fact there is an event next week, not one of mine, more of a party than an opening, the birthday of one of this year's more interesting young artists, so there will be a lot of the crowd there. Maybe we could meet for a drink first, if she didn't want to turn up on her own, maybe even get something to eat, then we could talk a bit more about how we could move her on from sending out brochures as soon as possible, maybe even get some of her painting seen more widely. And maybe, I add, hoping to dilute the fatherly tone, to entrench a sense of collaboration, of mutual interest, she could give me some tips on how to get Candida to see the value of using Mercury Associates to promote the gallery.

We agree a time and a pub in Clerkenwell, and she writes her number and email on the back of my hand. Her nails are short but even, rounded, lacquered to a flawless lustre; her fingers caress the pen, squeeze my wrist as she writes. Then she leaves and I kiss her awkwardly, tentatively, on both cheeks, firmly pressing my palm into the centre of her back as I do so. I can feel movement, the hint of her shape, through her coat.

...

We didn't make it to the party. My intention had definitely been to get there. I had wanted to show her off in front of people I barely knew, to bask in the warm ambiguity of our relationship: I had wanted to impress upon her my own importance, my potency, in being part of that circle, that edgy, youthful establishment. My every intention, as I sat waiting for Sophie Lamb in the little pub off Clerkenwell Green, had been to make it to the party, as a colleague, an accomplice; thick as thieves, but proper and immaculate. But in the end we became distracted.

She arrived just after on time, busy and buzzing into the bar, still cocooned against the November chill. I helped her unravel herself from layers of wool and cotton, placing her things in damp strata over my own coat, folded in the corner beside the little table. Beneath it all, a knee-length black skirt and a white blouse, each tailored to her suddenly revealed form. She seemed to flutter, to tremble with a private excitement, her body weightless and skittish, her breath rapid, shallow. Her lips, inconceivably redder now than last time, quivered in a nervous smile. Unable to think of anything cleverer to do or say, I indicated her chair with an extended palm, bowing slightly, and asked her what she'd like from the bar.

When I returned with her drink, along with a second for myself, she had settled into the evening, already deep dark at 6pm. Her earlier tremulousness had solidified into slow calm. She reached up to take her glass with both hands, as though a precious, heavy thing, and I fought back guilty thoughts of her nakedness. Still at that point, I had not admitted to myself what I was doing, what I was hoping.

She talked about her job, her work, her aspirations, her time at art school, and all the while the rain tapped at the window behind her. In turn, I talked about Mercury, how it had come to be, about art, about painting and the pointlessness of most of the work we promoted, about my stubborn refusal to deal with the conceptual crap; I talked about films I liked, places I'd been, about everything except my wife. She chose to leave the omission unchallenged, even as she glossed lightly over her own romantic disappointments.

Glasses empty for a third time, we had to make a decision about the party, about braving the still falling rain to walk ten minutes east. We pretended to debate the matter for a couple of minutes, both of us knowing that the dry warmth of the pub, and the first glimmers of intoxication, would win out. I returned to the bar, and watched Sophie looking around the room, vital and magnetic, perpetual motion in a pencil skirt. For the first time, I admitted to myself why I had approached her at the opening the previous week, why I had invited her to the party, why I had felt excited and nervous as I waited for her, why I had lied to Lainey about the evening.

'So, I take it you're married?'

Her enquiry, on my return to the little corner table, startled me. Masking my discomfort with a questioning, arched eyebrow, I replied that, yes, I was married, adding that it was an odd question.

'Not really. When a man talks for an hour without mentioning his home, his girlfriends, past or present, without talking about anything personal, it's a fair assumption that there is something he's hiding. Assuming you're not a serial killer – and I'm hoping not – then the most likely explanation, it seems to me, is that you're hiding a wife.'

I said that I wasn't hiding her, just that she didn't seem particularly relevant to the conversation. This prompted a small smile, a suppressed burst of laughter. She said that she thought my wife was, actually, highly relevant to the conversation.

'It's not a problem, you know? Actually, I have a little ambition, a thing to do before I'm 25: to have an affair with my boss. Of course, I had assumed that my boss would be a married man, rather than a neurotic spinster, so I figure I may have to tailor things a touch…'

She had leaned forward a little. Fixing me through her lashes with deep blue eyes, she had shrugged her eyebrows as her sentence trailed into unspoken expression. I felt a rush of longing as she pulled her bottom lip slightly between her teeth. Forcing down my weakness with a gulp, I asked her why, incredulous.

She was beautiful, could have her pick of men, why settle for being a mistress, the other woman? A laugh. It wasn't a lifetime commitment she had in mind, but a transient indulgence, something she could control because she knew its limits, its boundaries. It was an exercise of power, she continued, something important for a small, young woman launching herself in the world: subverting the power of a boss, of a wife, of a marriage. Moreover, she craved something fun, weightless. All her 'normal' relationships had fallen apart under the pressure of emotional commitment. And a man who had convinced another woman to marry him, had made it to a position of authority in a field she respected, stood a good chance of being rather more interesting than the single men she might meet, didn't I think?

Her eyebrows flicked up fractionally again, and she dipped her head solicitously. A pause. She asked if I had ever had an affair. No, I hadn't, I said too quickly, then, correcting myself, to clarify, not with my wife; I meant, yes, but only in previous relationships, not this one. I raced to regain control of my mouth, if not the conversation. I restated my position, that in previous relationships I had not always been faithful, but during my marriage I had been. I immediately regretted, then celebrated, my use of the words, 'thus far'. On the wave of possibility that flowed from my admission, that betraying Lainey was only a matter of time, an inevitability, I caught her hand, pulled her to me, and drew her into a kiss.

...

Leaving the station on Tooley Street, skirting the Saturday crowds outside the London Dungeon, I headed towards Bermondsey Street. A bright early December afternoon, cool but not cold. Terrified of meeting someone, anyone, I knew, certain that my betrayal was painted across me, I kept my eyes fixed to the pavement and moved as quickly as I could without scurrying. But the terror of discovery, mixed with excited anticipation, was exhilarating, delicious. I wanted to drink in great gulps of it, become intoxicated, inebriated.

Were I to be discovered, how would I explain this? Even I knew that she had not coerced me, that I was the author of my own temptation and fall. That she was comfortable with me being married did not create the infidelity, it simply made it easier for me, only having to lie to one woman instead of two. Through the adolescent thrill, I could dimly see that I wouldn't need to explain anything, that my wantonness was not yet a badge: why wouldn't I be walking on Bermondsey Street on a Saturday afternoon? What shame would there be in explaining that I was going to meet someone? What suspicions, given my profession, would be aroused by the admission that I was going to meet an artist, to view their paintings?

My cursory explanation to Lainey, weary that I had to work on a Saturday, had been largely honest. I had even said Bermondsey, protecting myself against the possibility of being spotted by a friend or acquaintance who might, innocently, cheerily, report that they had seen me here. I had only omitted the name and sex, claiming the artist I was going to meet was in his forties, unheard of, maybe an exciting new talent, but probably not.

I was not surprised at how easy lying to Lainey had been: it wasn't, of course, the first time I hadn't been honest with her. But over the past week I had been astounded at the ease of my conscience: my anxiety had been at the possibility of discovery, of the consequences of discovery, rather than guilt for the act of betrayal itself, for the wilful intention to continue and compound that betrayal by visiting Sophie's flat, on the knowing pretext of looking at her work. That night, after the party we never reached, after the fumbling in the dark of a Clerkenwell back street, I had returned home to Lainey wracked with what I assumed was guilt. But it had not been until the lights had gone out and I pretended to sleep, that I realised that it wasn't guilt that I felt: only fear, fear of being discovered, of being revealed to be something other than how I wished to be seen. From the facts of the betrayal itself, I took only pleasure, feasting on my hot, sticky sinfulness.

Indeed, my brazenness thrilled me, empowered me, justified me. As I walked into The Garrison, where I had arranged to meet Sophie, I was struck by a new thought: I deserved this. Not only did my affair – I named it for the first time – not trouble my conscience, I was proud of it.

...

I try to pull her back to me, but Sophie wriggles her way out of the embrace. She stands back from me, one hand on my chest, her pupils huge, her lipstick gone but for a pink wash around her mouth. She licks her lips, then laughs.

'You are impossible. You should definitely take more cold showers.'

I say that she doesn't normally complain, that over the last couple of months she has seemed to enjoy our stolen clinches. She says she isn't complaining, she just has things to do. She needs to be up tomorrow, and anyway, she doesn't much like doing this in a bar, even a very dark bar. I concede the points, and tell her I'll let her know tomorrow when and if I will be able to see her next week, maybe find somewhere less public. Then she is gone and I pick up the remains of my drink, take out a cigarette.

Through the first cloud of smoke, I see David. He is sitting on the other side of the bar, and I wonder how long he's been there, what he has seen. But his face, pale, outraged, unsure, tells me he has seen all that matters. I nod to him and, without waiting to be acknowledged, start across the room. He looks horrified, glances about the table, then holds his hand up to me; I stop abruptly, suddenly aware that Morag might be there. And if Morag, then maybe Lainey.

David shambles over to me. He is a cliché: brown corduroys and a checked shirt, beaten suede brogues; his beard has grown even longer since the last time I saw him. The isolation of the Borders, the exile of writing, has taken its toll on him. He seems dazzled by London, shocked by its brash intrusions and seething impatience. Tentatively, he holds out his hand when he reaches me; I clasp it and smile a hello. I ask if he is with Morag; he says no, just some chaps from the paper, work colleagues to be caught up with. He sits at my table, his half drunk pint meeting the table too soon, too fast, unforeseen. He jumps a little at the clash, and we both watch the glass for a few seconds, expecting it to crack and shatter in aftershock, spilling its contents across the table top, the floor, David's cords. But nothing happens and the clanging echo dissipates in the all too brief lull.

'Do you want to explain what that was?'

David's normal style is to skirt the issue, to ask after health and work, to share observations on the world's most recent events, before getting to the point. I am startled by his directness, the thread of steel running through the question, the challenge to make this right, explicable in terms that could be justified. I gamble on his directness and repay it, saying that it was exactly as it looked, that I am having an affair, have been for several weeks, that Lainey doesn't know, and that I'd like to keep it that way. David's face falls, his gaze returns to his pint and he exhales steadily through his nose in a slow sigh, resigned, almost as if he is disappointed that there isn't a better explanation, that it really is as bad as he feared.

'Look David, I don't expect you to approve of this, nor even to understand. I'm not asking you to be happy for me...'

His eyes shoot up at this, his face like granite.

'What are you asking of me, James?'

It strikes me that I don't know what I want from him, that I haven't even considered how this might turn out, what might happen next. I realise that, over the past weeks, I have abandoned concern for consequences completely. I take a moment to gather my thoughts, ask him if he wants another pint. He declines.

'I realise that, given your friendship with Lainey, god, given how close Morag and she are, you must hate me right now, must hate my betrayal of her…'

The word slid easily, lightly from my tongue, leaving no trace of remorse in my mouth.

'… and I know I can't ask any favours for myself. That's not what I'm after. In fact, I genuinely don't know what I'm after, what I want you to do. I'm not even sure I deserve any kind of consideration in this. I'm certainly not going to presume to tell you to damage your relationship with Morag to save my worthless skin; I know you're too close for that, that keeping something like this from her is not something you could do easily…'

David snorts and shakes his head derisively or maybe with something like deep sorrow. It is hard to tell, but his eyes are weary, sad, angry. He looks defeated, realising he is caught between the integrity of his marriage and the wellbeing of his friend. My sacrifice, my ready acceptance of culpability and the retribution that flows from it, has robbed him of a target for his anger, for his revenge.

'Well, what are you going to do about this, this situation, about this girl? Christ, man, she's barely out of school! What were you thinking? You've got to stop this, for her sake, as much as Lainey's. Does she know, even? That you have a wife? That she has no future with you?'

I nod, holding his eye, shrugging slightly as if to say, 'of course'.

'Christ, I don't understand you. Or her. But, look at me James, you have to end this. Put a stop to it. Today. Call her up and tell her this has been a mistake, that you owe it to your wife to stop being such a bastard. Good God man, you have a woman like Lainey, who's not just beautiful and clever, but has one of the biggest hearts I know, and you're messing around with some half-formed child.'

I begin to speculate on whether David merely settled for Morag, knowing he couldn't have Lainey, using their friendship as a way to keep her close to him. The thought that his righteous, pompous anger is as much to do with his own immoral longings makes me smile, and I can't quite smother it before he notices and explodes.

'This is fucking serious, James! You cannot keep this thing going. Lainey has already taken enough shit from you. Why she's put up with it, Christ alone knows, it's a mystery, but she has. But this would kill her. So stop it now. If you do, I mean really do, then I'll say nothing to Morag about what's gone on, nothing to Lainey either. Not for your sake mind; I owe you nothing here. It's just it would break Lainey's heart and she doesn't deserve that. I'm prepared to leave what's gone where it is. But I don't appreciate you making me complicit in this, in your betrayal. So end it. Today. So help me, if I find out you're still seeing the minx, I'll… You can't make this right, James, but you can stop making it worse.'

I tell him what he needs to hear, all the while stifling the laugh that is straining in my chest at his referring to Sophie as a 'minx'. I assure him that I will end the relationship, will stop making things worse, will make it up to Lainey, that I am grateful to him for saving Lainey from the pain of my indiscretion. I know he's right, that this can't go on, should never have started, that I don't know what got into me, it was my fault, not the girl's, certainly not Lainey's. David shakes his head as he stands to leave.

'You don't deserve her, never fucking have.'

...

The tug is a dirty blue and white, indistinct. Only the simple line of its fluorescent orange canopy stands stark in the grey dusk light, as it wearies its way against the flowing Thames, dragging refuse barges towards the estuary. The snub nose of each hull crumples the water racing in to meet them. The short caravan seems to hang motionless in the shadow of St Paul's, as the river moves past them. Minutes pass as the boats struggle their way beneath the Millennium Bridge. A tourist catamaran slides easily past, cutting the grey water effortlessly, carried on the tide upstream.

When the tug is finally beyond my field of vision, I check my watch, drink some coffee and watch the clientele despondently. Tourists arrive and depart, drinking a hurried latte in the gallery's café or coming simply for the view. Spanish and Italian women, their friends and boyfriends, teenagers and students, sporadically approach the window. The more intrepid test the door and step out onto the balcony. A chill blast of February air squeezes in past them. I feel an irritation towards them and their pointless pointing at buildings and places, their need to augment the visual stimulation of a hundred years of art with the City's dusky sky line.

I am impatient for Sophie too. She isn't late, but I had been fretfully early, installing myself at a corner table from which I can survey the faces of each new arrival, and ensure that I prepare the most impressive first impression possible. A book is propped in front of me, opened at a random page, insouciant camouflage for my anxious anticipation. I feel a rush of excitement, tempered only by a resentment that she is not already here. I have taken an afternoon off work, telling Gareth that I needed to meet up with some friends over from the States. He had too easily accepted my justification, not looking up from his monitor, simply grunting acknowledgement. He suspects, I am sure, but now that the work comes in anyway, he seems less interested in the impact of my romances on my professionalism. I have persuaded Sophie to take the afternoon off work too, so we can spend a couple of unrushed hours at her Bermondsey studio.

She arrives exactly on time. She is slightly flustered, flicking nervous glances around the room. Something like fear haunts her, inexplicable. I watch unnoticed for a while, taking in her shape, her movements. I wave, guilty at my voyeurism, and beckon her over, wearing my most relaxed and welcoming smile. The fear disappears, melting into air. I kiss her on both cheeks, formal, distanced, but catch her earlobe momentarily between my lips.

We chat for a while, catching up on the last few days, her eyes urgent, hungry, flitting across my face; she clasps my hand with both of hers, lightly, restlessly. She is eager, after five days of separation, to rediscover its geography, its texture, to hold it close so that it cannot disappear once more. Through the busy movements of her hands I can sense the movements of her whole body continually readjusting itself on the hard chair, and I marvel once again at her physicality, the delectable fact of her being. I scorn David for his pomposity; if he was capable of appreciating the deliciousness of the way she rakes her teeth across her bottom lip, he would never have dreamt to suggest I end this. He lacks imagination, he lacks soul.

'The other day, at the Coach and Horses, after you left, I ran into a friend. Well, not a friend. The husband of my wife's best friend. Had it been a friend, it would have been OK. Anyhow, he saw us. Together. I suppose we didn't leave a lot of space for ambiguity.'

She is transfixed with a giggling, excited horror. There is no embarrassment, simply glee at the gossip of which she is a central part. This is a game, and she is enjoying this latest phase of it, the thrill of falling into unknown territory.

'Oh god! What's he going to do? I guess he'll tell his wife. He has to really, doesn't he? Oh god, are you going to be alright? I mean, when she finds out?'

With quiet satisfaction, I consider Sophie's unwillingness to use my wife's name, but then the thought is gone and I tell her about the conversation with David, about my dread that Morag or Lainey might be with him, about David's anger, his description of her as a minx, about his eulogy to Lainey and my speculation that he fancies my wife. Then I tell her about the deal I struck with him, about my promise to end the affair, and his promise in return not to tell Lainey or Morag about what he had seen. Only then do I add that, of course, I have no intention of ending the affair. I realise, looking up, that she never thought for a second that I would, that she had simply assumed that we would continue and that if any relationship was going to end it was my marriage. And none of this was important, none of this mattered; it was simply exciting, thrilling.

She congratulates me on my cleverness and, moving on, bored now by the incident with David, says she wants to see the Joseph Beuys exhibition that has just opened. I say that I can't see why anyone serious, anyone with an informed interest in art, would want to see random collections of logs and fabric strewn around a gallery. She accuses me of being reductive, of binary thinking, of being a bit too serious, but says, OK, we don't have to see the exhibition, I'm probably right, she just thought that since it was here…

I tell her she should have more backbone, that if she wants to see the show, she should feel confident enough to set out her reasons, not just back down at the first resistance. I aim for a tone that is somewhere between contemptuous and patronising: she is entitled to like Beuys, she is simply wrong.

The ghost of something like fear shimmers across her face, then anger. But it is brief and melts quickly into a rising smile that breaks first in her eyes before spreading across her entire, glorious face. At the moment just before the grin, she is absolutely, completely, comprehensively beautiful. My irritability evaporates, and I am simply captivated by her.

'You're trying to war with me.'

I frown incomprehension at her.

'Pick a fight. Because of David. But I'm not going to let you. You're supposed to want to laugh with me, to be light as air with me, irresponsible. Not squabble. I'm your mistress, James, you're supposed to want to fuck me.'

As the 'F' forms on her lips, she remembers where she is, the ladies gathered in the café for tea and cake, a break from culture, and she lowers her voice, almost hissing the word, through a stifled snigger.

'If you want to fight, well, you've got a wife for that. If you want to fight with me, you're just going to have to make me something other than your mistress.'

She winks and, still smiling the most beautiful smile anyone has ever seen anywhere, she strokes the back of my hand, running her finger down to the first knuckle of my middle hand. She leaves it there, as she looks up at me through heavy lashes, twisting her mouth into something between a smirk and a sour pout.

'Shall we go?'

...

Richard was already drunk when I found him, sitting awkwardly on a bar stool, leaning heavily on his left elbow as he surveyed the room, easily maintaining an air of detachment to mask his blurriness. He didn't see me approach and almost fell from the stool when I clapped his shoulder, said 'hi'.

'What the fuck do you think you're playing at, Jim? You'll give an old man a heart attack. Or something.'

Then he clamped his arms around me, quietly telling me that

it had been too long, too long. And it had: in the seven years since the wedding, I'd only seen him twice: once at the housewarming, the other at an opening of a mutual friend's exhibition in the West End. Richard himself exhibited too infrequently.

He bustled a glass into my hand and asked what was new, eyes twinkling while I recounted the latest news of Gareth and the business, and ran through the important parts of London art world gossip. He asked about mutual friends, and as he told me about his latest preoccupations, how they were effecting his work, I struggled to catch him up on his progress through first one pint, then the next, then another.

I hadn't mentioned Lainey. A deliberate attempt to pique his curiosity, to prompt him to ask me how things were, so that I could tell him about Sophie without it sounding like braggadocio. Since my run-in with David, I had not spoken to anyone about my affair. It had continued unimpeded, of course, although I saw her more often in the privacy of her Bermondsey flat, ostensibly in the interests of discretion.

'Everything alright with Lainey? Married life still good?'

I started to equivocate, to prepare the ground for the revelation of my dirty little secret, my hidden, private sweetness, addictive and intense. I was certain that Richard, my Richard, would understand this, would be able to share my excitement, my happiness. He was not David, mediating life through a set of abstracted, implied imperatives: the 'oughts' and 'shoulds' of moral, social behaviour. Richard's connection with the world was raw, direct, visceral; you could see it in his art, you could see it in his face, in his fervent embrace of the world. He would understand why Sophie made sense.

But he was talking, telling me, then the barman, then the other drinkers within earshot, that of course married life was good with a woman as beautiful as Lainey. How could it not be? My wife was gorgeous, a sweetheart; marrying her was about as lucky as I was ever going to get. I'd be a fool to ever let her slip through my fingers.

...

'You haven't called all week.'

'It's been, uh… difficult. Work, you know. And Lainey. She has a lot on too, and she needs some attention, you can understand that, can't you?'

'What about what I need, James? Something always has to give, and it's always me. Why is it that she is never the one who gets let down? Ignored? Treated like an afterthought?'

'Sophie, honey, you're not an afterthought. Never. It's just difficult. You knew from the outset that I had a wife, and with that comes some responsibilities. Lord knows, I'm fulfilling precious few of them as it is, but she has a right to some support when work is being crappy like this. She deserves at least that. Plus there's stuff I have to get ready for, uh, um, later…'

'Your anniversary, you mean? For fuck's sake, James, I can't believe that you're choosing to not spend time with me, to not give me any attention, just so you can plan a hollow celebration of a dead marriage. It's not like you love her anymore, why go through the pretence?'

'It's not a dead marriage. And I do love her; I'm just not in love with her any more. What I have with you is different, better, but that doesn't mean that there's nothing left... this, us, was never meant to replace my marriage, you know that.'

'Look, I don't want to fight with you, I just want to see you, to be with you. I miss you. I hate not having you here, knowing you're with her. Of course, I know I just have to put up with it, but that'd be so much easier if I could have a little bit of you now. Can't you come to see me today? Just for half an hour. Maybe a bit longer?'

'Like I said, it's difficult. And today is just impossible. Sorry, really, because I'd like to see you too, very much, believe me. But it's not going to happen, can't. Let me see what's possible for next week and call you back later, OK, I promise. No, really, I promise. I will call you by the end of the day. OK, Sophie, I've got to go, I'm supposed to be seeing Gareth now. Sorry. Genuinely.'

10

Revolutions

The monsoon was almost over. For two days, there had been no rain. Intermittent breaks in the cloud revealed the sky's long hidden blue. He knew it was almost time to return to the forest, to reacquaint himself with Iravatha. The thought filled him with a dull heaviness and he was determined to make the most of the brief period of dry weather in the city. For six years the rhythm of Dasara had ingrained itself into him, the weariness of tedious repetition replacing the excitement, the glory, of leading the annual procession. Where once he had felt exalted, he now felt only duty, obligation. This was his dharma, and he had written it for himself. But this privilege brought only abstract pleasure now. Only the pleasures afforded by his position, as the keeper of the Maharaja's favourite elephant, brought palpable enjoyment these days.

Annayya pushed open the shutters, revealing the green and grey of the street outside his small house. The smell of dusty dampness still hung in the air and he breathed deeply. This time of year had once been his favourite, when there was a freshness to the world in counterpoint to the heat of summer and the oppressive weight of monsoon. This was the brief respite between the pervasive rain and the return of the pulverising heat. Others in the city found the air too cold for their taste, but he relished the space allowed by the receding sky. He breathed deeply, then called to the chai wallah making his customary way past the waking houses.

The tea worked its magic. The metallic taste on his tongue and the unsteadiness behind his eyes, remnants of last night, left him slowly. The mahout had once again spent the evening in the Khedda Lounge, buying drinks for his friends and for himself with what remained of his stipend, once he had sent money back to his family and paid the rent. The other drinkers had been pleased to see him as usual and listened eagerly to his stories of life around the palace, of Dasara, of the women he knew around the market. Annayya was the neighbourhood celebrity, and the workers and loafers who frequented the drinking den were never willing to let him leave until everyone was completely drunk, keeping him there to hear his stories and to drink his health until late into the night. Where once they had demanded tales of parades and maharanis, they now drank in the stories of Annayya's adventures with the painted ladies who boarded in the streets behind the Devaraja Market. Their jaws would hang low as Annayya recounted the lascivious details of his exploits, of the women's bodies, and of their willingness to pleasure him in ever more exotic ways. The bawdiness of his audience encouraged him to be still more explicit, to embellish, to hone his skill as a storyteller. During those evenings, when all hung on his words, cheering every tale and every round, Annayya felt himself to be a king amongst men.

But now the dull ache in his head coloured the morning light. Despite the freshness of the air, the stimulus of the tea and the memory of last night's exaltation, Annayya felt nothing but a lugubrious weight, a foreboding, the knowledge that his brief summer would soon be over, replaced by duty and destiny and dharma. His position as lead mahout of the Jamboo Savari brought him the comfortable life he enjoyed, but nothing more. He had long ceased to take any pleasure from the event itself, knowing he was trapped in his role, could not escape it. Had the word meant anything to a man of his class and time he would have known he was bored. Bored such that he had grown to hate the smell of elephants, even of Iravatha. He dreaded those first moments of reunion, when the two companions of so many years first saw each other after their months apart and he had to manufacture joy, pleasure and affection.

Yes, once there had been affection, real, visceral affection, an intoxicating infatuation even, but Annayya knew that the only affection he now felt was that which he carried in his memory.

...

When we were setting up the company, Gareth had told me portentously that George Orwell had written that revolutions fail when they have more to lose than to gain. He had read it when he was a teenager, and had precociously taken it as his motto, before it had been displaced by a swirl of lust and more fashionable slogans. At the time, I had ignored it, unable to work out its meaning in the context of our proposed business venture. I had concluded that it was simply one more example of Gareth seeking to appear cleverer than he was, using the words of others to define himself as the keeper of some deep counter-cultural insight, of an eternal wisdom beyond the rest of us.

But in the early spring of 2005, the aphorism began to make sense to me. It became clear that, like revolutions, relationships falter when they hold together more because of the fear of loss than the optimism of possibility. As daylight began its slow return to London, I worked the words around in my head, building their aptness daily, until they became a total encapsulation of what was wrong between Lainey and I. It was simply a new articulation for a standing condition, of course – the dawn of youthful bliss was long gone – but its long awaited articulation was coldly comforting none the less.

I don't actually remember when I stopped being able to see Lainey as the beautiful woman I once had. But I had lost the ability to see it, and I mourned its loss. She had looked like a film star, radiant, magnificent, and I had been able to spend hours simply looking at the line of her cheekbone, the curve of her lip, the soft delicacy of her skin. She had been the object of my desire, onto which I had projected my erotic imaginings; now I saw the flaws, the tired imperfections, and my familiarity with the whole made it unremarkable. There were times when my loss of her beauty almost brought me to tears. I had become blind to her loveliness to such a degree that it was only because everyone else still seemed to see her grace that I could believe it still existed, even if it was hidden from me.

Unprompted and unexpected, friends would comment enviously on Lainey. Some of my male friends came dangerously close to openly lusting after her, to the point where I would bridle possessively. Others were more sensitive, and merely expressed balanced, objective appreciation of a fine looking woman.

I usually accepted the honour graciously, although I could not escape the thought that friends were duty-bound to say such things in my hearing. But even when complete strangers congratulated me on my fortune or were overheard in their admiration, oblivious to my relevance if not my presence, I was still unable to detect the self-evident reality of Lainey's beauty. When the landlady of the small hotel in Aix en Provence had exclaimed on our arrival, '*Elle est si belle!*', nudging me, actually winking at me, and stood and stared in something like awe for a few moments, I had tried to follow the line of her gaze, to see through her eyes, to rediscover what I had once found so evident, so incontrovertible. But it remained elusive. I knew that Lainey was beautiful, because I had once been able to see it and because the world still did see it. But I was bereft, felt cheated, because I alone amongst men could not see it, could not take pleasure from its radiance.

I began experiments, to engineer opportunities to see her with strangers' eyes, to see without the astigmatism of familiarity. I would construct moments, situations, in which I might catch sight of her unexpectedly, at a distance, without her knowledge, to surprise myself by her presence. I would turn up a few minutes early at bars where we had arranged to meet, so that I might forget why I was there and create a facsimile of our accidental meeting in Waterloo, when she had looked like Greta Garbo. Once or twice she would see me first, and in her sudden form, saying 'hi' and smiling in front of me, I would have a fleeting sense of her as unknown, a beautiful unknown. But it was gone before I could savour it, before I could acknowledge it as anything other than a half forgotten memory, the trace impression of a consoling touch.

I spent a few weeks ambling pointlessly through the streets around her office at lunch time, looking up at the Barbican's towers or down at the traces of Roman walls, watching anything but the faces of the suited workers rushing to sandwich shops, to meetings, to assignations, to lunches. I saw her once, or thought I did. Copper curls gliding away from me, above the shorter figures filling the pavement. I started to follow, then checked myself, aware that I had already filled in the features of the unseen face, had robbed myself of the chance of an accidental glimpse. So I stood stranded among the swirl of lawyers and bankers and administrators, until I called her on her mobile, saying I was out on Berwick Street getting lunch and just wanted to hear her voice, just wanted to say hello, and her voice, fringed with bashful embarrassment at my touching act, was beautiful, and I had an ache of guilt for lying to her, for trying to trick her, for not being able to see her as she was, and being too arrogant, fearful, to confess it.

I gave up. The realisation that even if the perfect chance

encounter could be orchestrated, even if my stranger's eyes were able to see Lainey as she was, the moment would be so fleeting that it would give no pleasure, would simply feed my sense of loss. I came to realise that the reality was what I perceived. It didn't matter that Lainey was beautiful to every other person on the planet, if even the dogs and cats and birds saw her as the very Aphrodite. I had to accept that where she had once been beautiful, she was now plain. Never ugly. No, I could see clearly the elements of a balanced and well-proportioned face, could recognise that each individual piece was as it should be and more, that the physical composition of her cheekbones was that of a beautiful woman, that the arch of her eye and curve of her lip contained all the components necessary for allure. It was simply that those elements had been so closely analysed, so deeply drunk in through my eyes, that I could no longer read the beauty in their interplay. That seemed irretrievably lost to me.

So I had bargained with myself, trading the loss of sudden blithe pleasure in her face against the knowledge that the beauty others no doubt saw reflected on me, raised the value of my stock. I had resigned myself to a life of compromised acceptance, reconciling the diminishing returns of my future in a ledger bound tight in the memory of when that face had stalled my heart, left me immobile. That I had once had so much was the insipid compensation for my now settling for perpetual dissatisfaction.

My gradual withdrawal from her, though not unconnected, was not entirely a drawn out act of spite, of calculated vindictiveness. I did not see her as the author of my loss: I know that irrationalism on that scale would be close to paranoia. The progressive removal of myself from my marriage had deeper roots. Conversation between us became banal, aimless; the tone grudging. We had never really argued, not in a full-throated way, choosing instead to avoid confrontation, to bury discord; but fairly soon into the marriage we had stopped completely. Instead, we retreated into silent resentfulness. Every unspoken grievance lingered deep within me, spawning new animosities, phantoms, but potent nonetheless, making any disagreement impossible to vocalise. It was better to say nothing than to risk saying the wrong thing.

It was unnoticeable at the time, but is now obvious: this silence grew to include all but the most mundane topics, and eventually developed into a resentful secrecy. I began lying to Lainey about the evenings I spent out without her long before I needed to, before I had anything to hide. Lying became easy, forgetting also. Approaching the front door in Balham at the end of an evening became depressing, dismal. Before I ever met Sophie, I had lost the ability, the will, to see or hear Lainey. Even after the affair, when I had chosen, consciously and deliberately chosen, my wife over my mistress, the intimacy of trust proved impossible to recreate.

...

Even now, when I know there are but days left of us, she is perfect. In a shaft of late afternoon sunlight that has found the crack in the curtain, hung haphazardly across the tall window, she is dressing, slowly. The little spotlight picks out the curve of her hip as she, standing on one leg, pulls her tights over the other; the movements of flesh and bone under the skin of her back as she re-hooks the bra that I have so recently removed; it plunges into her cleavage before her breasts are obscured by the upwards march of her buttoning fingers. She wriggles the charcoal pencil skirt up over her thighs, her hips, and fastens it behind her. Then she looks over at me. Even fully clothed I cannot quell the lust that her eyes unlock in me; lust that would have seemed impolite, treacherous even, had I thought of Lainey in those terms.

On the bed, I suddenly feel very naked, exposed, and reach for my own things, hurrying to cover my ageing flesh, my decay all too apparent next to her youthful abundance. These Saturday afternoons will be what I miss most about our affair.

Her hand runs over my cheek, my ear, around to the nape, and she pulls me sharply down to meet her mouth. She breaks the embrace, and rests her hand on my chest: I try to stifle the cringe at this further reminder of my physical inadequacy. Looking up in the half-light, her huge eyes, her twisting mouth, are full of imploring mischief.

'Please have time for a cup of coffee.'

I do have time, but I know that I do not want to spend it talking to her. Words can only lead to one outcome, and I am not ready to break this spell just yet. The moment of fracture will come soon enough, it needs no hurrying. So I look at my watch, try to appear as if I am weighing the merits of being late for some imagined appointment. My nerve fails me and I smile and nod, and we move to her little kitchen, tucked into the corner of her studio.

Her completed pictures lean one against the other by the wall next to the window. Work in progress sits on two easels facing them. They are medium sized canvasses, maybe four feet tall, and one is still marked in charcoal; a jawline, sagging, is emerging in oils from the sketched lines. She is painting me. I wonder if she will ever complete it, once I have told her that I cannot see her anymore. If she does, will she do so faithfully, out of devotion, or will she distort my face to reflect her hot contempt for me? Or will she move on, disinterested, painting over the pigment and outlines, replacing them thoughtlessly with new concerns?

Sophie can't earn much at the gallery, but her studio is spacious, big enough for a bed and kitchen, a sofa and a bathroom, as well as room to work; high ceilings, a large window. Bermondsey is not cheap, despite everything. Her coffee machine is solid, German, and makes a good espresso. Her parents, I guess. I am suddenly amazed that in the eight months that I have known her, I have never asked her about her family. To me, she is a phenomenon, a simple fact without context, explanation, without history and without a future. All of my time with her has been spent in the present, in the here and now. Our encounters have been disconnected events. Like her paintings: there must be something that provides a narrative, a connection between them, but when I look at them, I see only discreet canvasses. A murmur of regret passes through me, that I have missed something of value by not engaging with those connections, with the story as a whole, that it is now too late to try.

The notion that there might be a future here, among her paintings and in her bed, hangs in the air with the pungent aroma of coffee. But I am good at ignoring these things. I have made my decision, or at least realised, that if I have a future anywhere it is with my wife. If the disruption were the only consideration, it would be enough to tie me to Lainey. But there is also the balance sheet of pain and duty: I owe Lainey more than I owe Sophie. I dare not unleash all of that, the practical and the emotional, for the untested potential of Sophie. I hadn't been able to confess to Richard even that I was having this affair: how could I tell him I had left Lainey over it?

'It's done. Come over here and sit down. It'll be nice to sit with you, chatting over coffee. I wish we could do that kind of thing more often.'

We sit. We drink coffee, and she tells me about her plans for the rest of the weekend, about the next steps for the portrait, about next week. I watch her, the movement of her mouth as she forms nervous, endless words, fitting her smile around them, her eyes never breaking contact, her hands like small birds flitting between coffee cup and her lap. And all I can think is that, even though I no longer have any desire for Lainey, even though it is Sophie's mouth I want to feel against my own, I have to leave here. Soon. Before real damage is done. Sophie didn't cause the death of my marriage. She is not culpable, she cannot be blamed. But even though my marriage is dead, I am not ready to let it end.

...

'Do you want to tell me what the matter is?'

Lainey fixed me with dead eyes from across the kitchen table. It was mid-morning, Saturday. We had been out late the night before, celebrating her birthday. Except it hadn't been much of a celebration, had turned ugly sometime during dessert. For whatever reason, I had been unreasonable, antagonistic, incessant far beyond the point where it had been obvious to both of us that I had already gone too far. I had picked the fight deliberately, if unconsciously, persisting up to the point where she had started to cry. Even then I had not relented. Some meaningless point that I couldn't recall, that I had selected as a battering ram against her, against her sense of self, her self-respect. As tears has started to gather around the edges of her vivid green eyes, like storm clouds heavy with rain, I had gone on, cold, relentless. Had I wanted to stop, to allow some respite, I don't believe I would have been able to; and I hadn't wanted to stop.

When she had left the table, hurrying to the bathroom, scraping the chair noisily across the stone floor, trying belatedly to cover her shame, her distress, I had called the waiter and paid the bill. We left the restaurant wordlessly, and the silence had stuck to us in the taxi and into the house. It stuck to us like a viscous corrosive, a caustic substance we had not been able to wash off. She had taken her share upstairs to bed, while I had wallowed in mine on the sofa, where I ultimately slept. Neither of us had found the will or the capacity to break it until then, in the kitchen, over a joyless breakfast, the champagne and pastries bought the day before untouched, unwanted.

Nothing, nothing was the matter. That was all that was open to me to say. The specifics escaped me, had melted into the darkness of the night before. And the substance, the reality, was too big to begin to unwrap, especially now, with the two of us locked in resentful antagonism, a bathysphere of distrust. To open that wound, to scratch and paw at it, risked bringing the whole edifice down, that flimsy were the foundations. Besides, it was an unformed thought, an agony as yet without words, names, description. The perpetual, latent fear of discovery that had weighed on me for the last few months was now bearing down on me ferociously. I was overwhelmed by the need for careful precision: I didn't want to lie, say something that I might be held to account for at a later date; but nor did I want, inadvertently, to tell the truth. So long as we didn't name it, we might survive. There was nothing to be said, nothing that could be said, in its own terms and for fear of the consequences.

Her eyes lingered on me for a moment, an eternity, longer, and I could hear the disappointment, bitter, crackling through the air between us. Still sitting across the table from me, she turned her head sharply and looked out of the window, formulating her next move, or waiting for mine. I simply wanted to move on, to get past this, to bring some mundanity in through the window with the sunshine. To thaw the ice that surrounded us with the prosaic elements of everyday existence, to replace the amorphous threat hanging over us with shopping and chores and a weekend schedule. To get back to the itinerary I had mapped out to mark her birthday.

I apologised, with as much sincerity as I could manufacture. I had been in a bad mood, stress with work I supposed, and something indefinite, beyond comprehension, beyond expression. She knew how I got sometimes, and I was just sorry that it had coincided with her birthday. I realised that was unfair, but I never set out to make her the enemy. This last was a lie and, there, then, I felt something like hatred towards her, for making me behave like this, for making me lie to her. Even though I knew full well that it was me who had been, was being, unreasonable, I believed that it was in fact her. In my head, a self pitying voice was repeating that it wasn't fair, that I couldn't believe she was being like this, that she was making me be like this, that she couldn't just drop it and let us get on with what I had planned. That she refused to look at me and kept her eyes fixed on something beyond the kitchen window was the height of childishness; it was unreasonable and petulant. She stood and moved towards the sink, her face to the sunshine, her back to me.

In exasperation, I lifted my hands towards the ceiling, sighed, sat back in my chair and ran my palms over my head until they came to rest on the nape of my neck. I shook my head, and said that I didn't know what else I could say, do, to put things right. I'd explained as best as I could. I didn't know why I'd been so unreasonable; no, she was right, so hateful. Something had just flipped and put me in an unpleasant mood. She should understand that, as she got in inexplicably bad moods too, withdrew, became confrontational. It wasn't just me. But it had passed now, and I really wanted to move on. As I stood and moved over towards her, I made a last appeal to reason: couldn't she accept that, and just forgive me? It was nothing. Really.

At this she swung back to focus on me, and I sought to ensure absolute control of my face, to give my subconscious no chance to betray me.

'So it was nothing to do with Sophie Lamb, then?'

I was immobile, a rabbit in her headlight stare. I stuttered some unconvincing prevarication, that I didn't know what she meant, who she was talking about, while I frantically tried to find the way out of this, the way to explain this away. That she knew Sophie's name meant this wasn't just some fishing trip: she had come with intelligence, reliable intelligence. And all I could think was what a fucking deceitful bastard David was.

'Oh, stop lying James, for Christ's sake. Do me that one courtesy, yeah? I know all about the stupid little bitch.'

No escape route presented itself. I wanted simply to freeze, stand motionless, play dead, wait until it had all gone away. I was sufficiently lucid to know that this wasn't going to go away, but I could find no words in any case. Instead I found myself focussing on the fact that she had described another woman in those terms, one she had never met, one who she might in other circumstances have viewed as much a victim as herself. I could not remember Lainey ever using that word before.

The word, or at least the sentiment it contained, must have come from David, from his contempt and scorn for Sophie. A seething, gnawing resentment at David's betrayal, at his pettiness, swelled around me, stoking a rising anger in my gut. How the fuck dare he? That he had deliberately gone out of his way to cause this trouble. That Lainey had chosen to use his betrayal to ambush me like this, after what must have been weeks of knowing. David would have told Morag, and she in turn would have been unable to keep it to herself, in fact she would have been gleeful in the telling, would have called Lainey as soon as she possibly could, and no doubt would have used the opportunity to destroy whatever was left of my standing with Lainey. She would have made sure that my wife thought less of me than dirt.

'Nothing? You have nothing to say about this? Do you really think that little of me? Fuck, James, you're pathetic.'

She had no right, no right at all, to take away what was left of my dignity. Anger, shame, guilt, impotence rushed through me, fizzing through my head, scalding my eyes. My right arm was raised, was drawn back across my chest to my left shoulder, was flying before I was conscious of the material facts of my own body, swinging through the kitchen air until the back of my hand struck hard into her right cheek. A dull slap, heavy, sickening. Strangely wet, organic, like driving a spade into fresh, moist peat. I felt her face turn, her frame give, as she slowly crumpled and stumbled, almost fell, catching herself on the kitchen work top, clutching its edge with unsteady hands.

For an eternity, she stood stooped over the counter, leaning heavily on her hands, head bowed, legs trembling. When she turned, the rage, the hurt, the shock had been contained, distilled, and she stared at me, her head tilted slightly to one side, her eyes fixed harshly, waiting, waiting for me to do something, say something. I could not hold her gaze and instead traced shapes in the grain of the kitchen floor boards. I had nothing to say, my mind a dry, terrified and vacant space. The anger of seconds before had been displaced and, instead of violence, my gut was home to a sickening emptiness. More than ever before in my life, I had no words.

Resisting the apologetic impulse was the easiest thing. The bitter tang of the word 'pathetic' lingered and it wanted no confirmation. In any case, my actions were unforgivable. There was no point in asking for forgiveness: to do so would be to underplay the significance, the permanence of what had occurred. To say 'sorry' could only be interpreted as self-regard, to believe that such a small word could erase the act, and the betrayal – my betrayal – that had led to it. So I stayed silent, for the want of anything meaningful to say. The seconds crawled by, neither of us speaking, moving, blinking.

'Get out.'

That was all. Such was my deficit, I had no choice but to obey. It was the least I owed her. Still silent, I turned and walked to the front door, pulling it to behind me, unaware then that I would only see Lainey once more, sitting silently in the kitchen as I packed my belongings and made my final exit from our house in Balham.

...

The door clicks shut, its implied resonance deadened by the

wooden frame. The almost-sound hangs in the air for some moments before it evaporates, leaving only its trace in her memory. She raises her hand to her face and recoils slightly at the first touch, then runs a whispered stroke along the cheekbone, over the already-massing glut of pain where his hand had struck. She becomes aware of the emptiness of the house, and can hear the molecules of air slowly bouncing into one another in the wake of his exit. She stops herself from rocking gently and moves slowly to a chair, the one he had vacated in order to hit her.

She is still stroking her cheek, pushing into the nascent contusion every now and then to release the pain, to remind her more clearly of what had happened only moments before. She is numb and needs this sensation, any sensation, to prevent her from collapsing into tears and regret. Why hadn't he said anything? The blow was unforgivable, but his lack of contrition, or even acknowledgement, had been crushing. His unwillingness to open to her, even at that point, had finally made it impossible to give him more chances. Ever since she had known about the affair, she had believed that there was a way in which things could be made right between them, if only he would acknowledge the wrongness of what he had done, and accept that they both needed to be part of putting things right. She had taken the fight in the restaurant as an indication that he wanted to resolve things, that since he was incapable of addressing the infidelity directly, he was provoking a fight into which the truth would spill. She had been prepared to forgive him ruining her birthday, as well as for destroying her trust, if that had been the intent.

But this morning, presented with the unequivocal reality of his affair and her knowledge of it, he had refused to try to save their marriage. Worse, he had chosen to hit her rather than talk to her. And then to say nothing, just to stand there, unable even to look her in the eye, to stare at his feet like a sullen school boy, smirking at his misdemeanours, expecting to once again get away with it. She had done her best, fought down the tears and the anger and the pain, to invite him to speak, to allow him a calm rational space into which he could start to make things right, to show he had an interest in doing so.

She struggles to remember him as he was in the beginning, to see if there had been any clues she had missed then to this heartless barbarity. Morag had been right about his weakness, his faithlessness, but she had not predicted cruelty, violence, brutality. She thought she knew all his flaws, had accommodated herself to them, but had never foreseen this. How could he have remained silent once again at such a vital moment in their relationship? Did it really mean that little to him? Had it always been worn so lightly? Only seven years of marriage. It sounded so slight to say it, that she could see how it would weigh so little to him.

She is crying now. The full density of the loss crashes down upon her and her steel buckles under the pressure. His departure, and the manner of it, robs her of more than a husband, more even than the superstructure of a life. She is a victim, she has allowed herself to be beaten, but worse, fooled, taken advantage of, betrayed. The entire story of herself, the story she has spent her life writing, is revealed as a sham. She is left unknown to herself. As the tears run unimpeded, slow and constant over her swollen cheek, she is struck by the terror of loneliness: not the loss of James, but the loss of Lainey. In the silence of the house, beyond the reach of any living thing, she starts to imagine that she is dead, that her existence has ended; more, that it had never even begun.

She wants to ask James whether he would have noticed, cared, if she had never been born, never taken the job in London, never met him. Knowing what he knows now, feeling as he feels now, would he rather have his seven years back? But, of course, he isn't there to ask, will never be there to ask again. So she is left alone, unreal, while that girl breathes and laughs and walks in the world of solid things. Is he on his way to her now, to this Sophie Lamb, she wonders? She starts to think of the email as a communication from the other side, some message from the land of the living to tell her she was dead, to finally alert her to her own nothingness. What made that stupid girl think she think she could do this to her? The affair she could understand; things like that happen, you could survive them, so long as you are honest and are willing to engage, to address the issue. But to send an email like that? It was beyond malicious. Stupid, stupid, stupid.

II

Hanging On

The girl was the first to see him. She was squatting by the side of the road, in the shade of the old Banyan, waiting. She didn't know exactly what she was waiting for, just that she would know it when it arrived. Her mother had shouted at her, chased her from the house and out into the dusty heat of the main street of the village. Her face flushing with impotent rage, she had sought refuge in the relative cool of the tree's shadow. And now there was nothing to do but wait. Something would come along to make everything right, to calm her mother, to take the drab dreariness out of the day. She just didn't know what it was. So she drew shapes in the dust, scratching lines and swirls with a stick, and she waited.

From the village, she could hear the babble of her sisters as they fetched water, swept the ground around the little house and made themselves busy, valued. Her brothers and father had left early for the fields: now that the rains had ended and the Kharif crop was ready, most of the grown-ups in the village were in the paddies, cutting the golden rice, threshing it against wooden boards, knocking the precious grains onto the large squares of coarse fabric that were laid out in the fields, under the sun, at each harvest time. The older children were holding sacks open to receive the shearing torrents of rice, or were tying the remains of straw into bundles for the animals. But the girl was too little to be anything other than a nuisance. She was not even able to gather firewood properly, so she doodled shapes that looked like they might be words and waited, keeping out from under the feet of those that had work to do.

She waited a long time. The day's heat was building, even though it was still early. Insects stumbled lazily through the air and the vultures soared high above. At first, she just noticed the dust above the trees that hid the road south of the village. Often there was dust, stirred up by ox carts carrying men, tools or animals, and the girl paid no attention, focussing instead on the ants running in the tiny trenches she had made in the dry earth.

Hearing something in the trees, she looked up, curious. An elephant emerged from the copse and walked along the road towards the village, its trunk swinging with each solid step. She stood up and shielded her eyes with her dusty hand, better to see the beast through the glare. Almost immediately, she was sure that it was the same elephant as last year. That elephant had passed through the village after the rains too. She could remember it clearly: there had been singing, and food, and her mother had been happy, had picked her up and swung her through the air. She had been able to stay up late into the evening to watch the grown-ups laugh and dance and sing. She had eaten and eaten and no-one had told her to stop; even her father had been smiling, had ruffled her hair with his big callused hand. It had been the best night of her life, and now the elephant was back.

She started forwards, breaking into a run, but then stopped abruptly. Her smile fell away and she squinted quizzically, her mouth twisted to one side beneath a wrinkled nose. There was no mahout. Last year, an old man had been walking beside the elephant, his dhoti hanging right to the ground, his bare feet flashing into the light at each step. But today there was no-one. She searched the trees for sign of the old man, anyone, who might be responsible for the animal, before deciding that he must be on his own. Like her.

Behind her, from the village, she heard the shout of one of the other children. An excited, impetuous shout. She realised that someone else had seen the elephant, would claim to have seen him first, would claim him for themselves, would ride high on the glory of spotting him, of alerting the others to his approach. It was too late now for her to shout, so instead she gathered all her courage and ran pell-mell down the road towards the solitary bull.

She pulled up a few feet in front of him. He paused as well, observed her curiously. She could hear the other children running from the village, but they were some distance behind: she would have a moment alone with him, when he was hers and no-one else's. She reached out her hand, but hesitated, was too terrified to touch the trunk which was hanging in front of her. The elephant had stopped, stood staring at the little girl, puzzled. Then he raised his trunk and touched her gently on the head, as he had done with hundreds of children before, at dawn each year on the morning of the big parade.

By now, the girl and the elephant were ringed by the village children and some of the grown-ups. All were too afraid to come closer. An old woman hissed at the girl to come away, it was dangerous, the elephant might kill her, might be a rogue; there was no mahout after all. Another exclaimed, almost fainting, that it was Iravatha, the elephant that had killed its mahout last year at Dasara. Someone else said, yes it was Iravatha, the King of Mysore, that he must be making his way to the city for the festival, out of habit. Another laughed that it was not out of habit that the elephant was walking to Mysore, but that he was making a pilgrimage. Other adults, the women and old men, had gathered now and were speculating about the elephant, how it had got here, why it had come, whether it was safe, who they should tell, whether they should fetch the police to shoot it. The little girl turned, emboldened by the majesty of the mighty bull. Speaking clearly and calmly above the hubbub, she brought their voices to a stillness. Yes, it was Iravatha, the brave and gentle elephant from last year, the noble beast who cried over the body of his dear, dead mahout. No-one should shoot him; instead, they should honour him. Like last year, they should give him some food for his long journey to Mysore, where he was going to look for his mahout, so that he wouldn't be lonely, so that the pain in his soul might be salved.

...

Date: Wed, June 21, 2006 at 10:53 PM

Subject: I am so sorry

Dear Lainey

I don't know if you are even aware of my existence, although we did meet once. However, I am sure that you will have your suspicions. James always presents you as an intelligent woman. In any case, I should introduce myself formally, to make things even, since I feel I know you quite well.

I am your husband's lover. For the past nine months, we've been having an affair. Those nights he had to be away, or was meeting friends, and those Saturday afternoon meetings: he was with me.

As you know, James is not a good liar, no matter what he thinks. So he must have given some clues. Or maybe he's now come clean and told you about us? I hope so, since he said he was ending our relationship to try to make your marriage work, and I think that to do that requires some honesty, don't you?

Anyway, whatever you've picked up, worked out, deduced, or been told, I thought you deserved to know for sure, to have the truth, openly and calmly. It will be up to you then to act as you see fit, once you have the facts.

I want you to know that I bear you no animosity, and I hope you can do me the same courtesy (although I realise that will be difficult.) That we both fell for the same man is nobody's fault and I hope that whatever happens in the end, you are OK and find a way to come to terms with this difficult situation.

With best wishes (really)

Sophie Lamb

She clicks 'send' and sits back, slouching slightly into the desk chair. It creaks gently against the shifting burden.

...

London is washed in the lemon light of a fine spring day. She is not working, although she can see the gallery through the trees on the Square. There is a gloss of incipient green at the branch tips, a herald of redemption, and the bright sunshine is playing among the breaking buds, framing each tree in verdigris. Sophie maps out the painting she would make of the scene, if she could find the energy.

Hoxton Square is busy with people hungrily absorbing the year's first warmth. Some are lying on the threadbare grass as if it were a beach. The terraces outside the few cafes and bars that ring the green are filled with the lunch time glut. She has failed to arrive in time to get a table outside, so she is inside, embedded in an armchair, its leather worn but accommodating. Around her, the slabs of cake, the thick tortillas and the impossible bowls of stews and salads await selection on shelves and side tables. She too is waiting, waiting for the boy with the improbable haircut and no sense of time.

That she is here on her day off, so near to the gallery, seems unfair. She had originally booked the day so that she could do some work, make some progress with her stalled project, the canvas that refused to make sense, no matter how much of herself, of her pain and joy and frustration, she poured into it. For months now, the portrait had brooded, intransigent, in the corner. At first, when its intractability had become apparent, unavoidable, she had thrown every spare hour at working and reworking the paint, trying to drag from its sticky ooze all that she knew she wanted to show, to express. The thought was real, definite, but it was inarticulate, formless. It floated inside her, clearly tangible up to the instant that she tried to grasp it, control it, shape it into something intelligible, communicable. Then it vanished like a ghost, leaving her questioning whether it had ever been real at all.

As the weeks passed, and she had got no further, she had given less and less of herself to the task. A grudging hour on a Sunday, defeated before she began. Maybe a Thursday evening of rational, planned realism, breaking down the elements into achievable, definable steps, things she could complete. But no matter how calmly, how systematically, how faithfully she compiled these elements, the whole still failed, and she would angrily resign herself to starting again, or to giving up.

Today, she had not even had the stomach to pretend to make a start, and when the boy had called and suggested lunch, she had rushed at the opportunity to avoid inevitable failure. Even when he had said here, on the Square, just across from the place she least wanted to be, she had not demurred, had been too happy to throw off the unbearable weight of unwanted obligation.

When had her work become an unwanted obligation? She had loved painting, revelled in the act of applying pigment to the flat, giving surface of canvas, of paper. It was the thing that marked her as special, the place where she was able to create, to be fully in the world. As a teenager, at college, it had never been an imposition, had never been difficult. It had never been a source of such anxiety. She had not had to suffer for her art, and had scorned the self-importance of those that claimed to have done so: how could the privilege of creating be suffering? When she had decided that this was what she was, what she did, it had taken on an importance. A weight certainly, but a weight that was reassuring; it had given her ballast, not drained her.

Even after the break up with James, she had been prolific. He had made her angry, sad, confused, but that had been fuel for the paintings, not an obstacle. In the months after that day by the church, when he had casually ended the relationship, she had produced some of her best pieces. His choice, not to choose her, had freed her to be herself and she had expanded to fill the empty liberty that that choice had created. The months immediately after the break up had been resolute and productive. She had discovered a rare diligence, a focus and determination that had kept her indoors for much of the summer and early autumn. She had still painted freely, without this crushing weight, this inertia, the aimlessness that gripped her now. Only the portrait refused to reach its conclusion: it had become a challenge she could not surmount, but one she could neither give in to, nor abandon entirely.

She gulps some coffee. The skinny woman opposite, with the long pony-tail and square glasses, looks over dismissively, as if offended by the sound of Sophie swallowing. She shifts awkwardly on the low sofa, making herself ungainly as she tries to maintain her dignity in the too short skirt. Sophie glares at her and, horrified, the skinny woman returns to her magazine, pulling at the hem of her skirt with her free hand.

The boy is late. In the swirling darkness of the club he had seemed weightless, lithe, pretty in a fashionable way. But in the bright fizzing light of now, he is merely late. James was never late, always gave her the respect of punctuality. Of course, because of his work and his wife, he had had to be fastidious in his timekeeping. Between his lives, he didn't have time to fritter, and being late for her would have meant being late for Lainey. She had wanted that, for him to be late for her, to mark out the respect he had for his wife as different, inferior, to that which he had for his mistress.

There had been a time, a short few weeks, when she had felt that maybe the balance had shifted, that it was with her, not Lainey, that his imagined future lay. She had been careful not to cajole him, at least not directly, in that direction. She had been patient, so patient. She simply had to have the courage, the strength, to wait. He had already left his wife sufficiently to take a mistress, to take her to bed, to lie consistently and repeatedly, thoughtlessly; surely the final step would be easier than that? Simply wait, and he would come to her. But then he had made his choice: Lainey. Crushed in the end by guilt and duty and cowardice, he had abandoned her, cheated her.

When she first heard the gossip at some private view or other that James and Lainey had broken up, she had been genuinely sad. She told herself that she had not wanted to be the cause of that, of wrecking a marriage. Even though, of course, she had. But her self-deception had not prevented her from savouring a pulse of guilty exhilaration that he had left his wife because of her. He hadn't left Lainey *for* her, of course, but she had delighted in the exercise of her capacity to affect lives beyond her own. She was no longer a child, subject to the will of others; she was not even simply the master of her own destiny; she could change the world around her through her actions, through her simple existence. James was no longer with Lainey because of his hunger for her. And because of her email.

To an outside observer, the reasons for sending that email would be obvious: spite, revenge, anger, bitterness. But she is clear in her own mind that her motives were not those. Of course, anger and heartache played a part: they were at least present in the room while she typed. But when she sat down that evening, a couple of weeks after the end of the affair, and started to draft the email, it was something much more grown-up, more dispassionate, that had shaped the words. She likes to believe that in some small way it was an act of compassion: Lainey had had a right to know the truth. And she had wanted to ensure that James actually did work at his marriage, really did make things right, so that her loss was not entirely pointless.

She had found Lainey's email address early on in the affair. Her curiosity had overtaken her once while James showered, leaving his Hotmail account open on her laptop. She had simply wanted to find out more about the people that were in James's other life, the friends she couldn't meet, and to taste the flavour of the way he spoke to his wife. As she had scrolled through his messages, she became feverishly anxious to weigh the tenderness in their day-to-day electronic exchanges, praying that there would be none, that they really were as emotionally remote as she hoped. And there it had been: Lainey's matter of fact response to a mundane request from her husband, sent from her office email address. Sophie had unthinkingly copied the address as the shower stopped running and James had shouted through something about a cup of tea.

Shame had flushed through her at first, with such force that she had been certain it had left a visible mark upon her, that James could see it painted on her face as he emerged from the bathroom. But her initial guilt dissipated over the following days. She had at first thought that she should delete the address, improperly acquired, but this too had faded and instead she had begun to see it as a secret weapon, one she guarded jealously. She thought about using it to reveal the affair while it was a going concern, to provoke the end of the marriage, freeing James for herself. She had rolled the idea around inside her head, examining it from each and every angle, as she lay in the darkness of her room after James had dressed and washed and left for the Tube to take him to Balham and to her. But she had resisted that temptation, knowing that it would have been cruel and selfish. And it would do her no good: James would not want her, knowing that she had deliberately set out to wreck his marriage.

After it had been sent, she had waited, braced herself for the storm, the shrill howls from her or from him. But none had come, only agonising silence. Lainey had never replied, had never risen to the bait, never poured out her anger and scorn and pain into an emailed reply. She had never unleashed a cauldron of undeserved opprobrium on her, to which she could respond defiantly, from which she could draw some sense of herself being wronged also. She had assumed that Lainey had been too devastated, too ashamed, to engage in any direct communication; his silence could only signal his terminal disappointment in her.

But when they met last autumn, months after the email had been sent, she learned that James knew nothing about it. Lainey had not mentioned it, leaving James to continue to blame David for a betrayal he did not commit, never questioning in his rancour how Lainey had known Sophie's name. Why Lainey had chosen not to say anything was a mystery, but Sophie was grateful for it: that James was ignorant of her transgression meant he could not blame her for it.

The boy has still not appeared. He has not even had the grace to text an apology. An anger rises through her. He lacks respect, he lacks maturity. He is vacuous and superficial. He doesn't even really like art. For him, only novelty matters, and he revels in the faddish and the fashionable. He finds his meaning in possessing the new, in being the first at the spectacle; to him, a work loses its importance, its value, when others know about it, appreciate it. Over the course of their three conversations, she has heard him redefine two shows from being the future of British Art to being tired and boring. Nothing has intrinsic value or meaning. Everything is sensation, everything is temporal. His pretended interest in her paintings, in painting *per se*, is predicated on a post-modern affectation with the kitsch, and the hope that it will get him into her bed once more. He is careless. Impetuous rather than spontaneous, predictable in his unreliability. His gauche youthfulness is no longer charming, but maladroit, coarse, unfinished.

And she, after all, is a year younger still than the boy, and just as formless. Even now, even after this year, even after James, she lacks elegance, control, finesse. How must she have looked to James then, when he had first seen her? When he approached her, at that dreadful opening in Shoreditch, she had assumed that he had wanted her first and foremost for her body. Men did that to her, saw her youth as an opportunity to exploit her physicality, to enjoy the firm ripeness of her form. She understood this, exploited it where she could, endured it most of the time. But with James there had been something more, something he had latched onto, drawn from her over and above sex. Maybe it was this roughness, this unfinished self, and the possibilities that that implies, that had drawn him beyond flirtatious fantasy and into faithlessness.

Of course, the premise for the affair, the relationship, had been the actualisation of physical attraction, but he had drawn something beyond base gratification. She had seen that in his eyes, before, during and after their increasingly reckless couplings. It wasn't simply desire for her flesh but a deeper hunger, need even. He was older, past his own prime, no longer as compelling as he maybe once had been. But there had been no vain, vampiric attempt to restore his corporeal youth through the consumption of hers. It was not her youth he wanted, but its companion: potential. He was boxed in, trapped by his marriage, his work, even his own character. He had run out of space for reinvention, and her open horizons provided a canvas for vicarious possibility. He craved her ambiguity, her uncertainty.

For herself, she had enjoyed his solidity, his wholeness. She understood the excitement of potential, but wanted to know potential realised. Despite his childish jealousy when they first met, shepherding her away from other middle-aged, predatory men, depositing her into the safe keeping of those two women, she had warmed to his mistaken belief in his own ease, his ability to lie to himself, to mistake delusions for convictions. He had asked her out at the end of the evening, and she could see that at least at the highest levels of consciousness, he actually believed that it was innocent, an attempt to help her get on in the industry. He believed honestly in his own virtue, which was as near to virtue as she had encountered in her life.

At that point, she had simply been amused, thought that at worst it would be fun. He was good looking, in that way that men can carry off as they get older, provided they don't put on weight, or grow beards, and dress neither like their fathers, nor their sons. A defined face, clear grey eyes. His dark hair cropped short, but still thick, cut in a contemporary but restrained style. Tall, athletic even: she had felt the strength of his arms as he had embraced her with a little too much familiarity when they parted at the end of their first meeting. She had not minded: he was cute and he had connections in the industry, could be helpful to her, as she could reflect some actual creativity onto his parched soul. With his contacts and her talent, they could take on the art world and show them that painting, the craft of putting paint onto flat surfaces, oil onto canvas, wash onto board, acrylic onto wood, was worth more than the frozen blood, the bottled piss, the piles of rubbish, wood and plastic, the detritus of the twenty first century, that masqueraded as art.

Walking to the Tube she had thought that his understated confidence marked him as a man who lived within himself, comfortably. She had smiled as the spectres of possibility rose and wove their ethereal shapes through her, imagined herself fully immersed in his embrace, the give of the skin on his neck under the weight of her lips, the moment of first contact, skin on skin, when he would take her hands in his and pull her into a kiss.

The first time they slept together, he had been twitchy, uncertain of himself. He was aware of his transgression, but more than that, he was alive with nervous excitement, an excitement he clearly hadn't felt for some time. She had understood that each was giving what was necessary to the other, and she had been empowered by that knowledge. When he had visited her studio, he had been genuinely interested in her work and, unlike the boy, had been happy to talk about art and brush strokes, until she was ready to pull him into her bed to lose themselves in physical immediacy, until it was time for him to return to Balham and his other life.

Something had changed over the Christmas. He had not gone to America with his wife, so they had been able to spend days and nights together, uninterrupted. On New Year's Eve, he had spent the evening with her at a party with her friends and, as 2006 began, they had been in her little bed in Bermondsey, frenetic in the cold grey of dawn. The words that she had not been supposed to say had slipped out, murmured in the half light, and she had held her breath hoping to smother them in silence. But he had not clenched, horrified, had not launched into a long explanation of why that wasn't true; he hadn't disappeared into himself, sullen and sombre, unwilling to dash, nor cement, her hopes with the clumsy words, a rabbit in headlights; all of this she took as a sign that the words did not scare him, nor disgust him, that he had maybe thought them himself. Instead he had pushed his face into the angle between her shoulder and neck as if her skin were an intoxicant and inhaled her, and she had pulled him closer to squeeze out any space between them and waited for him to say that he loved her too.

He never did. But the possibility that he might drew her inexorably closer to him, despite herself and her better judgement. As the old pattern of stolen hours, evenings and afternoons reasserted itself through the dark, cold months, she had felt herself falling for him. Each time she was left in her still warm bed, or bundled into a taxi outside some Shoreditch bar, it became harder to bear. That he had persisted with the affair, even after its discovery by his wife's friend, had made her begin to believe that there was an inevitable logic to their relationship, one that led to happily ever after. She waited for the explosion and the fall out, ready to be the angel who picked up the pieces. But the explosion never came.

By then, she already had Lainey's email address and she had

wrestled with the impulse to bring the whole phoney edifice down, to push at the walls, to fire the dynamite in the foundations. Instead she had chosen to wait, to wait until he came to his senses, until he realised that the situation was unsustainable. She settled into the rhythm of strangled evenings, furtive lunches and awkward encounters at openings and viewings, where she had to pretend to be just another contact at a gallery. She had even met Lainey once, at an event at her gallery in the previous spring. James had introduced her, his arm around his wife's waist, his hand resting lightly on her hip. Sophie had coveted the solid warmth on his hand, had longed to take the hand from her, to wrap it around herself, to feel his fingers resting on her hip in the full glare of everyone present. Especially her.

Lainey had been polite but cool, controlled, glazed with the elegance that Sophie knew she lacked; Lainey was classically beautiful, like a film star, tall and slender, a mass of red curls and irresistible green eyes. At that moment it seemed inevitable that she would lose, that Lainey would take James from her for good. She had made her excuses, and rushed off to attend to some important, invented task, realising too late that the balance of power in the relationship had shifted irretrievably away from her.

As spring turned to summer, Sophie had revised her ambitions to those of simply sustaining the affair as it had been. It was crazy; the marriage was clearly finished, only James was incapable of burying it. He had still thrown himself around her recklessly, had still crept his way to her bed as often as he could, drank her in with terrifying fervency. His physical self he had given to her absolutely, but Lainey had retained everything else just as completely. Even knowing this, she had crumbled when he had told her that he was choosing his wife, that the transaction was over, that it was time to part amicably. He had looked at her as if she should agree with him, understand. She had only retained what composure she did because of the numbing shock of it all. The final revelation of her folly, of her belief in his need for her, had washed over her, freeing her to feel again, unconstrained.

She knew that he would come back to her. He could not fail to. There had been such intensity to his immersion in her. She had seen the urgency and joy in his eyes when they had been together. He had evoked feelings in her that could not be attributed to artifice. He had withheld verbal confirmation, afraid of course of his situation, his position as a married man, but his eyes, his body had not been so coy. She knew.

...

The taxi seems to teeter on the brink for a moment, leaning precariously as it takes the corner too fast. I see it a little late, preoccupied, but manage to stop myself on the curbstone, almost coming off my unaccustomed heels. But I avoid stepping out in front of it, ending the evening before it has begun. More hesitantly this time, I cross to the traffic island, home to subterranean public conveniences and park benches but precious little that could be described as green: the four naked trees do nothing to temper the relentless landscape of tarmac, brick and stone. Clerkenwell Grey would be more fitting.

It is cold and I am almost late. He will be there already

of course, waiting for me to arrive. Unless he has changed fundamentally, now that he is no longer a married man. Well, not married in the ways that count. The piece of paper is not yet burned, but everything else is ashes. James is James now, not James and Lainey. And he's come back to me.

When he called, I couldn't catch my breath, didn't know how to react, how to sound. It had been so long, I'd pretty much given up on him, expected never to hear from him again. I had seen him around of course, at events, in town, but he was behind glass, a million miles from me, unobtainable, taboo. He'd made his choice, and there had been no point in trying to change that, trying to talk to him, to make him want me again. And of course, he would blame me for that email too, maybe hate me. But then he was on the phone, telling me that he and Lainey were finished, that he had his own place, off Essex Road, a different galaxy from Balham.

I'd known already, of course. Gossip goes around this industry just as quickly as it does in any other. James Townsend had been kicked out by his wife, was living in a friend's box room. He'd been having an affair with some young girl, some peroxide tart, and his wife, his saintly, glorious, gorgeous wife, had found out. She had caught them at it, and had thrown him out. Caught them. *In flagrante delicto.* In her house, in her bed. On her birthday, the bastard. I had had to listen to them gleefully making up salacious details, stood there, wide eyed, wearing my best interested face, saying that I wasn't sure if I knew him.

A part of me wanted to call him then. The part that is

melting now, in anticipation of seeing him. It's been so long. But of course I couldn't, not without losing every shred of self-respect I had left. It was his decision, his choice, that had created the months of silence, and only he could end it. So there was nothing else to do but wait, wait until he made a different choice. And now the waiting is over: he suggested this pub, the place where he fell for me, where I made him fall for me, where I slid into the space between his dissatisfaction and his desire, showed him a world of possibility beyond the confines of the trap in which he had found himself.

I pause at the door, my hand chill on the soft copper of the handle. This is not the end; the outcome is not yet sealed. He walked away from me, and he waited weeks before contacting me. Even then he had spoken with seriousness, talking about things that needed to be said. There was no excited urgency when he had said that he wanted to see me, as if meeting was a trial to be borne, rather than a giddy joy to be embraced.

I will be able to tell; as soon as he touches me, I will know. If he wants me, I am his. The anger and the hurt, the residue of his callousness in the churchyard, will evaporate and I will forgive him for making me a home-wrecker, a tart. He only needs to want me and that will be forgotten, become a historical irrelevance. Only to want me.

...

It had been too soon. He had still been mired in a sweaty stew of guilt and loss and fear. He had hung paralysed between regret and lust, available but consumed, able to express neither authentic contrition nor unequivocal hunger. At the end of an hour of desperate, nervous shadow boxing, of banality and half-formed, unnecessary apologies, she had left him sitting inert, impotent. One last look as she stood at the door of the pub, her eyes imploring him to go with her, to stand up and cross the room, to want her, to take her back to his Islington flat, to dissolve his fear and guilt in her body, to immerse himself in her soft pliability, erase all trace of Lainey against her skin and let her rediscover the man he was beneath the debris. But he had simply sat there unmoved, unable or unwilling, and she had left him, to wait for him to find his own way to the surface.

He had not called again, had sent no Christmas greetings, had not telephoned drunk in the early hours of New Year's Day. The snow had been and gone and still the silence deafened her, smothered her. His failure, to complete what should be easy to complete, weighs on her like concrete blocks on a drowning man. The effort of waiting, hoping, fills her dreams and drains her days. Only to want her. All she asks. She knows he desires her, that it would take only the merest movement on her part to coax him into pouring his desire into her, wrapping her in the certainty of her own centrality.

Simply a flicker of her eyes, a brush of hand on hand. She only needs him to put himself in the same space as her. To call, or email, or text. The merest effort; to stumble into her in a gallery, a bar. But he doesn't. He has shrunk away completely. She thinks it is odd that he hasn't seen him at events recently. No-one has any news of him, despite her cautious enquiries: James Townsend has disappeared. She wonders where he is hiding. She curses his pride and fear, and even as she does, she recognises in them her own. What if he isn't hiding, but living his life? What if he doesn't want her after all, what if he has already forgotten her, now that he has cleared his conscience, moved on to the next girl? Maybe it is she who is frozen, immobile, as the world spins on. Maybe it is she that wants him?

The boy is now thirty six minutes late. Draining her coffee, she waves to the girl with the bright blond hair and the dark blue apron, and pays. She will wait no longer for this boy, nor any like him.

12

VANISHING POINT

The place is quiet: it is a Tuesday evening, after all. The first crush of office drinkers has slackened now and the space in front of the bar is no longer bursting with raucous noise. I can see clear across to the papier-mâché head of a rhinoceros, hanging from the wall above the fire place, beyond which Sophie will appear at any moment from the outside chill.

I like this pub. I always have done, since I first started drinking here more than a decade ago. I find the dark warmth of its walls reassuring, comforting. Jess, or one of her friends, introduced me to it, before we had gone stale, had coagulated into torpid resentment. Subsequently I had brought Lainey here, in those bright, swirling early days, when our lives had been blurred across the London night. And this is where I brought Sophie that first evening, when latent desire had become kinetic. It's a place from which all the potentiality of London stems.

I knew also, of course, that Sophie would know where it was, would be able to find it. I still think of her as a tenderfoot, blinded by the bright lights. Naïve, even. She's not, of course. She has more sense of herself, of her place in the world, of her right to be here, than I do. But when I called, suggested we meet, telling her that things had been left unsaid that needed to be said, this had been the only place that had come to mind. Moral support, if you like.

I was surprised that she had agreed so easily, that I hadn't had to explain more, be more contrite. Maybe she just wants to see me squirm. Payback for the manner of our parting. I could have handled it better, I know. I knew at the time, but I had simply needed to draw a line, to cut her out of my life. If I was to have any chance at rebuilding a relationship with Lainey, I needed to cut myself off from complications, and Sophie, sweet, simple Sophie, had become a complication.

I had lost sight of Lainey before Sophie had appeared to take me further out to sea. She simply squeezed into the space created by the ebbing of our urgent intimacy: a symptom of the erosion of my love for Lainey, not its cause. That I still now do not feel guilty for my betrayal is simply evidence of how far I had fallen out of love with Lainey. But, despite the obvious hopelessness of it, I made a choice of which of the two half-formed relationships I wanted to make work.

Of course, none of this matters now. Lainey is divorcing me. It is done, David saw to that. Although why he waited so long is still a mystery to me. Malice aforethought. Maybe if it had been an unthinking act, in the first flush of moral indignation, rage, righteousness. But to wait so long, until I was actually trying to put things right, when I had chosen Lainey: that was cruel, bizarre. And it made my choice, my noble intentions, meaningless. Had I been able to make it right with Lainey, find some accommodation, a settlement, a way of living without that vibrancy, then maybe my callousness to Sophie would have been justifiable.

No, no matter what she said at the time, I was a bastard. Things had changed between us during the spring; our original ambition for a transactional, limited relationship had turned into simply a convenient pretence. I had hungered for the sensation of being in love, that urgent, joyous, vertiginous whirlwind, that all-consuming, stomach-twisting longing: the very feelings that had been lost from my marriage. So I had tried to synthesise them with Sophie. I knew that it was a simulacrum, simply an artifice without genuine content, a way to experience the thrill, free from the responsibility. Being in love without loving: the perfect counterpoint to my other life with Lainey, to loving without being in love.

But somewhere in my clumsy, frantic feasting on synthetic sensation, Sophie fell for me. I saw it happening, revelled in its sweetness, sucked every trace of authenticity from her swelling tenderness, her emergent need. And yet, somehow, I told myself that the old rules still applied, that the understanding that we had set out with was still shared. I maintained this tenet of absolution resolutely, for both my treatment of Sophie and of Lainey. For the one, a clean escape hatch; for the other, a demonstration that my betrayal was less serious, that it wasn't real, that it meant nothing.

Thankfully, I never got to use that excuse with Lainey, but to my shame I did use the escape hatch with Sophie. That afternoon, in St Giles's churchyard, I had cited the transactional pretence in making my excuses for choosing to go back, wholly, to Lainey. Under its cover, I conducted the ending of our affair with a matter-of-fact breeziness, for which I felt a growing horror in the days that followed. It gnawed at me during those last months with Lainey, consuming what conscience I had left, and once I had left Balham, it kept me sleepless as much as what happened in Lainey's kitchen, at the moment it ceased to be our kitchen. Neither of those facts sat comfortably with me. I am not violent, I am not callous, I am not a liar, a fraud. And yet I have acted as if I were.

A crushing hunger for a cigarette overtakes me and I curse my latest attempt to stop, my refusal to buy even a packet of ten on my way here. I will have to wait until Sophie arrives and even then wait, politely, until a reasonable time has elapsed before I can ask her for one. I wonder if she still smokes, what else might have changed. A sudden fear that she has met someone awakes in me another ambition, the thought that absolution might come wrapped in her embrace.

And it is now that she appears. The familiar flighty nervousness as she glances erratically around the room until she locates me. She is no longer blonde, and her clear blue eyes are now framed by a chestnut bob. With it she has gained an elegance that has made her taller, more controlled. I am suddenly aware that I am sitting at the same table, our table, in the same chair as I had been when I had let the words 'thus far' slip through my hungry lips. I try to convince myself that she will not notice the unintended symbolism of this, the recreation of the spatial arrangement of our inception; I try to interpret the little flash of discomfort across her face as exasperation at the Tube, relief at finally arriving, apology for being a few minutes late.

I hesitate fractionally before embracing her, suddenly unsure whether this is appropriate, whether I will be able to stay within the bounds of polite correctness, to know where and how my hands can legitimately fall. She sees, feels, the hesitancy and bridles into rigidity. We kiss the empty air beside each other's cheeks. I know her body so well but now, even at this proximity, it is buried behind glass, alien, proscribed, and my abdomen writhes impotently.

As she is taking off her coat, I ask her how she is, what she would like to drink, if her journey was alright; the formal blandness of my questions lies heavy on my tongue. Feeling the evening already spiralling beyond my control, I break a smile, tell her it's been too long and embrace her again, this time hugging her with the force and familiarity of an old friend, inhaling her scent heavily, my chin on her head, just above her right ear. Peeling us apart, she looks up at me and smiles tentatively, relieved that some of the awkwardness has dissipated.

'I regret it every day, you know? How it ended between us. How I ended it. You deserved more from me. I still think that the decision itself was the right one, even given how things turned out with Lainey. But I treated you…'

'Like a whore?'

The bitterness, the anger in her voice startles me; that she thinks that of me, more so. We had moved comfortably beyond the pleasantries and had spent an hour bringing each other up to date with our lives: she thought it was good that I had moved north again, that it clearly suited me, and getting a flat on my own was a sign that I was moving on with my life; I was glad that she had more responsibility at the gallery, I liked her hair, kept silent about there being no-one special in her life. Maybe taking that as my cue to launch my apology, my quest for absolution, had been a mistake, but her enmity hits me like dragon's breath.

She is saying she is sorry, that perhaps that was too harsh, but it's how it seemed to her, at the time, still. She'd known that there was never going to be a happy ever after, but to pretend that there were no feelings involved was stupid and dishonest: to treat her like an inconvenience to be disposed of, once I'd had my fun, was... well, how would I describe that?

I tell her I know, I know, that it is unforgiveable, that is why I want to apologise, to make things, if not right, then better. I want her to know that I don't think it was right, how I treated her, that I knew even as I walked away that I had been a bastard. But that there had been nothing I could do about it in the days, weeks, months that followed.

'The whole point had been to try to make my marriage work. Anything else, any contact with you, would have made that impossible, would have made breaking up with you meaningless. And it was hard enough to give you up: I never stopped wanting you.'

I have gone too far, over-played my hand. She shrinks back into her slender, perfect frame, recoiling from the stench of my desperate, clumsy neediness. She drains her glass, pivots to collect her coat from the empty chair beside her.

'Look, I've got to go. It's been really nice to see you, and I appreciate it, that you regret the way things ended. Thank you for having the courage to tell me that, and to my face. But, while I may be many things, I am not a consolation prize and I can't absolve your guilt. Get over your marriage some other way; get your life back together. You've got so much going for you, if only you could see it. Take care of yourself, James, and don't worry about me: it really is all OK between us, you know? When you're over Lainey, give me a call. Really.'

Her heels click across the floor. A fleeting, accusing glance over her shoulder as she reaches the door and I am gripped with a yearning for every woman I have ever kissed. The loneliness I have been suppressing closes tightly around me, choking out the certainties upon which I hang my self. I start to question who it is that I miss, if it is a person at all. I can sense my ability to do more than fall helplessly through time and space slipping beyond my fingers' length.

...

An aeroplane. Thirty eight thousand feet in the air. Below, a nameless smear of light slides past. Outside, darkness. The drone of engine and air-conditioning fills the semi-darkness inside, drenching the low babble of voices, of breathing, of pages turning. Seat 29A. A man dozes, his eyes closed against the limited visual stimulus of long haul flight, his mind wrapped in the embrace of airline Merlot. But he is not sleeping. Sleep remains out of reach, so he settles for chemically induced stupor and wilful blindness.

So he does not witness, only guesses at, the glances from the woman in seat 29D. She is also lost in her interior world, and this for now includes a facsimile of him. In four and a half hours he will be forgotten and she will return to her life: a senior representative of a communications conglomerate with offices in four continents. She is successful professionally, is popular socially, has three children she adores and a loving husband who provides comfort and stability and, each Valentines, brings flowers, roses, red, twelve, and leaves an unsigned card on the mat. But for now, in the semi-dark anonymity of flight BA0119, humming its way to Bengaluru, his face provides a harbour for her longing to be wanted, urgently, to be extraordinary. Maybe not classically handsome, but compelling all the same. A face of possibility, of potential, a reminder that she could change her life, reinvent herself, if she wanted to, if she had to. Even now, all was not yet set, fixed, permanent. She wraps herself in the comfort of possibility as she slips into sleep.

The girl too has surrendered herself to sleep, her terrified sobs of a few hours ago submerged in dreams, or nightmares. Would she remember on waking her parents' betrayal? Their cruel and unusual treatment of her in forcing her onto the flight, making her endure her worst fears in front of hundreds of irritable strangers, cold-hearted men and women who only wanted her to shut up, not to rescue her? But the hatred and terror and humiliation she felt at takeoff has melted into uneasy sleep. Maybe she will learn to love flying. Maybe she will never be able to fly happily, but will simply learn to endure it, to hide her terror, and the shame it makes her feel. And maybe she will forgive her parents, will rediscover the belief that, though not gods omnipotent, they do have her best interests at heart. Even when they force her onto aeroplanes against her will, or suggest she loses weight, or slowly shake their heads at her school reports, understanding rather than chastising: maybe she will feel the warmth of their love, rather than the chill of resentment at their presumed disappointment.

But thinking about the girl does not distract him for long. Instead he finds grim comfort in naming his own terror, his own melancholy. Suddenly, he envies the Germans their *zerreissen* – to disconnect, sever, rupture, shred, to tear apart; a violent, lingering, definite separation. A sense of tearing, a slow rending of human tissue. Like ham-fisted surgery. Flesh scored by a bread knife, fingers reaching into the fibres, pulling apart the sticky confusion of mortality: a numb, jagged agony.

The ragged faces of the two pieces hardening with each passing moment, distance solidifying the parts, but like shapes in an atlas, like the unseen shapes below him, retaining the remembrance of the whole that they once were. With time, the details along the join become eroded, making a seamless reconnection impossible, even if the tectonic plates could reverse their trajectory. Impossible, even if the impossible were to become possible. He feels very alone in the darkness of space, high above clouds that seem more solid now than the world they obscure, the land and sea and cities buried in the dark depth below. He opens his eyes, in a slow panic, to check that the woman in 29D is still present, that he is not completely lost. But the seat is empty and has been for the last four and a half hours, since take off. He realises that there never was a woman in seat 29D, much less one who could find anything comforting in his face, who could see in him possibility, the merest chance of reinvention, of changing the direction of tectonic plates, of trying again, one more time, to see if he could get it right at last.

Zerreissen. A satisfying, horrific word. The prosaic 'separation', limp in comparison, unable to describe the shape and depth of the gap to be filled by this journey.

...

The slow red, brick red heat of the day quivered in each fragment of dust. The town baked, was microwaving itself. James stood at the roadside, his bag in the dust, looking out across the street. Despite the chaos of the bus stand behind him, the world seemed to pause, the stifling air hanging at that still point between inhalation and exhalation, waiting, while his imagined Badami of memory converged with this present reality. That it had been eight years, almost to the month, since he had last been there seemed inconceivable. That everything had happened in only eight years.

The intervening time had not done much to tidy up the town. The air was still filled with dust, of course; the sewers were still open, still the playground of ugly grey pigs. Malodorous and deafening, everywhere dirt and decay. With precious little in the way of charm to compensate, Badami conspired to be both sleepy and chaotic. He remembered his first arrival here, the initial disappointment, the slumping dread of having made a mistake, the cannoning impetus to turn around and leave. But he also remembered that that had melted away, that Badami had become a favourite place, and not just because of the cave temples, their pink and pristine wonder. And this time he was on his own, without the constraining need for order, for tidiness, for comfort and cleanliness; he could drink in the chaos, his senses unmediated by Lainey.

He became aware of, then unnerved by, the staring macaques perched in the tree above him. James hauled up his backpack and dodged his way through the traffic, towards the hotel that faced the bus stand. The pink marble and mirrored glass of the façade suggested that there had been some ambition for the place when it had been constructed, ambition that had not been realised. But the young man at reception had been pleasant enough, had been happy to find a room for him, a deluxe with *en suite* and air-conditioning, had shown him up to the second floor, and into the room, halfway along a dark, undecorated concrete corridor. As with the town, so with the hotel: everywhere dirt and decay, all of which, despite himself, he could see only through Lainey's eyes.

The last of his hardiness melted on seeing the dilapidated room. But he hesitated a moment too long, only nodding, smiling, while the porter showed him that both the AC unit and the empty fridge were functioning, that there was indeed a bathroom, of sorts, attached to the room. It was only after he had been left alone in the room that he finally, categorically, decided he didn't want to stay. But he realised it was too late, and he resigned himself to one night at least in the unloved, mildewed room.

He looked around. The bed seemed solid enough and the sheets, while not exactly clean, were not entirely dirty either. There was mosquito netting behind the windows. The bathroom had at least a Western-style toilet. It would not be so bad.

Beside a small and fragile coffee table there was a well-used armchair, upholstered in thick corduroy. It was the colour of pond water. He sank into the tired but accommodating seat and took out his cigarettes. He smoked three while he decided that the temples could wait until tomorrow and he tried to work out what to do instead with the afternoon. The town, he remembered, offered little else in the way of distraction.

After all, he had not intended to be here. Not yet, at least. His loosely structured itinerary had included a number of stops between here and Mysore: the temples at Belur and Halebeedu, the ancient city of Hampi. His sudden, unexpected presence in Badami was some way ahead of his plans. He chose not to interrogate the reasons for his precipitate arrival: he was too tired, too unsettled. The preceding thirty six hours had been dreamlike, a frictionless transition through the towns and fields of Karnataka. Like a ghost, fading, receding. He could barely recall Hospet, where he had slept the previous night: only the pigs in the street and the foetid light of the dhaba where he must have eaten something, before giving up on the evening. The morning's bus ride into Badami was already lost; his journal entries were like reports from a distant land, another time.

He lit a fifth cigarette in a seamless, continuous movement from extinguishing the fourth in the wide shallow glass of the ashtray. The little table wobbled as he twisted the stub into cold inertia, its energy dissipating through the wood and into the marble floor tiles. He knew of course that he had come back to the place where he and Lainey had been happiest, where she had agreed to marry him, where things between them had been right. Better than right, perfect. He knew because everyone had told him, warned him about returning, about the dangers of becoming trapped in the past. He could not capture the echoes of happiness simply by revisiting the places where they still resonated. Happiness could only be found in the present: memories of past happiness could only bring sadness, regret; anticipation of future happiness, longing and dissatisfaction.

He had known this also, and had tried to explain that he hoped to find something other than the faded happiness of his marriage, but had been unable to articulate his need, his want, to reclaim India for himself, to retrace his steps and make associations, memories, that were his alone. To retake photographs without her in them.

Now he was here, he wondered whether things would have been different, had they stayed here back then. Had they not returned to London, to work, to a world that shaved slivers from each of them, every day, relentlessly, whittling away their available attention, their desire, would they have retained the undoubted happiness they had felt together then?

Pointless. Conjecture like that was meaningless. There would, in any case, have been other distractions, temptations. No, Badami was no Garden of Eden. Its potency, he realised, was in the possibility it symbolised in his memory. He had not merely been happy here, but had felt capable, transcendent; he had possessed entirely the certainty of his potential to find meaning, to shape the world. From the top of those cliffs, the view stretched off to the wide, far horizon, cloaked in a haze that hid Goa and the Arabian Sea and a universe of possibility. The last months, years maybe, had robbed him of that, left him suspended in a sticky ocean of pointlessness.

In the aftermath of the break up, when everything else fell apart, he had found himself returning to places where it had once appeared that there was a viable way of being, of becoming. Looking for a future in his past, all the while neglecting to occupy his present. In the six months since he had walked from the house in Balham, numb, the knuckles of his right hand still slightly stinging, James had become stuck, frozen, unable to find a satisfactory way to remake himself. The inescapable, inexplicable fact of his striking Lainey, that external, alien act of sudden violence, clung to him like a noxious smell. He had spent hours excavating the single second of that heavy, dull impact, trying to stitch together the man that he had been with the man he had become at that moment.

So he had hidden in the chaos of Gareth's spare room, in the reliable fug of whisky and cigarettes. When he had found a flat of his own, it had been to escape the embarrassment of his hosts and business partners, rather than to start to rebuild. When he had returned to the Balham house to pick up his belongings, it had been to remove the physical traces of himself from Lainey's home, rather than to reassemble himself. He had felt himself start to recede, to disappear, and rather than resisting his waning, he had welcomed it, immersing himself in its warmth.

That afternoon in Balham, Lainey had barely spoken to him, had not looked him in the eye. She had sat at the kitchen table, in the chair she had occupied on the morning after her birthday and had stared into the past as he threw clothes and toiletries and books into black bin liners. When he had finished, had loaded the relics of himself into his car, he had returned to the kitchen, had tried to say something that would make her world even a shade less bleak and, failing, had simply put his keys down onto the table and left, for a second and final time. The letter from the solicitor had arrived at his office a couple of days later.

The divorce progressed elsewhere, observed but outside the universe he inhabited. He worked with reasonable effectiveness, and Gareth did not have to weigh up the needs of the business against his sympathy for his friend. He saw friends, the few he had left. He saw his brother for the first time in years, a stranger, a man without sympathy, without empathy, absorbed in duty and responsibility for his own wife and kids. And there had been that abortive, unrequited, lustful hour with Sophie Lamb.

Another cigarette.

He felt sick. He had smoked too many cigarettes. Eleven filthy, twisted stubs made a paper pyre in the grey remains that filled the ashtray. Gazing at them, the slow nausea crawled through him again and thin, acrid saliva filled his mouth, sliding over the metallic taste that refused to be washed away. The peeling apart of the gummy lining of his throat when he swallowed sickened him further, and he became acutely aware of the horror that was his body. It hadn't always been so present, and its recent, grumbling announcement of its discontents still shocked him. A weary lethargy sapped the strength from his limbs, and a shiver of cold sweat ghosted his whole body, despite the heat. He resolved once more to stop, to overcome this compulsion to self-destruction, to finish this packet, then no more. He inhaled the last of the twelfth and extinguished it in amongst the debris.

He looked around. The room was wreathed in a yellowing pall of nicotine smoke and the stale tang of rubberised plastic made breathing unpleasant. The sun had fallen low in the sky, its orange light forcing its way into the room, casting hard shadows onto the wall facing him. He was gripped with a bilious claustrophobia, with the sudden need to flee the confines of the room, to find some air. Meeting the stairs he chose to climb rather than descend.

The fluid intensity of the redness of the cliffs, incandescent in the light of the setting sun, occupied him for fully ten minutes. He stood on the roof of the hotel, among the drying laundry, the plastic water tanks and the forsaken, gnarled curls of steel, while the wall of sand stone reared up over him. There was no-one else there, and he was not sure if he was allowed to be up there himself, strictly speaking. He had simply continued up the flights of stairs, towards the light and air cascading down to meet him, until the walls had disappeared and the scrappy rooftop had spread out around him. Certainly, it did not appear to be part of the guests' facilities offered by the hotel. Half-used cans of paint, their contents shrivelling, contracting, crusting, were clustered in small groups, mingled with the other debris of haphazard maintenance: warping planks and metal rods; a set of step ladders; a trolley with only one wheel; a glass-less window frame. He sat on the broken trolley and drank in the view, absenting himself from it, erasing his unauthorised presence from the banality of the rooftop detritus, from the dusty chaos of the street below and from the majesty of the rocks above.

...

He felt uncomfortable sitting alone at the little table. He'd at last found his way into the walled garden from an unpromising side street, which slid off the main road and into the darkness. The young man behind the desk at the Rajsangam Hotel had told him about the restaurant with a shrug and an indistinct nod indicating the direction he should head. He had turned off the main road, still clogged with dust, luminous with the sporadic headlights of trucks and buses, and started down the unlit alley. In the quiet gloom, his hopes for a decent meal in clean surroundings had evaporated entirely: he had resigned himself to another indifferent rice and dhal at the sticky dhaba by the bus stand.

His lack of faith was unfounded, however. He had found the doorway, marked with a small blue sign, exactly where he had been told he would find it. Once inside, he'd been greeted by one of the waiters and pointed towards any of the empty tables. Sitting with his back to the wall, facing the garden, he felt very alone. The isolation of his solitary journey had crept slowly over him as he had sat smoking, thinking, in the mossy arm chair in his room. Now that he was here, companionless at his table for two, his separateness, his loneliness, weighed still more heavily on him, was made more real by the presence of witnesses. The other diners were all European, and he could almost taste their pity, their distaste at his aloneness, hanging in the pleasantly cooling air. Everyone else was in a family or larger group; the other lone travellers banding together into temporary, portable families to avoid confronting themselves in the darkness.

On one table, the largest in the garden, were about twelve diners. They spoke English but with a variety of accents and ability: where two or more nationalities are gathered anywhere in the world, it seemed, the *lingua franca* was now this simplified, bastardised English. A new variety, distinct from North American and Australasian English, as much as from the British, with a grammar and vocabulary of its own; recognisable, comprehensible, but definitely of itself. A complex creation, the default second language for Europe's young and mobile.

Most of the people at the table were French, with some Dutch, a German woman and a couple of indeterminate Scandinavians. Conversation bounced back and forward, up and down and across the table, but it was anchored on the exploits of a Frenchman in his late-twenties, who had been everywhere, knew everyone, and consumed life with an insatiable hunger. He had a lightness and self-certainty that had all the young women around the table captivated, the men cowed.

His beard, in particular, annoyed James. Even before the Frenchman had looked over and, with good grace, offered a space at the large, convivial table, he had seemed insufferable. James declined the invitation of course, perhaps a little too dismissively. Turning back to his disciples, the would-be host reflected loudly on the English reserve, the haughty exclusivity of their company, of their desire to keep themselves to themselves. The table laughed, and James felt more alone than he had felt for years, unable to think of anything to do or say other than to say nothing and to look anywhere but at the table in the middle of the garden, the people arrayed directly in front of him.

The arrival of the bottle of Kingfisher, and then the food, gave him something to do, somewhere to look. That he was alone was no longer an admission that he was friendless and forsaken; instead his solitary state became a badge of honour, marking him out as intrepid, unconstrained. He too had been everywhere, knew everyone, but didn't need an audience to justify himself. For the first time that day, he smiled.

This was his freedom, his independence. It was what he had come here to demonstrate. It had had to be here, because India was his totem of self-determination. Alongside the trip with Lainey, as well as the proposal of marriage, it had been here that he had declared his independence, stated his authorship, at key moments of his life. He had had the courage to make his journey alone, without the prop of companions or guides, becoming himself through finding the path without assistance, without reassurance. He defined himself without mediation. While others painted on canvas, his great creation was himself: he wrote his own destiny.

His defiance melted as he remembered hitting Lainey. It was an act which lay entirely outside his own narrative of himself. His infidelity he could incorporate as an act of positive choice. Selfishness certainly, but that in itself was not alien to who he believed himself to be. But that single act of violence had been a betrayal of a different order and could not be reconciled; it was external to him, even while self-evidently his. It was horrific, and was not him, at least not the him he believed himself to be. In that one act he felt the mask had slipped, that he had revealed another, more authentic, James Townsend. One he did not want to exist, one beyond his capacity to create or destroy. His faith in his authorship melted, with it his self sufficiency. His aloneness once more turned to loneliness. He craved another to tell him who he was, to tell him he existed, but with deepening terror, he realised there was no-one left. Until the boy in the park had told him the story about the elephant. In those few minutes, James had seen a way to rewrite himself, once again; write himself into something noble, something worthwhile. He had clung to the elephant as tightly as he could, all the way across the plains of Karnataka. His grip was fragile, but it was all he had, all that was left.

...

He was sitting on the low steps of the temple. A man in his early forties, his face sagging in the sun's glare, the skin bowing under the weight of sleepless nights. Despite the wear, he retained some suggestion of earlier good looks: not pretty, nor strikingly handsome, simply well-proportioned and even. His slight frame still hadn't spread as far as could be expected for a man his age, thickening only at the waist. And his hair was still dense and evenly coloured, although dusted a little at the temples. His grey eyes were absent under heavy lashes, staring off to the horizon beyond the town, evidently lost in thought, adrift in an interior universe.

The red stone of the temple where he sat was smooth, eroded by a millennium of rain and wind, yet it still retained the abstracted forms of dancers and lions and elephants. These latter were carved from the living rock of the plateau and the man too seemed to emerge from the rock, as immobile as the carvings that surrounded him: the wind, gently pulling on his shirt, raking his hair, provided the only movement in the scene.

Below him, the dusty town breathed its staccato rhythms. The birds of prey, drab, brown, menacing, hung suspended on the up draughts of the cliff. Maybe ten minutes passed before he moved.

Reaching into the canvas shoulder bag which lay at his feet, he pulled out a newspaper parcel, some 20 centimetres square, flat; the paper worn and supple, but intact. Carefully, as if for the thousandth time, he unwrapped the package, smoothing each fold of paper on his knees, until the brilliant green of the scarf was revealed. Holding it up, his arm extended, he let the folds and creases fall away so that its full length fluttered like a flag, a standard, a shroud. He gazed at it for a moment then pulled it in to his face, as if to inhale its absent fragrance, nose and eyes and mouth buried in its softness. The moment passed, and he again held the scarf up to the sky, this time releasing it to the wind so that it floated lightly on the billowing air. He watched it disappear over the cliff edge before solemnly resuming his vigil.

Jagganath studied him for a while from the path. He had paused from his morning walk, so struck was he by the man's calm stillness. He was a European, maybe French – there were a lot of French in the town – but Jagganath hoped he was British. The British were so much easier to get along with. Jagganath felt an affinity with them, despite the history. He was a good Indian, a proud Indian, and he knew that throwing the British out had been an important moment in the long history of his country. But he wasn't sure everything had gone all that well since they had left, that things hadn't started going to the dogs shortly after independence. Partition, of course, but so much more: corruption; incompetence; moral decay. So meeting an Englishman, a Britisher, speaking English with someone who knew how to use the language properly, not like the above-themselves merchants in town, that was always a pleasure.

'Hello there, sir. I hope I am not disturbing your peace?'

Jagganath stroked his thick moustache uneasily, running thumb and forefinger out to his rounded cheeks, making a mental note to have the thing trimmed later in the day. The Englishman looked up, raised a fatigued smile, and said not at all; he indicated with his palm the space on the step next to him. Jagganath hesitated – he had not intended to sit with him, simply to pass a few pleasantries – but feared now that any standoffishness might be interpreted as bad manners. Warily he sat down.

To maintain some degree of formality, Jagganath introduced himself, extending his right hand. The foreigner reciprocated.

'Ah! Like the King and his Bible! A fine name, a very fine name, sir. And you are visiting for the first time?'

The Englishman explained that he had been in India frequently, and in Badami once before, years earlier, with his wife. That all seemed such a long time ago now, so he had wanted to return, to see India, to see Karnataka, again. He had especially wanted to see the temples once more. He couldn't think of anywhere he'd been that was more remarkable. His eyes focused into the distance, across the lake, across the horseshoe of the cliffs, to the caves.

Jagganath's next question, about his wife, if she was with him, or if she had stayed in England, maybe to care for the children, seemed to puncture the Englishman like a skewer, startling and deflating him simultaneously. He sat paralysed for a second or two, without bearings, unable to respond.

'She's dead. My wife is dead.'

His voice carried no bitterness, no rancour, only deathly emptiness. Jagganath felt the roundness of his cheeks sink, as the smile he had been wearing since the conversation began drained away. His horror at his question, at the awkwardness he had caused, discomforted him greatly. He didn't know how to begin to react to this, to the Englishman's grief, his own *faux pas*; he could not imagine what the right thing to do was in such circumstances.

He stared at his feet for a moment or two, embarrassed by the gnarled and yellowed toenail that was suddenly all too visible. He wished there was something he could say that would make this unpleasantness pass, or at least extricate himself from it. He understood now the ritual with the green silk shawl and he felt a wave of sympathy for the Englishman, but had no idea how to express it appropriately: matters between a husband and a wife, even a dead wife, were for the couple alone, certainly not for strangers. He thought of his own widowed brother, with whom barely a word had passed about his sister-in-law in the three years since she had died. Was it conceivable that he should share a moment of grief with this Britisher, this stranger, but not with his own younger brother? He quietly offered his commiserations, apologised for his insensitivity, all the while looking at the red stone in front of him. He hoped that, despite his forwardness in offering a seat before they were introduced, the Englishman still retained some of his countrymen's reserve.

And so it seemed he did. In fact, he appeared more embarrassed by the revelation than was Jagganath. Gazing at the patch of rock immediately to the left of where Jagganath was staring, he thanked the Indian for his kind words and said hurriedly that it was all in the past, had happened some time ago, that there was no need to apologise, he himself was sorry for saying anything about it. Jagganath warmed immensely to the Englishman's stoicism, unaware of the guilt that was ravaging James for telling so big a lie to save such little face.

...

Malathi made the tea in the kitchen, while Jagganath looked on proudly, impatiently. She recognised this expression: he was pleased with himself, but anxious that his triumph would as quickly turn to dust if everything was not just so. Often the speed and accomplishment with which she made tea, fried the snacks, or greeted the visitors seemed to be critical to how long his triumph would last. Such was the case today, it seemed, and she tried as always to do as he asked.

Quite why he had brought this Englishman home with him, she couldn't fathom. He had done similar things before, of course, but not for a couple of months, after that German couple. They had sat sullenly, disinterested in her husband's stories and explanations, had eaten all of the Bourbon Creams, and had over-stayed their welcome. As he had said, he was fed up of these bloody foreigners making themselves at home in his house, eating his biscuits and showing no respect; never again, they can buy their own bloody tea. But here he was with another one: he'd found him up at Shivalaya Temple, where they'd talked for a little while, about the caves, about the town, until it got too hot under the late morning sun, and he had suggested a cup of tea at home; had felt sorry for him, thought he needed the company, some intelligent conversation. Malathi realised that by now Jagganath was talking of himself: he had never found a way to fill his time since he passed the plantation on to their eldest, Ranjeet. She smiled at him indulgently as she poured the tea into the porcelain cups set out on the little tray next to a plate of Bourbon biscuits. She followed him into the little parlour, carrying the tray, her eyes lowered, watching the heels of his feet padding across the tiles.

'Please, take a biscuit.'

Jagganath pushed the plate across the table an inch or so towards his guest. The Englishman sat somewhat uncomfortably on the settee, seemingly unsure of his right to be there, wrapped in a haunted, hunted air. Jagganath was pleased when he declined the biscuits, instead taking up his teacup, silently sipping the hot sweet brew. Malathi lowered her eyes and smiled gently, discreetly.

For the benefit of his wife, Jagganath asked what it was that he did for a living in Britain, where he lived. He was delighted to find that it was in London, a place he could locate on his mental map of the United Kingdom; he was intrigued by the talk of art, of painting. Jagganath nodded knowingly to Malathi: you see, a cultured man! Emboldened, he asked how James thought the economy would fare in the coming period; whether China was a military as well as an economic threat; what he thought about the sentencing to death of Saddam Hussein. He ignored the tutting of Malathi at this last question, and leaned in slightly to study the other's face as he gingerly formed an answer as fragile as a baby bird, as precarious as Philippe Petit between the Twin Towers.

Jagganath sighed. He agreed, it was a frightening and dangerous world these days. Everything was changing, and not always for the best. Independence, for example. Of course, the British had to leave, if James would forgive him for saying, but the Indians had not always made correct decisions since decisions had been theirs to make. The injustice of land reform, for example: it had been difficult to maintain the profitability of the plantation, as parcels of land had been sliced from the estate that his grandfather had built up in the early part of the twentieth century. His son was making the best of what remained, but he doubted that his grandchildren would still be in the business of growing cotton.

So much had passed, was passing. It was important to maintain those things that could be maintained. Five thousand years of religious and cultural tradition was a good basis for preserving those things that were worth preserving. Those traditions were more solid to Jagganath than the stones of Badami's temples; the Indian sat back in his chair, holding out his cup for more tea, looking absently through the window, lost in nostalgia and anxiety.

James accepted the tea that Malathi offered. He took the opportunity presented by Jagganath's reverie to move the conversation on from potentially contentious subjects, and onto the more eternal, spiritual aspects of Hindu identity. Jagganath warmed as much to this theme as to the previous topics, and spoke energetically about the tragedy of the separation of man and nature.

'What about cows? I mean to say, why are cows held in such high regard? You see them everywhere, in the street, everywhere.

What is it that makes them sacred?'

'It is not exactly true to say that cows are sacred, you know? More that they are taboo. We do not kill cows, even people who are not vegetarian. We honour them as the givers of life: they are the source of milk, of curds, for food; they are the givers of light, from browned butter which used to be used in lamps; and the givers of heat, from their dung, which village people still use to fuel for their stoves. All the products of the cow are used in puja, in worship, so we revere the cow. Some used to say that killing a cow is like killing a Braham, but I don't believe this. Cows are not the equal of man.'

Jagganath's enthusiasm spread once more, as he had the opportunity to explain the world to this Englishman.

'You see, we believe that there is a hierarchy of all living things, with man at the apex. Cows are near the top of this hierarchy, because they give life, because they help man. Elephants too, because of the help that they give to man, and because of their intelligence, are held in high esteem.'

The Englishman leaned forward, seemingly animated by this idea. Encouraged, Jagganath continued, explaining that the work elephants were able to do, on account of their size and power, was invaluable to men in the past, before machines and motors. And of course their renowned intelligence was also highly regarded. They were very clever animals, almost as clever as men, and their remarkable memory, together with their great age, meant that they were able to understand many things, far beyond the capability of other animals. The old adage, that elephants never forget, was true. They could remember everything that had happened to them.

At this, Jagganath too leaned forward in his seat, his voice dropping to a conspiratorial timbre. A sly smile spread across his face.

'Do you know how elephants are trained? The mahout takes charge of the elephant at a young age and spares no discipline in his instruction. To bend the giant to his will, he has at his disposal an ankus, a steel hook with two points, mounted on a wooden pole. Elephants, of course, have thick skin, but it is very sensitive, especially around the mouth and inside the ear. To persuade an elephant to move in a particular direction, the mahout will push the spiked end into a sensitive part of the skin, or use the hook drag the elephant by the ear. Not enough to draw blood, of course, simply to cause pain, so that the commands are learned and the animal will respond.'

Jagganath sat back, taking a mouthful of tea and loading a Bourbon Cream into his mouth. His moustache wriggled as he chewed, his left hand slowly chopping the air to ensure his flow was not broken. Brushing away the crumbs from his knee, he continued.

'As I said, elephants have tremendous memories. Well, it is not a surprise that they also remember these acts of violence against them. They will often hold a grudge against their mahout for decades, maybe even for their whole lives. Of course, they are made to fear the hook, and will do as their mahout demands.'

'I heard a story about an elephant. In Mysore. The elephant pined away for its dead mahout. Surely that is a different kind of memory?'

The Englishman's voice was flat yet insistent and, Jagganath thought, the grey eyes contained a desperate hopefulness. He nodded enthusiastically, eager to deliver the anecdote's coup de grace.

'My friend, there is no inconsistency here; it is simply a matter of perspective. Often there is a strong bond between the elephant and his mahout, it is true. As strong as a marriage, perhaps, despite the harsh treatment. But it is widely believed, and there are cases to demonstrate it, that an elephant, given an opportunity, will take their revenge for what they see as the wrong done to them. Sometimes, you know, an elephant will even kill their mahout if they have the opportunity.'

At this, the Englishman rose and made his precise, colourless farewells. Something had changed in him, and he seemed smaller in his leaving than he had on his arrival. Jagganath watched his shallow steps until his guest had disappeared from view completely.

...

He feels the slipper slide on the stone. All these years, and still these shoes torment him. He has only looked up for a moment, to trace the origin of the shout in the crowd. He is sure it is his name, that someone in the crush beside the road has called his name, but the faces are anonymous, blank. Maybe he has imagined it; maybe in his desire for recognition he has personalised a random sound among all the other random sounds that surround him. Then he glances up briefly at the yellow eye of Iravatha, and his foot slips, just a little, less than an inch, but in that fragment of time and space the whole world shifts beneath him, infinitesimally but sufficient to bring the universe crashing down.

The street is rushing up to meet him before he even begins to extend an arm to break his fall, a half-hearted, absent-minded gesture, ineffectual. His chest, his chin, crash into the asphalt; a sudden, wet pain grips his right knee, engulfing him, immobilising him. The immediacy of the roar of the crowd envelops him, dwarfs him, his senses are swamped by its indifferent vastness. He is an old man, and he has borne so much in his life. The aches in his bones each morning, the grudging muscles in his arms. Lying here is so much easier than trying to stand up yet again. He barely sees the feet moving past his face only inches away.

But he feels the brush of the trunk tip against the side of his head, swinging low in time to the music, and he feels a momentary pride in the training he has given Iravatha over all those years. The trunk's glancing kiss pulls him back into the world long enough for him to remember who he has been and to feel the terror of its passing, as the flat pressure builds on his temple, drives down irresistibly, a relentless force against the immovable asphalt. A million headaches burst in his skull.

Searing pain. The grinding of flesh on stone, the rending of fibres and tissue and bone. Then the sudden release, the receding flow of matter and spirit, as the world vanishes from Annayya or Annayya vanishes from the world. In this last moment of life, he no longer knows which it is, only that it makes no difference.

13

A Shade

I have become aware of myself as a composite; an indefinite thing. My edges are blurred and my skin is fractal. It reflects everyone I have known, no matter how fleetingly. Their faces, their fears, hopes, the long lost traces of love and disappointment. All of these reflect back, each onto one another, onto those around me, diffusing my presence in the world so that I have lost all sense of self. Where do I start and where do I end? If I am only a creature of the gaze of others, known and unknown, met and unmet, then do I have a substance of my own?

When I was a child, I believed myself to be bad; I believed myself to be evil. As soon as I had properly grasped the concept of evil, I co-opted it as my very essence. At my core, beneath the onion layers, I believed absolutely that I was bad. I never knew if this was an act of complete self-loathing or an act of self-love: a desire to own entirely this truly powerful force, to define myself as a unified being, something coherent, connected, continuous.

No-one else knew, of course. I didn't need to keep my black heart hidden like a secret: my evil nature was unrealised, unrevealed, not yet acted upon, latent. My badness did not shape my behaviour, was not a description of how I was but who I was. Even unseen, I knew it was there, my essence, awaiting its moment. It made no material difference to how I was in the world, but yet it defined me and that was sufficient. And now that the conviction of my badness has faded, I miss the certainty that it gave me as being a discrete entity in the universe. Clear edges and a solid core.

Where did it come from, this conviction? How had I become so certain of my badness? The Bible? My parents? Television? It didn't matter. It no longer made sense to think in terms of cause and effect, agency and purpose. You simply needed to recognise events, accidents, all of them without meaning, without intent. The patterns you could see between events, they were all your own work, were only real in your own head.

When our relationship had ended, it was simply another event, consequent of course upon our having started. That, in turn, was consequent upon earlier events, such as my moving to London, and the choices that I made once I had arrived there. An accident, at the end of a long line of accidents. An accident that seemed to have happened quickly, almost unseen, barely anticipated. That it had happened was sufficient; there is no need to search out explanations, or to assign blame.

14

THE PAINTED VEIL

It is early spring, March. There have been some sunny days and already the hedgerows are washed with green. The colour is returning to the face of the country after the sallow months of winter. The sky is blue once again and although the sun carries precious little heat, its mere presence warms me despite the air's chill. Down in London, you can go out without a coat already, but not here. Here, the buds are staying tightly shut, biding their time. The sheep too: the lambs have yet to come, even though the ewes look like they're good and ready. But they're going to have to wait a little while longer, I think, unlike their southern cousins. On the drive up, lambs with elastic band legs were shaking in almost every field through Lancashire and Cumbria.

Out here, there is just the wind and my breathing. A bird, some kind of hawk, hangs high above the gorse-clogged gully. He is motionless on the breeze, patiently waiting for his breakfast to emerge from the sharp yellow. I am grateful for his peaceful company, for the silence. Since I arrived, Morag and David have been nothing but hospitable, concerned, lovely. But they still treat me as if I am damaged, vulnerable, even after all these months. As if the divorce was a mortal blow, rather than a release. They walk on eggshells, speak calmly, carefully, and indulge me far beyond the limits of friendship. And it's so claustrophobic. So I crept out early this morning, before even Fergus was awake. Across the fields and onto the moorland, onto the big wide open, up on this hill. James would've had some fancy word for it – some geological, topographical, elaborately pointless word. But to me it's just a hill. And that's enough.

Things are just what they are. They don't need interpretation or classification. Their power lies in their simplicity, not their elaboration. People load so much meaning onto simple facts, so much so that they strain under the weight, lose their capacity to be. Meaning and significance and potentiality are all extraneous, and things lose their own selves in the swirling mass of annotation that people insist on bringing to them.

Here, among the green and blue, the rise and fall of earth and rock, the slow shifting shapes of grass and gorse, the invigorating freshness of it all, there is no need for explanation, interpretation. Gorse isn't more gorse-like because we name it. The air is cold and clean because it is; and it makes me feel more alive than any words or abstractions ever could. Certainly more than any painting.

Every friend I ever had, and even James – especially James – has built for me an intricate container, classified me consciously or unconsciously, rather than simply letting me be. They have put me in boxes, defined me with a few short sentences, shaped me so that I fit the gaps they see in themselves. I don't think it was malicious, at least seldom, just that they had no other language in which to think of me. But they couldn't let me just exist. Even daddy, who always made a big point of telling me that I should be my own person, that I should have the courage and confidence to defy definition. Yet he defined me as beautiful and clever and precious before I was out of diapers. By making me his princess, he stopped me from being a railroad engineer, or whatever else I might have been. I don't want to be a railroad engineer, and I know that his categorisations came from the deepest, most helpless love. I know that he believed he was giving me something valuable. So I can't, I won't, blame him for it, as if I were some inadequate on the psychotherapist's couch. I have worked out where the responsibility lies for who you are.

And I got over blaming Morag; it took some time, but I got over it. When she had said that she thought James was having an affair, or was thinking about having an affair, was on the verge of infidelity, she necessarily cast me as the naïve victim. By warning me, she assumed that I couldn't see what was in front of my eyes, much less get out of the way of the car crash. She made a victim of me just as much as James did in the end. It just took a while for me to realise that I did not have to accept the definition, from either of them.

...

'You don't know what you're talking about. Why would you say this?'

The evening was supposed to be different. With James out,

seeing an old friend, it was supposed to be Morag and memories and gossip. But somewhere in between the conviviality and confidences, a darker narrative has emerged, winding itself around us, tying our hands, taking up residence in the corners of the living room, under the table, the sofa. We are powerless now to escape its venomous logic. My best friend can be only relentless in her attack on my marriage, my husband.

Before this, I had thought that she liked James. If anything, I had been occasionally uncomfortable at how comfortable they were together. Her seal of approval had been a reassurance during the early uncertain weeks and months when James was crashing through my life without restraint. That she liked him made saying yes to his proposal possible.

Until the second bottle of wine had been uncorked, we were as we always are, sharing irrelevancies before unwrapping our hopes and fears under the cover of fuzzy intoxication. We had been doing this since college, had never tired of the ritual. Always Cabernet Sauvignon, always bold enough to offend, knowing we never could. Until now.

It had started with the by now familiar discussion of children, the whether and when of starting a family. We had rehearsed our fears, our doubts, all the while using the presence of the other to temper the naïve excitement we have both felt for years, but cannot admit. We know that it will not be simple, painless, easy, and that saying otherwise out loud will underline how complicated, demanding and difficult it will be to bear and rear a child, so we do not.

That Morag should drop her bomb in the midst of this reassuring landscape made it only more destructive. From the safety of our shared, pretended anxieties, she had confessed her real misgivings about my having a child with James; that she would not, strictly speaking, trust him. More certain of her ground, her voice slightly but appreciably louder, her eyes looking past me, fixed on the book case behind me, her doubts about James's faithfulness came tumbling out into the thickening air of the living room.

Rigid now, I stare coldly at my friend, waiting for some kind of explanation. I can hear the anger, the terror, pulsing behind my eyes. The room hangs for an age and I am caught between outrage and fear. I struggle to formulate a response to the imminent revelation of my husband's betrayal, now that Morag, my anchor through so many years, is no longer my ally, but the carrier of my misery.

But it is simply that she suspects; nothing more. A way he has about him. Something about some girl from his office at our housewarming, about them smoking and talking, flirting maybe, about her walking out into the garden to find them sitting on the wall, heads together; their embarrassment at her arrival, the girl running off as quickly as possible. And again, sometime in the previous summer. She had been down in London, had been at the *Guardian's* offices and had seen them together again, on the street one evening, his arm around her, him flagging a cab. She'd known that I was out of town on business, had tried to arrange to meet me, and there he was, getting into a cab with that girl.

I laugh a short, bitter laugh. I know Daisy, have met her at work events frequently, have had her in my kitchen, chatting, nervous and sweet. More than that, I know my husband. Of course he's charming and friendly and open: that was part of the attraction. I trust him, know he wouldn't cheat on me, especially with a sweet girl like that. He's not like that, we're not like that.

'Oh, for god's sake Lainey, listen to yourself! You're not a bloody Smiths' record.'

I look blankly back at her, my anger and hurt stilled momentarily by the unfathomable absurdity of this.

"This one is different because it's us'? Christ, where were you in the eighties? Anyhow, it's not different. It's exactly the bloody same. They're exactly the bloody same. All of them. If they're not already cheating on you, they're fantasising about it. It's just a question of how long before their dicks win out over their guilt and fear. Bastards.'

Morag's eyes spill over as she spits this last expletive, and she glowers like a wounded, terrified animal. I already know what this means, can feel the horrific force of her hidden agony reshaping her before my eyes. I will her to spare herself this, but she continues anyway, dragging her secret shame and still-raw anguish out into the unforgiving light, shredding it through her cracked throat.

'Yes, even David. Even bastard David, butter wouldn't melt, bookish, boring David. Not even two years! We'd not been wed two years before he'd started with some bit of a girl at the paper. And I didn't see it, completely bloody oblivious, complete bloody fool. Yeah, I trusted him, I knew he wouldn't cheat on me, too. Bastard.'

I want to comfort her, tell her I never knew, to tell her that I understand it is a terrible thing, that she could have talked to me. I want to ask how they survived it, and only now do I understand the sudden move to Scotland, the abandonment of the temptations of the capital. But I can't say anything comforting or normal. I am too incensed that she would attempt to damage my marriage, to seek to sow doubt, to make me unhappy, simply to slake her thirst for revenge, to reassure herself that she is not alone, that she didn't choose any worse than I did. I pity her for what happened to her, but I cannot forgive her for trying to make me pitiable too. I am too incensed to hold my tongue, to unleash my empathy instead of my anger, to be a friend where she has not, and I tell her this, without mercy, without comfort.

As she leaves, a whirlwind of hurt anger crashing out of the front door, I cannot recall how many times I called her sad, pathetic, selfish; how many times and in how many ways I told her that maybe if she had shown any warmth to David he might not have gone looking for it elsewhere; only that it was too many. The stillness of the house without her crowds in around me, the emptiness suffocates me. I empty the last of the wine into a glass, and swallow the dense notes of ruby fluid in one, before numbly seeking out the Scotch James hides in the bookcase.

...

Morag will be up by now, making tea, fussing over Fergus, shouting instructions at David. David, the meek, mild man that

I can now only see as a hypocrite, a liar and a cheat; since Morag's confession I haven't been able to look at him without seeing his dirty weakness. For all his moral posturing, his Presbyterian rectitude, he is as steeped in the sins of the flesh as any of the philanderers at whom he sneers, even now. Like James. He reserves a special vitriol for James, which goes beyond any simple defence of me. I suppose James's infidelity simply reminds him of his own, makes him complicit in man's betrayal of woman all over again.

Morag has forgiven him, in her own way. She kept him, had a child with him, she looks at him in that secret way that says 'I love you'; when he comes into the room, she strokes his arm from her chair without looking up, no need to see him to know where he is, the shape he forms. Of course, she dragged him away from the city he loves, made sure that there were no temptations nearby, that his office was clear of twenty-something girls with ideas and energy and ambition: just a box room with his wife and child downstairs. But she had forgiven him, as I had thought I might forgive James for his twenty-something girl with ideas.

She had been wrong, of course. About Daisy, back then. But somehow she had been able to spot in James the seed that would grow into his infidelity. I still didn't know if her insight was simply the suspicion that grew like moss around David's betrayal, and the consequent mistrust of all men, a refusal to believe that she had made an especially poor choice, an understanding that all men will cheat. Or had there been, even then, a specific tell, a mark, an aura around James that was invisible to me?

I had been ready to forgive him, just as Morag had forgiven David, and I wouldn't have taken us away from London: I really would have forgiven him. I believed that he loved me, despite everything. What that stupid girl didn't realise was that he had left her, had chosen me. With all her crowing, vindictive gloating, she had failed to notice that, when it came to it, he had come back to me. He could just as easily have chosen her, if that was what he had wanted, if she was what he had wanted. But he hadn't. If that had been all there was, it would have been easy to forgive him.

But it had not simply been the affair. There had been everything else that meant forgiveness had been impossible from the start. God knows, I had given him the time, after receiving the email, to start to make amends, not simply to give her up but also to find me again. James had disappeared long before Sophie Lamb appeared, before she had taken advantage of his vacancy. I had finally realised the futility of forgiveness in the kitchen, my cheek still numb, the unwanted tears building, burning behind my eyes. The echo of the impact still ricocheting up and down my auditory canal. At first I had wanted to believe that the shrill ringing was the reason I couldn't hear him, but it became clear that the silence was his alone. His silence again, like his silence in the hours, days and weeks after I lost our baby.

That was the point at which his silence began, and although the banality of noise and movement filled the space between us, the empty stillness was deafening. It had been as if he had decided at that point, when the baby died, that the relationship had gone as far as it could, was all it could be. That his life with me from then on would be stasis, simply repetition and tedium. There was no space left for progress, no potential for growth, for change. He seemed to believe that he had become fixed in a place that would become narrower every day until finally it asphyxiated him. It was as if he had pulled himself into himself to wait for the inevitable, leaving me outside in the lonely cold. But I could have forgiven him that, like I forgave him for deserting me to my grief, if only he had wanted at least to try, or to pretend to try, to be with me. I think sometimes that I could even have forgiven him for hitting me, for the simple unmediated act of hitting me. But I could not forgive him for once again saying nothing. Even then, acting as if my pain did not matter to him. Something cracked and I knew we were over, that I no longer loved him, that I just wanted him to disappear.

But to the world, I became a victim. I am the woman who was left, abandoned, betrayed; subject to events beyond my control. When Morag tells me he was a bastard and that I'm better off without him, she takes from me my right to responsibility for my own life, for my choices. When Mom asks if I need anything, she is expressing condolences and, even across 3000 miles of ocean, the pity in her voice does not lose its subtle intensity. I've stopped trying to explain that it was me who threw him out, me that ended it. It's pointless: even Morag doesn't know the reasons why I threw him out, so I am fixed in her imagination as the victim of James's treachery. The story is written, even though it is a fiction.

...

A group of men is gathered on the corner, outside the bookmakers, in the last of the year's sunshine. One is angry and anxious, his loose jeans masking a thin, deformed leg that is only apparent when he walks the two steps to shout abuse into the face of one of the others. He is caught between his pride and his fear, advancing and retreating in a stuttering, quaking cycle. The other, a whole head taller than him, is calmer, more confident. He juts out his jaw towards his tormentor; he puffs his chest, his straightened arms tensed downwards and backwards, his clenched fists slightly behind his puffa jacket. He too is speaking, but the sound of the whole exchange is lost behind the glass, drowned in the noise of traffic from the High Road, by the distance from my window. And his words are too indistinct to lip read, unlike the shorter man's simple, repeated 'fuck you'. He punctuates this refrain with occasional flecks of spit, some intentional, some accidental, that fly in the direction of the taller man.

One of the spectators ensures that they are never close enough for long enough to launch a punch. He alternates his peacekeeping activities between pushing against the lame man's chest, his head turned away, and pulling at the other's shoulder, whispering something in his ear. But he does not seek to end the confrontation. No-one else intervenes, and the shoppers simply tack around the volatile obstruction.

From my vantage point, the whole exchange seems abstract, absurd even, a silent choreography staged on the moon. It is utterly fascinating and terrifying, and all the more fascinating for the terror the scene provokes. It lasts maybe three minutes, before the lame man backs off, still screaming 'fuck you' over his shoulder. As he limps down the street and past me, flicking anxious seething glances behind him, the men watch his unfinished form recede and they laugh. When he has disappeared completely, they go back into the bookies and the High Road swallows up the echoes of the scene.

This street was never threatening before. Before James left. It had always seemed safe here, even though Balham, like London itself, is often the stage for confrontations like this, the habitat of barking men and malevolent, rat-faced teenagers. Like New York City too of course. Is it my age that has turned what James would call edginess into latent threat? Or simply that I am here alone, unguarded? The house has always creaked too, but it is only now that I hear footsteps on the shifting boards.

The confidence I once had in myself drained into the kitchen floor in the moments after James hit me. That was the moment I realised that the control I believed I possessed was a mirage, a lie. I had pretended to make myself, to write my own story, but in that moment, the pretence fell away. There is a comfort in ceding responsibility. James did this to me. I am afraid because of those men. My friends chose other cities, other countries.

Even my job. I am a professional woman, successful, respected. I define myself in what I do. It is mine as much as these hands are mine. In as far as I believe in myself, I believe in this. But even my career, the last anchor of selfhood I own, even this is just the product of someone else's plan. Daddy teaches law in school, I studied law in school; Mom is a professional woman, self-sufficient, a good wife but dependent, and that is what I wanted to be. I took it and tried to make it my own, to nurture my plans to use my training for something useful, something noble.

I had wanted to change the world, right wrongs, comfort the poor and weak, bring down powerful villains. At the very least, I had thought I might be able to make a difference, the smallest, most modest difference. But the need to pay the rent overtook me, corrupted even this. An accident, unintended, temporary. For years I lived with it, endured James's dismissiveness, certain that my disappointment, my dissatisfaction, would pass once I found the energy, the opportunity to start the life I had intended, becoming the champion of human rights that I knew I should be. And so I'd spent my adult life waiting, on hold, rather than living it.

The street is empty now. Just the parked cars, the bare trees dotted along the sidewalk. I have seen them all a thousand times before, and the view from the window pales, bores me. The sofa beckons, welcomes me into its folds. I sip tepid coffee while I plot out the course of the rest of this Saturday, struggle to reassert my presence in the inertia enveloping me. Shopping maybe, or cleaning up the house.

I still notice the spaces where his things used to be, even though it's been months since they left. The picture I hung over the fire place is smaller than the one it replaced, and the shadow of the former occupant still ghosts the wall. A dirty memento in the whiteness. The prospect of decorating flares briefly and I wander over to inspect the grubby rectangle. There, among the forest of objects on the mantelpiece, a small, smooth, wooden elephant, the ghost of an elephant. Holding it to my nose, its supple shape nestled in my palm, there is still a trace of its heady aroma, the memory of the richness of sandalwood, a whisper forceful enough to provoke longing, but no more. Almost gone. And I realise that James, as he rushed from the house with his plastic sacks and shame, must have left it, abandoning our past as well as our future. A shudder of regret. Memories I have set aside are carried back unbidden on the exotic scent.

Lost, I let the lithe form slide from my fingers; the flash of its descent catches that other sight, primal, instinctive, alerting me to its movement, and I catch only its subtle leap as it bounces from the hearth rug near my feet. For a moment there is only silence and the stillness of the empty house. The elephant stares back at me from where its eyes should be and I watch it, feel my sadness and ache harden, inhale the last of the sandalwood on my hand. With unexpected clarity, I press down my foot, harder, shifting my weight onto my left-hand side, until at last I feel the sudden give of the wood, feel it crack and splinter.

'Fuck you.'

Looking up, inhaling, I can see my reflection ghosted in the picture glass above the fire. The calmness of the face surprises me: there is none of the madness or rage I had expected to see. I study the broken image of myself that emerges from the shapes and colours of the print, chosen in the days immediately after James had left, and test its reliability. I am surprised by the smile that spreads across my reflected face.

I do not want him back. I am glad that he has gone, that he has freed me to myself. These are things of which I am certain now. And yet, I do not know what to do with this freedom. My excuse, that I will begin to fully occupy the space I have been given once the divorce is through and all the legal issues have been resolved, is just that: an excuse. It is easier to slide through life, avoiding friction, avoiding culpability and the responsibility for who and what we are.

...

Fergus is playing airplanes down in the paddock behind the house. He is running in looping circles, his arms outstretched, pretending to fly. The sound is lost on the wind, but I am sure he is making that neee-ow noise that little boys instinctively know is how an airplane should sound. A five year old's world is filled with certainties, with possibilities; it is a place where certainty does not constrain you, where possibility is not a threat.

The paddock where Fergus is lost in clouds of imagination is where James and I consummated our marriage on our wedding night. Alone and freezing, drunk, under the stars. Just us. He was different then. Charming, silly, a little pompous maybe, but there was only possibility, possibility and certainty, and there was no sense of constraint or threat. Could it have been different? I've asked that question a million times, but can find no answer to bring me comfort or vindication. That night I was so hopeful; beyond hopeful, certain that we would go the distance. Lost in the dampness of the grass, it felt as if we owned the whole world.

But today, watching Fergus, the grass of the paddock no

longer belongs to that night, to James and me. It belongs to my godson. It is no longer my wedding bed, but his playground. The memories and meaning of it he has claimed for himself, and I happily grant them to him. The boy is precious to me, almost as much as to his mother. I was pregnant with my own child when I stood in church and became his godmother and as he grew, he filled the space left both by the receding James and by my own gnawing hollowness. As he wheels around in the bright spring light, running and stumbling, dropping to his knees, then setting off again, unperturbed, unimpeded, a sweetness and warmth fills me, and incipient tears bulge behind my eyes. My voice, like a stranger's, struggles above the sound of the chasing air, saying 'thank you', the words bursting out unbidden, autonomous.

A sudden wind rips across the hillside, and the ragged air seeks out the slackness in Morag's coat, driving my fists into the sanctuary of its pockets. I should go back now, let them know that I've not disappeared, wandered off into the night. Morag will hand me a cup of tea on the doorstep, hot and strong, and will look at me with eyes that still harbour the anxiousness that my absence will have created. We will sit, the two of us, while the boy plays out and the man busies himself in the background, knowing that this is time for the two of us, that he is not part of this. I will hear his keyboard clicking in his study, and I will hear the long pauses, as he stares out across the moor, all the more loudly. When my mug is empty, Morag will pour more tea from the big brown teapot and look at me to tell me it will all be OK.

What is it with tea? I've been here for a decade now, and I

still don't understand the British and their tea. As if no crisis is too large to be beyond the restorative powers of a half pint of hot water, some dried leaves and a splash of half-fat milk. Why do they think that every problem can be solved with some kind of beverage? David went straight to the whiskey when I arrived on Friday night and poured me a glass, an offering of commiseration, of consolation. Before I moved to Britain, I never drank whiskey, didn't like it. James would say that that was because we didn't have proper whiskey in the States, just bourbon and rye, not proper, real, Scotch whisky. That's bullshit, of course. Manhattan is full of single malt. But there is something about the damp climate here that means the earthy smokiness and salty tang of Scotch makes sense.

Maybe, just like you shouldn't drink rum except in the Caribbean sunshine, whisky's peculiarities don't translate. Or maybe it's just that the longer I've lived on this damp, dark island, the more I've absorbed its flavours, developed a taste for them and, little by little, learned to love them. I mean, each time I've gone back to the States I've missed this place a little more, and landing at JFK has felt less and less like a homecoming. Mom asked at Christmas if I wanted to come back home, now that James and I are over. But London is home, Britain is mine. It's not something loaned to me by James, something I need relinquish now that we're not together, like his fucking Eames chair. He's not taking this too.

Nor is he taking this hill, the house down there, nor that stretch of grass where Fergus is flying, free of all this gravity. His ghost is not welcome here, in the grass and the stones and the air. But I do not need to chase the apparition out: it has already left, of its own accord, melted into the air, powerless. Tomorrow, I will return to London, back to my house, my home, ready for work on Monday morning. But I'll come back here soon. Soon and often. This place, these people, are mine.